Jasmine reached across Zoey and snatched the cup from Shay, giggling as she peered down into it. "Yes, it's right there. I see the *P* . . ."

Her words were broken by a bout of raspy coughing. "I . . . I can see it . . ."

She coughed again, but this time her voice was strangled when she tried to speak.

"There's the . . ."

Her face turned bright scarlet. She clawed at her throat and let out a sharp gasp. Her eyes rolled back.

Then she fell forward, hitting the table with enough force to rattle the teacups and send spoons flying . . .

Books by Lauren Elliott

Beyond the Page Bookstore Mysteries
MURDER BY THE BOOK
PROLOGUE TO MURDER
MURDER IN THE FIRST EDITION
PROOF OF MURDER
A PAGE MARKED FOR MURDER
UNDER THE COVER OF MURDER
TO THE TOME OF MURDER
A MARGIN FOR MURDER
DEDICATION TO MURDER
A LIMITED EDITION MURDER

Crystals & CuriosiTEAS Mysteries
STEEPED IN SECRETS
MURDER IN A CUP
A SPIRITED BLEND

Published by Kensington Publishing Corp.

LAUREN ELLIOTT

Murder IN A Cup

Kensington Publishing Corp.
www.kensingtonbooks.com

KENSINGTON BOOKS are published by

Kensington Publishing Corp.
900 Third Avenue
New York, NY 10022

All Kensington titles, imprints, and distributed lines are available at special quantity discounts for bulk purchases for sales promotion, premiums,
fund-raising, educational, or institutional use.

Special book excerpts or customized printings can also be created to fit
specific needs. For details, write or phone the office of the Kensington
Sales Manager: Attn.: Sales Department. Kensington Publishing Corp.,
900 Third Avenue, New York, NY 10022. Phone: 1-800-221-2647.

KENSINGTON and the KENSINGTON COZIES teapot logo Reg US
Pat. & TM Off.

First Kensington Hardcover Edition: December 2023

First Paperback Edition: September 2024
ISBN: 978-1-4967-3521-8

ISBN: 978-1-4967-3524-9 (ebook)

10 9 8 7 6 5 4 3 2 1

Printed in the United States of America

Chapter 1

We all have our small daily rituals. They range from a must-have, take-on-the-go morning cup of coffee or tea to double- or even triple-checking the front door to make certain it's locked behind us. However, whether we recognize them as rituals is another thing. For Shayleigh Myers, certainly no workday could commence without her spending quiet time in the second-floor greenhouse of Crystals & Curiosi-TEAS, her tea shop in Bray Harbor, California. Although, if you referred to this part of her morning routine as a *ritual*, she would totally dismiss it and tell you she just enjoyed the peace and quiet before she started another busy day peopling.

She would climb the spiral, wrought-iron staircase to the second floor; pause at the top in the entrance to the small alcove office; and immediately close her eyes. This part—blocking out the sight of all the paperwork that screamed at her daily from the desk—was a *must*. Then she'd reach around behind her with her left hand and grip the handrail to keep her bearings—stumbling blindly down the staircase was not her idea of the perfect start to any day.

She'd draw in a deep breath, and because she had done this every workday morning for the past year, she would take exactly four steps to her left until she was well past the handrail and steep stairs it surrounded, and then she'd slowly blow out that initial cleansing breath. After that, she'd slowly inhale another deep breath and savor the pungent, earthy scents of recently watered soil and the accompanying spring-like fragrance of the plants and herbs growing in the planter boxes that filled her second-floor conservatory. Next, she'd open her eyes, smile at the vast array of greenery that surrounded her, and take a seat on the bench beside the potting table, where she would sit for precisely thirty minutes to reflect on and give thanks to all in her life that had brought her to this moment in time.

On occasion, her tranquility would be threatened. It would start with a churning in the pit of her stomach, and fleeting images would pop into her mind of her cheating, thieving ex-husband, who had ruined her career and her reputation back in Santa Fe, New Mexico. She'd quickly draw another deep breath, releasing it along with her pent-up anger toward him. Then remind herself that sometimes when things fall apart better things fall into place, and if Brad hadn't done what he had, she might well not be sitting here today.

She would then give thanks not only to him for his infidelity and scheming behind her back, but to Bridget Early, the woman who by her bequeathment had led her here and given her this new lease on life. The mother

Shayleigh would never get to know except through the journals and letters she'd come across living in Bridget's cottage and running Bridget's tea shop.

Without fail, tears would well up in her eyes. Yes, this tea shop had been a new beginning and had led Shay down a path she never thought or knew existed, but it hadn't been an easy road. Far from it. It had tested her resilience this past year for certain. The warming of the amulet under her blouse against her chest was a constant reminder of the powers it awakened in her. Not to mention the confusion that followed on the rare occasion she had opened not only the pouch encasing the amulet but also the door that by doing so opened up in her mind.

On that reflection, a shiver would race up her spine and settle at the base of her skull. Yearning to speak with Bridget not only in spirit but in body, with tear-filled eyes, she'd once again scan the opulent greenery that surrounded her. There were still too many unanswered questions, and she had no idea where the answers lay.

Like clockwork she'd hear the reverberating ping of footsteps on metal. She would hurriedly wipe her damp cheeks and then hear her sister Jen asking in a cheery voice, "Shay? Are you up here?" as she reached the top of the stairs and came around into the greenhouse. "I can't believe you *always* manage to beat me in. Here's your morning coffee," Jen would say, and given the day, her blond hair might be a single long braid that hung down her chest, giving her the appearance of a Norwegian Viking queen, or it might be tucked up in a high ponytail like the cheerleader she had been back in high school. Shay never knew what version of her sister she would encounter, but it didn't matter because every version of her sister reminded her why she loved being back in Bray Harbor after a sixteen-year absence. It meant she was reunited with the only remaining family member she had in the world.

Then Jen would take a seat on the bench beside Shay. Her forget-me-not, pale-blue eyes would sparkle as she'd say, "I just love that we take a few minutes every morning to sit and drink in all this." Jen would then wave her hand toward the expanse of the green-house. "But best of all, I'm glad we still have our morning coffee before a day of tea services." Then she'd giggle at their naughtiness and take a sip from her steaming take-out cup from the coffee shop across the street.

Shay would nod and smile, then take a sip from her cup and silently give thanks for the opportunity to work side by side with the person she loved most in this world. Even though she'd never had the heart to tell her sister that she purposely arrived thirty minutes before their prearranged meeting time, just so she could have all this to herself while she had her morning chat with Bridget.

No, this wasn't just a daily routine or even a ritual. It was Shay's way of keeping in touch with her new life and the new her. It was a time to quiet and separate her erratic thoughts from her heightened senses. The ones that meant she could sense other people's energy. Inky feelings is what her sister called them, and Shay would smile with Jen's description, but most important to her, no matter what they were called, was that they had served her throughout her life. Even though there was still so much about her abilities she didn't understand. She hoped this part of her morning routine would bring a kind of enlightenment to her because the secret to harnessing her power was here, somewhere. She was sure of it. Why else would Bridget, the mother she never knew, have left all this to her if not to teach her . . .

However, today something was off.

There was a disturbance, an unusual static buzzing in the air, disrupting the greenhouse's usual reassuring setting. When the static level increased and found a home at the base of Shay's skull, she tilted her head, much like Spirit, the dog who had claimed her, did when he sensed something. No matter how she positioned her head, she couldn't detect the origins of the odd sensation prickling her skin. Instinctively, Shay reached over and gently squeezed her sister's hand in hers.

"What brought that on?" Jen turned to her, a puzzled expression on her face.

"Just because . . ." Shay shrugged and weakly smiled.

"Ah, Sis, are you having one of those moments again? You've been thinking about Bridget, haven't you?" Jen gently cupped Shay's cheek in her hand. "You know that just because we discovered we aren't related by blood, it doesn't mean our bond isn't strong, right? Because I've told you a thousand times this past year that the lifetime bond we have can never be broken, as it goes deeper than blood ties ever could."

Shay shook her head. "No, it's not that. Something

in the air is off, and I can't quite put my finger on it." She took another sip of her morning elixir, but instead of a sense of contentment rushing through her, a shiver tingled across her shoulders. She scanned the rows and rows of waist-high planter tables veiled with pots of flourishing vegetation that grew like weeds in the protection and warmth of the greenhouse. Whatever was wrong was here, in front of her somewhere in all this greenery.

Her overall sense of uneasiness narrowed in on the closest table, and the amulet in the leather pouch she wore around her neck, tucked discreetly under her blouse, grew warm against her skin. She rose to her feet and took a step toward the planter. However, in that moment, Spirit, her pure white German shepherd companion, skulked around the end of the staircase rail, crept over to the same stand Shay was eyeing, sat back on his haunches, and let out a low, woeful howl.

"Did you let Spirit into the shop when you came in?"

"No," said Jen, rising to her feet. "Didn't he come in with you?"

"No, he didn't. After I let him out of the cottage this morning, he took off down the boardwalk."

"Well," Jen gulped, "someone let him in."

"Did you lock the door behind you?"

"Of course I did."

"I know he's smart, but"—Shay cocked her eyebrow at Spirit, who looked at her with puppy-dog eyes—"he doesn't have a key."

"This . . . this is no time for jokes," said Jen, choking out her words. "Someone let him in, and no one other than us is supposed to be here now." On tiptoes, she unsteadily crept to the top of the railing, peered down at the main floor of the shop, and cocked her hand to her ear. "I can hear someone moving around," she hoarsely whispered.

"It must be Tassi," Shay said, coming to her side.

"It can't be. It's nearly nine. She'd be in class by now."

"Tassi, is that you?" Shay called.

"I tell you, it's not her because it's not a school holiday."

"What?" Shay's young part-time assistant's voice echoed up the staircase.

"See, I told you. Tassi," said Shay.

"I sure hope her Aunt Jo didn't see her come in. We'll never hear the end of it if she's skipped school to come into work," snapped Jen, and then added as she trotted down the steps. "Something must be wrong."

Shay glanced back at Spirit, still beside the planter table. When he lay down and whimpered, a cold hand gripped her chest.

"Yes," whispered Shay. "Something's wrong for sure."

It was clear that Spirit sensed the same shifting energy in the air, but what wasn't clear was why he had singled out that particular planter table today. It had been months since Madam Malvina, the owner of Mystical Gardens in Monterey, had swept through the greenhouse like the whirlwind that she was, pointing out several questionable plants Bridget had used in her healing treatments. Then she'd casually strolled out of the conservatory with a good-bye warning to Shay, declaring that although parts of the herbs and plants she had pointed out had healing properties if harvested and used correctly, the subsequent dried tea made from them in the hands of a novice could also be deadly.

Since Shay considered herself just that when it came to the healing properties of plants, naturally Shay had panicked at the woman's parting words. Wanting to take no chances, she had immediately set about separating the questionable plants from the ones she knew she could safely use without inadvertently poisoning any of her customers. Then to be extra safe, she had cordoned off the entire table and placed a warning sign on it, CAUTION: POISON, and called Dr. Mia Harper, an area botanist, with an urgent plea for assistance. Shay had met her last year by way of an introduction through her old friend Dr. Adam Ward, the local coroner, the day he'd announced to Shay that he and Mia were soon to be married.

Since Mia had made it clear from that first introduction that she was itching to go through the greenhouse, she'd jumped at Shay's invitation. Mia's years of experience as a college professor had showed in her ability to explain, in layman's terms, the properties of the plants in question. She'd even offered Shay some of the textbooks used in her classes so that Shay could do some extra reading.

Shay had then spent the better part of most days reading everything she could about her plants and what parts were safe to use and what she should discard. Some, like tansy, with its fragrant ferny leaves and bright yellow flowers, could be safely used in small amounts as an external wash or poultice for sprains and bruises. However, ingesting it in large amounts could be deadly as the essential oil in the plant was toxic. Others like cinnamon, jasmine, fennel, clover, lemongrass, and rose hips were safe, and these plants or parts of them could be extracted and dried for tea. On the other hand, nutmeg was great for cooking and baking, but it could be deadly when brewed in a tea.

The never-ending lists of the plants whose stems or flowers were safe but whose leaves and berries were poisonous, or vice versa, had caused Shay's confidence level to plummet. The more she read, the greater her doubts grew in her abilities to distinguish between what was safe and what wasn't, and she'd expressed her hesitancy to Mia.

Mia had completely understood and suggested that once she got settled into this new school year and had time to screen her graduate students for the brightest and best, she would have them remove any of the plants Shay wanted to donate to the college's botany program. Shay had been thrilled, as her biggest fear was that she might accidentally poison either herself or an unsuspecting customer.

"Shay!" Jen's shrill voice rang up the stairwell, pulling Shay back to the present. "I think you'd better come down here, now."

"Did you hear that, boy, we're needed downstairs."

Spirit raised his head but didn't move. She had learned long ago that he also had an uncanny sense and she shouldn't question him or his actions. If he felt the need to stand guard by the poison table, she'd let him be, at least until she knew what was going on with Tassi.

"Okay, you win, but I will admit you're kind of freaking me out this morning." Shay took one more look at her protector lying prone on the floor and shook her head. "That planter has been there for months. What's so different about it today?" she muttered as she trotted down the stairs.

When Shay reached the bottom step, she hesitated. Tassi was seated at the round table in the back room, her gaze averted to the wooden-planked floor. Jen's face was contorted in her best stern mother expression as she hovered over the girl. It was clear that Tassi had done something Jen, a mother of two, didn't approve of.

"What's up?"

"Are you going to tell her or should I?"

Tassi shook her head and looked up at Jen, then over at Shay. The whites of Tassi's gunmetal-gray eyes were streaked with red, and her smudged charcoal eyeliner dripped down her cheeks.

"What's wrong?" asked Shay, hurrying to the girl's side.

"She cut class, that's what's wrong," snapped Jen, crossing her arms over her heaving chest. "If Joanne finds out about this, it will be the end of her working here, and do you want that?" She glared down at Tassi.

"No." Tassi's bottom lip quivered. "But I did go—"

"Then why are you here now?"

"Wait a second, Jen. Let her explain. Something clearly happened," said Shay, pinning her gaze on Tassi's pale face. "Is that right? Did something happen when you got to school?"

Tassi nodded, tears leaking from the corners of her eyes.

"Take your time." Shay sat next to Tassi and held the

girl's hand. "Just take a deep breath and tell us what upset you this morning."

"I . . . I got to school, and Spirit was sitting by the bike rack—"

"Like he was waiting for you?" asked Jen skeptically.

"Yeah, it was weird. He's never done that before, but, anyway, I locked up my bike, and I heard Spirit growling behind me. I turned around to see what was going on, and my *dad* was standing there."

"Your dad?" said Shay in astonishment.

"Your aunt's never mentioned him dropping by before," said Jen doubtfully as she eyed Tassi.

"He never has. I've barely heard from him since he and Mom got divorced. I always thought it was because he was mad at me for embarrassing him back home. You know, when I got into so much trouble at school and then with the police."

"Yeah, which led to you coming to live here with your aunt Joanne, right?" said Jen, taking a seat at the table.

"Yeah, so she could straighten me out, I guess." Tassi said, casting her gaze downward.

"So, how do you think your aunt is going to react to you cutting school today?"

"I had to, though." Tassi looked back up at Jen. "He was just standing there, grinning at me."

Jen opened her mouth but Shay sent her a warning glance. "What did he want?" Shay asked encouragingly.

"He wanted to introduce me to his girlfriend, and he

insisted that he'd pick me up after school to take me out to dinner so she and I could properly get to know each other."

"You're kidding." Jen's usual pale blue eyes flashed sapphire. "He blindsided you at school when you were heading to class to introduce you to *that* woman?"

"Yeah, I guess, because there she was, sitting in his car, waving and smiling at me with those dark red puffy lips and fluttering her butterfly eyelashes like I'd be all happy to see her."

"What did you say to her?" Shay asked, inwardly cringing at what Tassi might tell them next.

"Nothing to her. When she started to open the door to get out, Spirit leapt at the side of the car and stood snarling at her through the window. She slammed it shut and stayed put."

Shay quietly let out a sigh of relief. Sometimes Tassi's seventeen-year-old internal filter was lacking, and she could often make a bad situation worse with an outburst. A lesson the girl was slowly learning, it appeared.

"Then Dad yelled at me about controlling my dog. I told him it wasn't my dog but obviously he was protecting me from something. Dad blew a gasket and shouted that I didn't need protection from him or the woman who was going to be my *new* mother. I told him I already had a mother and didn't need a new one."

"Good for you. I bet he couldn't say much after that," said Jen.

"Nope, he did. After he stopped laughing, he said"—Tassi dropped her voice to mimic her father—"'Yeah, you've got a great mother, don't you? She shipped you off to live with your aunt the first chance she got and look at you with your crazy dyed hair. What are those, rainbow streaks? I thought it was bad enough when you hacked it off and then bleached it white. Now you look like one of those little pony toys you played with as a kid, and what's this I hear about you working at that witch's store after school?'"

Shay dropped her mouth open in indignation, ready to give her two cents' worth, but she took one look at the tears forming again in Tassi's eyes and quickly snapped it shut.

"Then he said"—Tassi's bottom lip quivered, and tears she'd been holding back streamed freely down her cheeks—"'Well, I'll tell you, little *Missy*, this is all going to stop. You'll be coming to live with me and Jasmine and have a proper family life from now on. Mark my words, Tassi, you haven't heard the end of this. You and that mother of yours—if you can call her that—will be hearing from my attorneys, and I'll make sure you never set foot in this town again. You belong with me and Jasmine, and you'd better start getting to know her because, unlike you, she isn't going anywhere.'"

Shay and Jen gasped a collective breath.

Spirit then silently meandered past Shay and rested his head on Tassi's lap, his sorrowful whimpering sending shivers up Shay's spine.

Chapter 2

Shay closed the door into the back room behind her, glanced over to the sales counter, and gave Jen a weak smile.

"How's Tassi doing?"

"Better," said Shay. "She freshened up and is just finishing her tea before she comes out."

"Good. As you can see, we don't have any customers yet, so while you were calming her down, I locked up and went across the street to Cuppa-Jo and told Joanne what happened."

"Is she upset about Tassi cutting class?"

"Not at all. As a matter of fact, she completely understands and is going to call the school to tell them Tassi is having *girl issues* today—"

"Girl issues?"

"Yeah, they're less likely to ask many questions with an excuse like that. She feels it's up to her sister to fill them in on the details if she needs to. Anyway, she was giving Karen a call when I left to tell her about Peter's latest antics and find out what she wants her to do now."

"It's just not fair to put Tassi in the middle like this. I would love to have two minutes alone with that man." Shay glanced over her sister's shoulder to see what she had in her hand. "What's that?"

"These are the posters for the Fall Harvest Wine and Artisan Festival. Joanne gave me a couple, one for inside the shop and one to hang in the window."

"Yikes, I forgot all about the festival coming up."

"Are we going to have a table on the sidewalk again?"

"I can't see why not. Giving away tea samples at the town events seems to be the number one way we're gaining new customers." Shay scanned the shelving units of gold-bagged, premade tea blends she had prepared. "But I can see a few busy evenings topping up our inventory between now and then if we're going to."

Jen's gaze followed her sister's to the half-empty shelves, and she nodded. "Yeah, who'd have thought a year ago when we were struggling to make a name in this town as the premier tea shop and not the witch's weird store that it would actually work and be such a success."

"Oh ye of little faith," laughed Shay.

Jen shook her head. "It wasn't us I doubted. It was the people in Bray Harbor. You know, between the bizarre junk collection Bridget had stacked up in here for years and the dead body on the greenhouse roof, I really thought we'd never gain a foothold in the business community, and now, we can't keep up with the demand."

"I think the new décor has a lot to do with that."

Shay cast her gaze around the tea shop and smiled. Pride swelled in her chest at the work she and Jen had put into bringing the musty old space into the twenty-first century with its linens in soft hues of green and cream and the large potted plants around the room's perimeter that brought life back into the space. "Yeah, we've done good, Sis, but don't discard all the other stuff Bridget used to do. It is the reason a lot of our customers come back."

"I know your afternoon tea leaf readings have been a hit."

"I only wish I knew more about all the stuff I read about in Bridget's journals. Like how to read crystals and palms. To learn just by looking at someone what ails them and then finding the right tea solution to ease their ailments. I've only touched the surface on what we could be offering our customers."

"I thought you could already do that. You know, with those inky feelings you get."

"I can to a certain extent tell when something is wrong, but I want to be able to look at someone and just *know* what it is instead of just sensing they have an issue or ailment."

"I thought you wanted nothing to do with all that *other* stuff."

"I don't. Well, not really, but the more I read in Bridget's journals, the more intrigued I am, and it makes me wonder if perhaps there is more to it than I thought."

"What about Madam Malvina? You've been spending a lot of time with her. Hasn't she been some help with all that other 'woo-woo' stuff?"

"It's not 'woo-woo.' It's about learning to get in touch with and channeling energy."

"Is that what she told you?"

"No, that's the conclusion I've made on my own."

"You mean she hasn't been dispensing any pearls of wisdom during her visits?"

"Not really."

"Then ask yourself why not. Could it be because she's afraid you'll steal her secrets? After all, you are her only competition in the area."

Shay shrugged, recalling how evasive Madam Malvina had been the last time she popped in for one of her fly-by visits. Jen might be more right than she knew. Shay already suspected that Madam Malvina's visits were actually recon missions to see how far Shay had come with her lessons in Bridget's journals and if Shay's abilities were a threat to the woman who proclaimed to be the best and only *real* psychic on the Monterey peninsula.

If Malvina only knew that Shay had no intention of making that claim. Shay was not, as far as she was concerned, despite the "inky feelings," as Jen had called them, a psychic. She was a scientist, originally trained as a geologist, which had ignited her love of gemstones and eventually led her to establishing her high-end jewelry design shop in New Mexico. That was, until it was stolen out from under her.

She took a deep breath, pushed the image of her ex's betrayal from her mind, repeated her mantra—*When things fall apart, better things fall into place*—and re-

minded herself that any results Bridget had produced
with her healing herbs and readings had a plausible
scientific explanation. As a scientist, that's what she
was interested in studying and evaluating.

"I think her visits have more to do with her son,
Orion, wanting to spend time with Tassi. They seem to
be kindred spirits, don't you think?" said Shay.

"I don't know. I don't trust the woman. I think everything about her is phony, and I wouldn't put it past her
to be using Orion's feelings for Tassi as an excuse to
keep tabs on you."

"Maybe, but she was a big help in identifying the
toxic plants upstairs that, if used incorrectly, could kill
one of our customers"—she swallowed—"or us."

"Yeah, but that's all she said. Then she left it up to
you to figure it out. All I can say is thank goodness for
Mia and her training."

"Speaking of Mia, I should give her a call to find
out when she's sending her students by to pick up those
plants for the college. The longer they stay upstairs the
longer I worry about having them around here, and
Spirit's behavior this morning really has me on edge
right now."

"What do you mean the way he was behaving, was it
weirder than usual?"

"I thought so." Shay then replayed the dog's actions
regarding the planter that morning after Jen went
downstairs to check on Tassi, and she involuntarily
shivered with the image. "So, you see, something has
changed with those plants. I was about to inspect them
to see if they were causing the edginess I'm feeling,
but then he showed up and his actions sent my senses

on high alert, and then the crisis with Tassi erupted and well . . ."

"Hmm," said Jen as she taped a festival poster on the glass door. "We're not busy yet. Maybe you should take a few minutes and run upstairs to check it out. Who knows, perhaps one of them has flowered and the fragrance is deadly?"

"According to Mia, henbane and angel's-trumpet are guilty of that, but I don't have any growing upstairs, thankfully."

"Are they the only ones that even if you smell them they can make you sick? You said yourself that you have a lot of creepy stuff up there according to Madam Malvina."

"They're the only ones both her and Mia warned me about." Shay shook her head. "Although, if some of the flowers on the other ones are ingested, they are deadly, but as far as just smelling them, no, I don't think so."

"Well, as you said, something is bothering Spirit today. It wouldn't hurt to check it out now that things with Tassi have settled down."

"Did I hear my name?" asked Tassi, coming out of the back room. "Did Auntie have a fit about me cutting class?" Her eyes widened. "Is she going to send me to live with that horrible woman?"

"No, not at all," cried Jen, rushing to her side. "Joanne completely understands. She's even going to call the high school and excuse your absence." Jen rubbed her hands up and down Tassi's arms when the girl's shoulders shook. "Don't you worry, she and your mom will make sure his threat is just that and nothing comes out of it."

Tassi nodded and sniffled as she glanced toward the window. A low gasp left her chest, and she pointed. "Then what's he doing at Cuppa-Jo now?"

Shay swung around to look just as Spirit bounded out of the back room, raced across the tearoom, and leapt at the door, planting his front paws on the glass. His lips pulled back in a snarl.

"Spirit, down," commanded Shay.

The hulking canine sat back on his haunches, turned his crystal-blue eyes on her, and let out a gruff whine, showing his disapproval.

"I know, I know," Shay whispered, joining him at the door. "You'd like nothing better than to bolt out of here, snarling and snapping, to chase that man down the street in order to protect Tassi, but"—she patted his head—"we have to be smart about this, or we'll end up losing her for sure."

Spirit let out a low, whining whimper.

Shay cringed when a well-groomed, salt-and-pepper-haired man she assumed was Tassi's dad, Peter, took a step toward Joanne and wagged his finger in her face. She slapped his hand away, and after planting her feet, she leaned into him and shouted something into his face so forcefully her bobbed dark hair quivered. He flung his arms up, spun on his heel, and took a step toward the main sidewalk, but Joanne grabbed his arm and spun him back toward her. Clearly caught off guard by the feisty woman's actions, he stumbled into one of the street-side patio tables and his face turned beet red.

"Tassi," Shay called nonchalantly, hoping her voice did not indicate her panic over the situation she was watching go down, "Jen and I were just talking about preparing for the Fall Harvest Wine and Artisan Festival and how we need to top up our inventory." She glanced over her shoulder to where Tassi and Jen stood by the backroom door. "Since you're going to be here today, perhaps you could get a start on gathering some of the plants we're going to need to dry. The list of blends we make regularly is in the file folder upstairs on my desk."

Tassi started toward Shay. Shay gave a slight shake of her head and hoped her eyes telegraphed, *Don't let her come over here*, to Jen.

"I'll help you look for the list, and we can get started on harvesting," said Jen, grabbing Tassi's hand before she got too close to the window. "Come on, it'll be fun."

Tassi craned her neck to try to get a better look past Shay, but Shay did a little bop and hop in the hope of blocking her view of the scene playing out across the street. "Now that does sound like fun," Shay said. "I'd join you, but someone has to look after the shop while you guys play in the dirt," Shay added with a laugh that she hoped came off as sincere.

Tassi's shoulders dropped when Shay bounced to the spot Tassi had been trying to see out through. "Are you okay? I've never seen you so jittery. Is my dad causing a scene over there?"

"No, not at all. Jo has everything under control. I'm fine. I'm . . . um . . . just excited by the prospect of your teaching Jen how to harvest the chamomile flowers and mint leaves."

"Okay . . ." said Tassi, an edge of skepticism in her voice. She eyed Shay and attempted once more to see out the window, but Shay blocked her view again. "Since I'm here, why not? But if it gets busy, call us so we can wait on tables."

"I will for sure. Best to take Spirit with you too, though. Sometimes some of the customers are intimidated by his presence."

Tassi took another questioning look at Shay, slightly shook her head, showing her skepticism, and retreated into the back room.

Jen stared blankly at her sister and whispered, "What's up?"

"Look." Shay gestured toward the heated scene still playing out across the road. "I couldn't let her see her aunt Jo and her dad going at it like two cats on a fence."

Jen scowled and then winced. "And I'd say it's about to get worse. Look, that woman he's dating just got out of his car and she's heading over here."

Shay spun back toward the window in time to see the woman she presumed was Jasmine tottering on her spike heels across the cobblestone surface of High Street toward the tea shop. "Great, just what we need."

"I'll make sure Tassi's kept busy upstairs. You take care of *that*," Jen said as she disappeared through the backroom doorway.

"Gee, thanks," grumbled Shay.

Chapter 3

Shay plastered a smile on her face as the overhead doorbells tinkled. "Good morning, may I help you?" She pinned the woman who was destined to be Tassi's stepmother, or so it seemed, with the sweetest smile she could muster.

"Hmm." The woman shoved her sunglasses up onto her head and scoped out the shop. "This isn't what I expected at all by the signs on the window. It's . . . it's rather nice in here."

"What exactly *were* you expecting?" asked Shay, knowing her question came out a little more biting than she'd intended. "I mean—"

"Where's all the witch stuff Peter told me about? You know, the cats, caldrons, and the skull candleholders." The woman visibly shivered. "You know, the witchy stuff." She flipped her head back, sending her long dark hair cascading over her shoulders, and continued to scan the shop. "It's just"—she shrugged her slender shoulders—"normal in here. The green napkins and cream tablecloths even complement the window curtains and all those plants." She waved her hand about. "I really can't see what all the fuss is about."

"Fuss? I'm sorry, you are?" Shay fixed what she hoped was a naïve expression on her face.

"I'm Jasmine Massey, Peter Graham's girlfriend. You know, Tassi's dad. He told me all about it and the goings-on in here."

"I see." Shay nodded, pensively replaying Jasmine's words. "That's funny, though, because I don't recall him ever being a customer or even coming into the tea shop."

"He's heard stories, I guess, and he said he was worried about his little girl getting involved with witches and magic and all that stuff." She glanced around again. "But it looks normal to me." She paused when her gaze settled on the closed door leading into the back room. "That is, unless you have the other stuff back there," she said excitedly and took a step forward.

"No!" said Shay, bounding in front of the woman to block her path. The last thing Shay needed was for this woman to see the hundreds of crystal pendants hanging from the ceiling. "That's off limits to customers. It's the kitchen. We can't let people wander in and out. Health code and all that, you understand."

"Right, of course." Jasmine looked down her perfectly refined nose, glanced back at the window, then locked her gaze on Shay. "Do you offer *any* of the services you advertise on there, or is that a scam to get people like me to come in?"

"It's not a scam, I assure you."

"Okay, then I want you to read my tea leaves and my aura. Where should I sit?"

Yikes! This was the last thing Shay wanted to do. Reading the woman's aura was not an issue. The energy surrounding her was flashing an array of neon colors, everything from red to orange to yellow and even black. However, Shay knew if she didn't get the woman out of her shop now, Peter could well storm through the door any minute, looking for her, and then the shop would be filled with a dark energy for sure, especially if Tassi happened to come downstairs.

"As much as I would love to," cooed Shay apologetically—she hoped, "I'm afraid I'm completely booked up for the day." That wasn't exactly a fib. She did have a tea leaf reading on her schedule for later that afternoon.

Jasmine raised her perfectly waxed brows and glanced around the empty shop.

"As a matter of fact, my first client is here now." Shay smiled and waved at Zoey Laine—a local veterinarian and the girlfriend of Liam Madigan, the owner of the pub next door to Shay's tea shop—when the overhead bells tinkled out their greeting.

"Zoey, you're just in time. Take a seat, and we'll get started on your reading right away."

Zoey tucked her sunglasses up against her jet-black hair, which was piled in a high messy bun, and stared vacantly at Shay.

"Did you want chamomile for your reading today or should we be a bit bolder and *play it by ear*?" Shay fleetingly glanced at Jasmine, then locked her gaze on Zoey's.

Zoey's gaze darted to Jasmine, and a flash of comprehension filled her eyes. "Sure . . . let's play it by ear. What do you suggest?" she said, taking a seat at the table closest to the door.

"Hmm." Jasmine pursed her noticeably enhanced ruby lips and gave Zoey a quick once-over, her expression showing great disdain for Zoey's natural striking beauty enhanced by her exotic olive skin tone. She huffed again, tugged at the hem of her miniskirt, shouldered her diminutive handbag, and looked back at Shay. "I still want a reading."

"Sorry, as I said, I'm all booked up today." Shay motioned to the door. "But if you're ever going to be back this way again, you can call ahead and book an appointment. Bye now, it's been lovely meeting you." Shay opened the door just as Peter stormed out of Cuppa-Jo's street-side patio and marched across the street toward them. Shay glanced back at Jasmine, still lingering in the spot where she'd been standing. "Really, you'll have to go, *now*."

Jasmine wiggled her body in indignation, harrumphed, and sauntered toward the door Shay held open for her. "I'll be in town for at least a week," she said over her shoulder as she sashayed past Shay. "Peter has some business to look after, so if you get an opening in your schedule, we're staying at the fancy hotel on the beach." She tossed her mane of hair just as Shay closed the door behind her but not before Shay heard Peter bellow, "Where is she?!"

He stepped up onto the curb in front of the tea shop and glared down at Jasmine. "Where's my daughter? Is she in there?"

Jasmine shook her head and said something to him as she ushered him back across the road toward their car.

Shay laid her forehead on the glass of the door and slowly let out a pent-up breath.

"That was entertaining." Zoey chuckled and stood beside Shay.

"Yeah, I bet it was."

"Mind telling me what it was all about, or shouldn't I ask?"

"*That* was Tassi's father's girlfriend, and Tassi had an altercation at the school with them this morning. She's upstairs now with Jen and seems to have calmed down, but I was afraid she might walk in when Jasmine was here and everything would be set off again."

"What did you just say her name is?" asked Zoey, peering out the door.

"Jasmine, Jasmine Massey. Why?"

"It's just that she looked familiar." Her gaze focused on the two getting into the car across the street. "No," she shrugged. "I don't know the name, though."

"Hey, thanks for going along with my little ploy to get her out of here."

A mischievous glint flashed in Zoey's forest-green eyes.

"What?"

"Perhaps you could return the favor?"

"Okay . . . ?" Shay eyed her guardedly. "What can I do for you?"

She hoped that the favor was something simple like a neighbor wanting to borrow a cup of sugar or even her lawn mower. Since Zoey had made the big step to

move into Liam's Crystal Beach cottage a few months
ago and put her own condo up for sale, Zoey had taken
Shay's neighborly hospitality to the max already and
was always asking for a favor. Shortly after she'd
moved in, Liam had received a call that his grandfather
in Ireland had passed away. Since Liam's own father
had passed a couple of years ago, he was the last close
family member. It was only right that Liam go and help
his gran take care of business and personal matters.
That left Zoey on her own in her new home and in her
new surroundings with most of her furniture in stor-
age. According to what she'd told Shay then, she wanted
to make sure the living arrangement would work before she downsized any more, and was keeping her options open.

Shay liked Zoey. She was practical, intelligent,
friendly, and until Liam had gone away, she had seemed
a fiercely independent woman. But with Liam's depar-
ture something had changed. Since Shay's cottage was
across the lane from Liam's, Zoey had become some-
what of a permanent fixture on Shay's doorstep most
evenings, and most days too, as she'd drop into the tea
shop for a quick chat before or after work. However,
the gleam in Zoey's eyes and the sparks of energy that
zinged through the air around her told Shay this might
be more than her neighbor wanting to borrow a cup of
sugar.

"I need you to do a reading for me now. It's important."

"Right now?" Shay asked, glancing at the clock on
the wall behind the back sales counter. It was almost
ten, and her usual morning tea group would be arriving

shortly. They were the most punctual group of customers she'd ever had, and they converged at the shop for tea around ten. They'd have their visit and then leave just as Shay's lunch-hour rush began at noon. It was perfect, and Shay couldn't be happier that the group had selected her tea shop as their daily meeting place since the group consisted of over a dozen ladies who were on the who's who list of Bray Harbor's most influential people.

"When I said now, I meant today." Zoey glanced at her watch. "I have to do surgery on a pet pig in half an hour, and then this afternoon I'm doing my biweekly shift at the animal shelter. But I can drop by after that if that's okay?" Her eyes darkened as she implored Shay.

Shay sorted through the mental card catalogue of her schedule. Her mind flashed to the plant table upstairs and the image of Spirit lying beside it. The amulet around her neck once again warmed against her skin. "Um . . . today might not—"

"Please," Zoey said, holding her hands in a prayer pose. "It's really important. Remember, I told you the other day that because Liam's family pub had sold, he was packing up Gran's personal effects and flying back with her to San Francisco later this week so he could get her settled in with his mom?"

Shay nodded, recalling how Zoey had talked relentlessly about Liam finally coming home. News that made Shay's heart do a little flutter, if she was being completely honest with herself.

Not that she harbored any real romantic feelings for Liam. But she had to admit she did miss that impish grin of his and how his electric-blue eyes sparkled when he teased her. More importantly, she missed him because he was one of the few people in the world she could talk to about their experiences last year and how that shared experience had bonded them together as friends and, in his words, made them kin as both their ancestors were from County Claire in Ireland. But still, this didn't stop her from daydreaming from time to time about what *could* be.

"Well," Zoey said breathlessly, "he phoned me this morning and told me . . . he has a big *life*-changing surprise for me when he gets back this week." She squealed with excitement. "So, you see I just have to have a reading done now."

"A life-changing surprise, you say?" Shay quirked a brow as another daydream bubble burst right before her eyes.

Chapter 4

Shay glanced up at the wall clock, scanned the street view outside one bay window, then the other one, and checked the time again.

"Relax," said Jen, as she arranged the tray of Scottish scones that Muriel Sykes, the owner of the Muffin Top Bakery, had dropped off earlier as part of her regular morning delivery. "They're just running late. I'm sure it's not easy to wrangle over a dozen ladies together and have them all arrive at a precise time and location."

"But it's well past ten, and every day this month they have been here within a few minutes of each other. I'm just afraid that we're not their favored café anymore. You do the books. You know that their coming in Monday through Friday also brings in a lot of *wannabes* who are hoping to be invited to join their prestigious group, and it's really boosted our daily sales."

"Did you say prestigious group?" Jen stifled a chuckle. "Is that what you call a bunch of ladies who traipse around town wearing little white gloves and having tea and scones five days a week?"

"Gentry ladies perhaps. Is that a better description?"

"I guess if you think donning dainty white gloves and paying homage to the nineteen fifties is that, then yes."

"Don't be so hard on them, Jen. You know full well they do that so they can help recapture a more peaceful, gentler time in history than what's been happening in this day and age."

"I guess," said Jen, covering the tray with a sheet of cling wrap.

"Be careful," mocked Shay, going to the window and scanning the street in both directions. "It's starting to sound like you're a little jealous that *you*, the sheriff's wife, weren't invited to join the group and Julia Fisher was."

Shay heard her sister's exasperated purge of breath behind her and turned. "You have to admit that your constant comments of disapproval for the group are beginning to sound a lot like resentment or jealousy."

"You have to admit, though, that the reasons for my disapproval are exactly why the Little White Glove Society isn't the prestigious group they think they are. If they can allow a double-crossing, crooked real estate agent to be a member and not me, then it just goes to show they actually have *no* class at all." Jen flashed Shay a smug smile, spun on her heel, and disappeared into the back room with the tray of goodies.

"While you're back there, can you go upstairs and check on Tassi and see how she's managing?" called Shay.

She no sooner got the request out when a loud crash resounded through the second floor.

Shay dashed to the back room and found Jen already halfway up the spiral staircase. With two long, bounding steps, Shay was right behind her sister when a series of animatedly uttered curse words drifted down toward them.

"Tassi!" hollered Jen. "Unless you're lying in a pool of blood, there's no excuse for that kind of language." She reached the top, looped around the handrail, and stopped short.

Shay popped up behind her sister and did a quick assessment of the scene before them. The large potted rosary bean plant, which had been isolated on the table with the other highly poisonous plants, was lying on the brick floor in a heap of dislodged earth, and its pot lay in shards around it. "What happened?"

"Him!" Tassi pointed at Spirit. "That's what happened."

Shay glanced at the hulking white dog standing between Tassi and the mess on the floor. "I don't understand."

"I was gathering the mint leaves from this table." She pointed to the planting box directly behind the roped-off table labeled POISON. "I'd just laid my gloves and pruning shears down on the edge of the poison table so I could collect the leaves I'd snipped off, and he started yipping at me. I couldn't figure out what the problem was, but then he leapt up from where he'd been lying in front of that table, planted his front paws on my shoulders, and I stumbled back and slammed into the table and . . . well, you can see what happened."

Jen glanced at Spirit and then at Shay. "He's never done anything like that before. Is this what you meant by him acting weird today?"

Shay surveyed the spilled rosary plant and noticed that a number of the highly poisonous beans had fallen off in the mishap and were scattered over the floor. "I'll deal with Spirit later and try to get to the bottom of his behavior, but first we have to make sure we pick up all the loose beans. They're the toxic part of this plant, and we can't risk them inadvertently ending up somewhere they don't belong."

Jen cocked her head at the sound of constant tinkling of the doorbells. "It sounds like the ladies have arrived. I can go and get them set up if you and Tassi want to deal with this."

"No." Tassi threw her hands up. "I guess it's *my* mess." She glared at Spirit. "Since he hasn't learned to use a broom and dustpan yet, I'll just clean it up myself. It's going to take both of you to keep that group happy." She grabbed the broom from beside the potting table.

"She's right," said Jen, from the top of the stairway. "Especially since you-know-who is bound to be with them, and I try to avoid serving whatever table she's sitting at."

Shay inwardly cringed at her sister's parting comment, bit back the words that first formed in her mind, and took a deep breath. "Don't you think it's time you let this thing with Julia go, Jen? Leave it in the past, where it belongs."

"Yeah, but the past keeps invading my present, doesn't it?" Jen scoffed as she headed down the steps.

Ever since Julia had tried to swindle Jen and her husband, Dean, in a real estate deal, and even though they had caught on before any damage was done, Jen had wanted nothing to do with Julia. Sadly, even though Jen would eventually forgive someone for a personal transgression, she would never forget, and that person, no matter if they had been best friends growing up, would basically be dead to her from then on and well into the hereafter.

"Tassi, don't forget to wear your gardening gloves when you're handling the beans," called Shay as she headed downstairs to join Jen. "Remember what Mia told us. They are deadly if their shells are cracked or scratched in any way."

The next hour flew by. Jen handled serving the pots of tea and scones, while Shay traipsed along behind her, pushing the serving trolley and setting out the condiments the ladies insisted on having with their morning treat. There were the usual plates of lemon wedges, a creamer pitcher, and a honey pot for each of their three tables, but that's where the similarities to a normal California tea service ended. When the Little White Glove Society had their morning tea, it had to be authentic and include an assortment of fine jams and jellies—in genuine British jam pots, of course. Shay had to order these specially from England, along with the small jars of Devonshire clotted cream—a thick white spread similar to cream cheese but sweeter and creamier—which, according to the ladies, was a must-have and very popular in England.

Needless to say, sales might have increased with the extra traffic in the shop, but as it turned out having the ladies five mornings a week was expensive. Their special requests all had to be imported, which Joanne had been kind enough to help out with by ordering the required import items through one of her coffee shop suppliers who gave her a high-volume discount rate, which she had thankfully passed on to Shay. Since there was also the matter of a surplus of napkins Shay had to stock and keep stacks of on the trolley for one particular new member.

The latest addition to the group reminded Shay of Dorothy, the character in *The Golden Girls* television show, in her stature but definitely not her demeanor since she constantly adjusted the placement of her cup and saucer and persistently wiped her teaspoon with a napkin. A few weeks ago, when Shay first noticed the woman's conduct, she had tried to ease her fears about dirty utensils, assuring her that all the dishes and silverware had been washed in an approved industrial dishwasher. However, as Shay handed her the fifth napkin of today's tea service, she realized the woman couldn't help herself. It was a compulsion.

As if all this weren't enough, Shay had to field questions about why the scones were different this morning. To which Shay explained repeatedly that these were authentic Scottish scones made with rolled oats from a recipe dating back to the 1500s. Thankfully her explanation garnered a lot of oohs and ahs and seemed most satisfactory to the society ladies.

When the lunch hour approached and the ladies signaled they were done, Shay was relieved. As much as she appreciated their business and the sales, today was not one of those days. While she tallied up the group's bills and then made the laborious rounds accepting their individual payments, she repeatedly had to brush strands of her long red hair from her damp forehead. All morning she'd found it difficult to focus on each of their individual requests because her thoughts kept flashing between Spirit's odd behavior regarding the plant table and Tassi's altercation with her father, which had led her to mix up their orders and constantly apologize for her errors. She just hadn't been able to focus, or shake the feeling that since Spirit did nothing without intent, these two earlier incidents must be related. But how?

She learned very quickly after meeting Spirit that he was far from a normal domestic dog. He had an uncanny sense of situations and future occurrences. His actions could be a warning, signaling that Tassi's father was more of a threat than they thought. The idea of losing Tassi and her having to move back to Carmel gave Shay a queasiness in the pit of her stomach. Yes, this day had gone from weird to truly bizarre, and the edginess that still niggled at the base of her skull told Shay it wasn't over yet.

Soon the tea shop's regular lunch customers along with a number of tourists began rolling through the door. It was perfect timing as Tassi had obviously completed her cleanup task and reappeared to retrieve the serving trolley Shay had been using, take it into the back room, and return with the trolley laden with a collection of tiered serving plates. Tassi proceeded to wheel the cart from table to table, allowing customers to select their choice of goodies from the assortment of sandwiches and dainties.

With the hectic tempo of the morning settling down, Shay popped upstairs to double-check Tassi's cleanup of the toxic beans. Even the minor spill this morning had her senses still running on high alert. Until Mia removed those plants, she knew she wouldn't be able to truly relax.

When Shay stepped into the main greenhouse, the amulet pouch resting on her chest grew hot against her skin and the fine hairs on the back of her neck prickled more intensely with each step she took.

Spirit pawed at the brick floor where he lay, and Shay edged toward him. He whimpered and pawed again. A single red bean rolled from beneath his paw toward her. She leaned over to get a better look, and in a flash he leapt to his feet, growling at the space under the planter. Shay dropped on all fours and eyed the underside of the table. It seemed Spirit hadn't discovered one stray bean Tassi missed in her cleanup but a number of them.

Mia's words about the properties of the rosary bean plant, also known as rosary pea plant, jequirity bean, gunja, crab's eyes, and Indian bead, echoed through her mind: *Jequirity beans have been used for hundreds of years as beads in rosaries and other ornamental jewelry. But don't let it fool you. The problem with the plant is the beans or seeds contain high amounts of abrin, which is similar to ricin, and thousands of jew-*

elry makers have died over the centuries from handling seeds that were broken, cracked, or scraped because abrin is one of the most fatal natural poisons on the planet.

"One of the most fatal natural poisons on the planet," she whispered to Spirit as she stood up with a shiver.

Chapter 5

The uneasiness that had overcome Shay in the morning continued to grow as the day progressed. The sensation she'd been experiencing could only be equated in her mind to that of a blanket surrounding her, and when pulled off, it would reveal a truth she didn't know if she wanted to face.

"Zoey, are you certain you want to have your leaves read now? I mean, you must have so much to do at home to prepare for Liam's return," she said hopefully, then added, "Like groceries to stock up on, and ... well, you know, all the little extras that would give him a nice homecoming after being away for over two months."

Zoey eyed the empty white teacup Shay had set before her and nodded. "Yes, I need to be prepared because if he's going to ask me what I think he is, it's something I want to be able to consider fully before I give him my answer."

Shay paused pouring hot water into the teapot and

studied Zoey. "Does that mean you're having second thoughts about him?"

"No!" Zoey's head snapped up, and she stared at Shay. "Not about him or me, only if . . . I really want that kind of commitment right now. I've been down this path before, and it ended badly, and I'm thinking what we have right now is pretty good, so why change it, right?"

"Okay," said Shay, filling the teapot. "Then ask yourself this. What if he's not about to pop the question, and it's something totally unrelated? Will you be disappointed?"

"No . . . yes . . . maybe?" She looked at Shay uncertainly. "I don't know. That's why I need the reading. If he does ask me, I want time to prepare and to think about what my answer will be and not just come out with the first thing that rolls off my tongue and then come to regret my decision. I love him, and I don't want to lose him, so . . . yes. We need to do this reading so I have time to think." She pursed her lips and nodded firmly. "Yes." An unmistakable expression of resolve lit her eyes. "I need time to consider all the options before I blurt out an answer, and if it's not what I think it is, then anything else will be a moot point, and I can deal with it."

"As you wish," Shay said, disregarding the heat intensifying from the amulet and ignoring the churning in the pit of her stomach while she continued to prepare the tea and cup for the reading.

Ever since the small blue bottle she wore inside the amulet pouch had come into her possession, her lifelong ability, what Jen called her "inky" feelings, which allowed her to experience energy vibrations, had sharpened. On the few instances when Shay had been brave enough to actually remove the bottle from the pouch, hold it in her hands, she'd discovered it wasn't only people she could read, but the overall energy around her. Everything took on a crystalline appearance. Even colors become so vibrant they radiated a scent. The scents were so vivid that she could taste and feel the texture of them on her tongue, which ultimately opened new doors in her mind.

However, given Shay's scientific training, the experience was something foreign to her, and until she worked out the exact properties of the mixture inside the bottle surrounding the blue diamond—those accompanying effects of her direct contact with the bottle were clearly the result of some kind of chemical reaction—Bridget's blue bottle would stay securely confined inside the pouch.

The simple act of wearing the amulet inside the leather covering, however, still seemed to work as a warning system. She'd learned that when it heated against her skin, trouble could be brewing, or, at the least, changes were coming, and she should be wary of her surroundings or of a particular person or event. The warming was a signal that something was off and for her or others to take precautions.

She'd tried to rationalize this effect, thinking the unidentified liquid surrounding the precious blue gem secured in the bottle was acting as a beacon for her nervous system and reacting to her skin's own fight-or-flight response. An external magnifier so to speak of her own nerve endings and not some psychic phenomenon, or so she concluded. Either way, when heat radiated from it, it made Shay wary, especially considering the reading she was about to perform.

This was why she could never claim to be a psychic. She couldn't tell if she was actually sensing her client, the surroundings, or her own emotions. Truth be known though, *she* didn't want to know the answer to Zoey's question.

With the steeping and pouring of the tea into Zoey's cup completed, Shay said, "Now drink the tea, and leave only about a tablespoon of liquid in the bottom along with the tea leaf sediment, then when you're done with that—"

The backroom door burst open, and Tassi, with a sheepish look in her eyes, peered around the door frame. "Sorry to interrupt, but I think you'd better come out here, Shay. Someone wants to talk to you."

"Can it wait? We're just going to begin."

Tassi pressed her lips together and shook her head. The sheepishness turned into a mischievous glimmer, and she grinned. "I think you should come out here."

As much as the interruption aggravated Shay—when she was conducting a private reading both Jen and Tassi knew better than to interrupt—she bit her tongue when she realized that maybe this was the way out of performing a reading she didn't want to do in the first place.

Shay leapt to her feet. "Okay," she said to Tassi and then glanced at Zoey. "Hold that thought. I'll go see what this is all about, and I'll be back in a minute."

Shay entered the tea shop and started to pull the door shut behind her, but when her gaze settled on the tall, dark-haired man leaning against the bookshelf in front of the sales counter, she froze and a gasp caught at the back of her throat. In a flash, she was transported back to the first time she had been caught up in this same set of electric-blue eyes made more striking by the frame of tousled raven-black hair. The look that had caused her to go weak in the knees then appeared to have the same effect on her still, judging by the burning on her neck and cheeks. That wasn't an end to the similarities to their first meeting. It was clear she was also dealing with a sudden attack of her red-mottled-monster disorder, leaving her looking splotchy and diseased. Oh, how she wished now more than any other time that she was a pretty blusher like Jen. But no, she was cursed with alabaster skin that transmitted her emotions in flashing neon.

"Liam!" she cried with far more enthusiasm than one would deem appropriate for greeting a friend. She dug her toes into the soles of her sandals to fight the urge to run to him, throw her arms around his broad chest, and hug him until neither of them could breathe.

"*A chara,* 'tis a fine thing to lay eyes on ye again." His sun-kissed cheeks darkened with what Shay could only assume was a blush since he, for the first time since they'd met, was the one to break eye contact. "I trust ye've been well?" He looked at everything but her.

What was he looking for, or who? Shay followed his sporadic gaze as he scanned the tearoom. A diminutive white-haired woman chatted with Jen by the wall of preblended teas. Four ladies sat at one of the tables drinking teas, and Tassi was measuring out some dried lemongrass for a customer at the counter. Then it hit her. Tassi must have told him Zoey was here, knowing he'd want to see her and that was the reason for his blush. He was excited by seeing the love of his life after being away from her for over two months . . . his flush had nothing to do with Shay.

With a forced zest she didn't feel, she turned to fetch his true love from the back room. "I'll get Zoey—"

The door behind Shay burst open. "Liam!" squealed Zoey as she darted past Shay and did exactly what Shay had wanted to do except she not only jumped into his arms but wrapped her legs around his waist and planted kisses on his face all while giggling and crying. "I can't believe you're home early, and I . . ." She kissed him fleetingly on the mouth this time. "I can't be happier. I've missed you sooo much."

Liam tenderly unwrapped Zoey from around him and gently set her down on the floor. "Zoey, I didn't know ye were here."

Shay's brow rose at that.

"As soon as I heard that singsong voice of yours through the door," cried Zoey, "I couldn't believe my ears. I wasn't expecting you until later in the week, and I . . . oh no, I don't even have anything prepared for you at home." She glanced at Shay. "I guess I should have listened to you."

Shay shrugged and smiled weakly. Well, at least one of her hunches was right, but this situation hadn't come up on her internal radar. But what bothered her now was that niggling sensation still very much present at the base of her skull. It told her the surprises for the day weren't over yet. Judging by the way Liam took

Zoey's slender hand in his and brought it to his lips and tenderly kissed it, she feared he was going to ask her that life-changing question right in front of her, and she had no idea how she would react. Zoey, on the other hand, regardless of the waffling she had done in the back room while talking to Shay earlier, would, by the look on Zoey's face now, shout yes without a second thought.

Shay needed to collect her thoughts about Liam spending the rest of his life with the beautiful raven-haired wood nymph she was slowly coming round to calling a friend. "I'll leave you two alone to celebrate your reunion."

"No," said Liam. "I came by to see ye and having Zoey here is a bonus because I thought she and I would be seeing each other later, and then I could—"

"Aye," said the diminutive white-haired woman, who fixed her gaze on Shay as she came to stand at Liam's side. "Ye are a sight for these old eyes."

"Pardon?" said Shay, taken aback by the intrusion and the words from this most peculiar woman.

"Shayleigh, how nice to finally meet ye," said the woman as she held out her gnarled hand. "Did ye know that name means fairy princess in Gaelic?"

Shay looked questioningly at Liam, then at the old woman.

"Shay, Zoey, I'd like you to meet Granny Madigan. She's come to live in Bray Harbor."

"Oh?" Confusion laced Zoey's voice. "But I thought she was going to live with your mom in San Francisco."

Shay held her breath as the old woman's eyes locked with hers and a warm, peaceful sensation crept through her. It was as though she knew this woman from a different time and place, but, nonetheless, they were connected, and the energy that passed between them couldn't be denied. This woman knew her too. Shay could feel it, and she wanted to hug her just as she had wanted to hold Liam close to her. *This is what kin feel, isn't it?*

"No, Zoey."

Liam's voice broke the spell and the hold the woman's blue eyes had on Shay's soul.

"Gran's decided she wants to help me run the pub, so she's going to live with us at the cottage."

"With us?" Zoey said, her voice strangled between shock and amusement. "You can't mean the three of us are going to live together in that little cottage?" Zoey looked at Liam in disbelief, while her eyes remained hopeful as a half smile teased the corners of her lips. "Surely, you're joking, right?"

He shook his head.

"Is that the big *life*-changing surprise you had for me?"

Liam nodded. "It'll be grand, ye'll see," he said with an impish grin.

Chapter 6

Shay massaged the bridge of her nose, exhaled, and took a deep whiff of her cup of lavender, chamomile, lemon balm, and honey tea, a blend that Bridget swore in her journals would aid in stress reduction and induce a relaxing aura of well-being. Shay crossed her fingers. After the past few days, that was exactly what she needed.

She took a sip and sat back, relishing the ambiance created by the red and orange streaks of a perfect autumn sunset made complete by the sporadic squawking of seagulls overhead and the waves lapping gently on the shoreline.

"It's been a crazy few days, hasn't it, boy?" She smiled down at Spirit, lying at her feet.

The shepherd raised his head, let out a groan, settled back down, and rested his head on his paws.

Shay chuckled. "Well, I'm just glad Tassi's mom finally came from Carmel to run interference between her aunt and her dad because I've missed you." She bent over and gave the silky fur on the back of his neck a scruffle. "I know you were protecting Tassi, but I had some pretty wild evenings too." Spirit let out an *oomph* and flopped onto his side. "I did, really." She cradled her teacup. "You know, running inference between two alpha females isn't easy." She glanced down at her snoring friend and smiled. "But thankfully, I think by the peace and quiet this evening, Zoey and Gran must have come to an understanding about what belongs where in Liam's cottage and peace has been found on all fronts."

As good as the evening was, the best part was no Zoey on her doorstep filling Shay in on the latest saga in the ongoing feud for household dominance between her and Gran. She didn't envy either woman. They both clearly loved Liam and wanted the best for him, but both women had very different ideas as to what or how to make that happen.

At least, that was one thing that didn't involve her. She nestled into her chair, took another sip, savoring the moment of a perfect fall evening, and released a sigh of contentment. By the rhythmic thump of Spirit's tail on the porch boards, he couldn't have agreed more. However, when a mini gust of wind whipped at her hair, leaving in its wake a velvety whispered voice on a waft of warm air as it brushed across her cheek, *Open the door for Gran and let her in,* he let out a low, mournful bay that shot a shiver rocketing from the base of Shay's spine to the top of her head.

* * *

The whispered words from last night echoed in Shay's mind as she prepared for Mia's students' arrival. Even though Bridget's ethereal messages had been right in the past, Shay wished they didn't come cloaked in riddles. Had Bridget meant it literally that she should open the door and ask Gran to live with her, to help relieve the strain of her intrusion into Zoey and Liam's new life together, or was the meaning of her words deeper than that? Shay never knew until the entire situation started to unfold.

Gran intrigued her, and Shay did want to get to know her, but she wasn't certain asking her to come and live with her was something she was ready for. Since their initial introduction, Shay had actually been avoiding her. That twinge at the base of her skull hadn't gone away, and combined with the way Gran had locked eyes on her and the feeling that had surged through Shay at the time, she wasn't certain she wanted to spend any alone time with the woman, just yet. Enough secrets had been revealed to Shay this past year to serve her a lifetime, and the look in Gran's eyes had forecasted that there might be many more to come. Right now, Shay wasn't sure she could handle any more big reveals, because her senses told her that when Gran's came, they would hit like a bombshell when they landed.

She shook off the possible scenarios that flashed through her mind's eye. She didn't have time to dwell on the *what–ifs* today. When the time was right, and she was ready to hear it, Gran would reveal her truth. Until then, she had real-world problems to deal with. Mia's students were on their way to pick up the plants, including the depotted rosary bean plant, which she'd had to make certain was properly secured in a plastic bag with sufficient water to keep it alive long enough for today when it got transported to the college.

After the incident with Tassi and Spirit and the plant along with its deadly beans ending up on the greenhouse floor, Shay had wanted nothing to do with it, including its repotting, so plastic bag it was. "Leave it to the experts," she murmured as she closed and sealed the bag, placing it on the table with the other questionable plants Mia's students would be taking, and hopefully making her one step closer to getting rid of the spasms that had made their home in her neck.

She headed downstairs to the tea shop only to find her sister in the small kitchen frantically refilling the three-tiered cake plates they used for serving with what was left over on the large trays Muriel and Joanne had dropped off earlier.

"Are we almost sold out?" Shay asked, scanning the dwindling selection of finger sandwiches and dessert treats on the sheet pans.

"It's chaos out there, I tell you, and you know there's one thing in this world I can't tolerate: chaos," Jen snapped, then grabbed the gold ring on the top of the tiered cake plate arranged with sandwiches and wedged it between the dessert cake display and a large pot of steaming tea. "This is my third refill of the plates in the last fifteen minutes. At this rate, we'll run out before noon. Then what are we going to do?" She huffed and bustled through the door with the cart.

Shay followed her out the door and stopped short. "Whoa," she whispered as she surveyed the full house.

It appeared Jen wasn't kidding. There wasn't an empty seat. Not only had the Little White Glove Society numbers grown to fill four tables instead of the three they started with, Mia's college students took up a table of four and wouldn't let Jen and her serving trolley pass without taking a number of every item.

"We need more food." As Shay turned to dash back into the kitchen to put out a distress call to Muriel and Joanne, a woman with a familiar face seated with the Little White Glove Society ladies caught her eye. She blinked. It couldn't be, but there she was—Jasmine, Tassi's father's girlfriend, sporting her dainty little white lace gloves and all.

Shay glanced at Jen, who was refilling teacups at her table, to see what her reaction to the latest member of the group was, but judging by the wild look in her sister's eyes, Jen wasn't seeing faces right now, only a blur of images before she made her way to the next group of four.

Then Shay spotted Gran. Her white hair pulled high on her head like a dollop of whipped cream, she was seated at the table for two in the far corner beside the window cheerily chatting with a group who occupied the table beside her.

This was crazy. Since Gran had been in Bray Harbor, she'd set a routine. After the lunch rush was over in the pub, she'd stop in for tea before heading back to the cottage for an afternoon nap. Her timing had nicely coincided with the teashop's afternoon lull and meant—because Shay wasn't quite ready to have any more secrets revealed—on the premise of having to harvest, Shay could discreetly disappear upstairs to the greenhouse, easing any guilt she had for shunning Gran. Their routine had been working just fine. So what was with the change in routine today of all days?

Then Shay realized that although Gran chatted with the group at the table beside her, Gran's focus was directed toward the four college students seated across the room, and it hit her. Zoey or Liam must have mentioned that the stock of deadly plants was being picked up today and Gran, an Irish woman of some abilities in that area, had only stopped in to see what all the fuss was about.

There, mystery solved, and it was a good thing too. She didn't have time to worry about how she was going to avoid Gran with this change in routine, and dashed back to the kitchen. Her very real-world problem right now was to figure out a way to replenish their food stock and soon. If not, they'd have to close their doors before lunchtime.

She knew calling Muriel and Joanne was a long shot as they would both be busy with their own midmorning rushes, but she didn't know what else to do. There wasn't time for her to go grocery shopping and make up trays of sandwiches. As for the baking—pfft—that had never been her forte. If she feared she'd inadvertently poison her customers with a tea ingredient that might be deadly, serving her baking would definitely kill them off.

Reluctantly, she pulled her phone out of the back pocket of her cropped jeans. Even though her friends might be swamped themselves, at least they had sandwich ingredients on hand she might be able to borrow. Something she was going to have to rectify for her shop in the future. Memo to self: *Keep kitchen well stocked for emergencies*.

"I hope there's enough left to get us through this rush," puffed Jen as she raced the cart to the kitchen counter and frantically began restocking the tiered cake plates again. "Those students of Mia's are cleaning us out."

"I'm just going to place a distress call to see if Muriel or Joanne can help us out in any way, fingers crossed." Shay's thumbs tapped across the small keypad.

A series of cheers and hoots rang out from the tearoom.

"What the . . . ?" Jen poked her head out the backroom door to see what was going on. "Yes! Mia just arrived," cried Jen, returning to the trolley. "Maybe she'll put an end to her students' gluttony, and we can still salvage some of the food for lunchtime."

There was a soft knock on the open door, but before Shay or Jen could respond, a red-faced Mia stepped through. "Shay, I'm so sorry about my students," she said, then walked over to Shay, beside the food dehydrator, and shoved something into Shay's hand.

Shay glanced at what Mia had tucked into her hand and gasped. "What's this for?"

"To pay for my students and their belief that a serving trolley means all-you-can-eat buffet."

"I can't accept this. You're doing me a big favor." Shay thrust her hand out in an attempt to return the hundred-dollar bill to Mia.

"Nonsense." Mia put her hand up in a stop gesture. "They arrived early and misused your hospitality, and it's only fair that you be compensated for what it appears they ate."

"No." Shay emphatically shook her head. "I can't accept this. You and they are doing me a favor and feeding starving college students is the least we can do to show our appreciation." She ignored the faint gasp that came from Jen's direction.

"You're the one doing me a favor. The plants you've been kind enough to donate to the college to use as part of my teaching program will save the department thousands of dollars in this year's budget." The petite woman smiled and turned. Her grin widened when she locked eyes on the young woman who appeared in the doorway. "Shay, I'd like you to meet Lilly Sullivan, my new teaching assistant for the year and the person who will be taking the lead on the removal and transportation process."

Shay reached her hand out in greeting to the young woman. "Hi, Lilly, nice to meet you, and I'd say you have the perfect name for a botanist, don't you?"

The girl rolled her eyes, flipped her head of pulled-back chestnut-brown hair, and flashed a smile that didn't quite reach her eyes.

Shay inwardly sighed. Perhaps Lilly had heard that comment once or twice before. "Anyway," said Shay, "welcome and thank you. If you're ready, I'll show you where the access to the back alley is as it's probably the best way to remove the plants, and then I'll take you up and show you what's to go."

Shay pulled back the heavy black curtains that surrounded the back room and exposed a door that led to the restrooms and alley exit. A gangly young man wearing dark-rimmed glasses that matched his slicked-back, dark hair joined them and Mia quickly instructed him to take the van around to the back of the shop.

"There, they should be all set now, but I have to run. I've got a class in forty minutes. If you have any questions, Lilly is a dream and so knowledgeable. I couldn't have asked for a better TA. Thanks again, Shay," Mia said with a toss of her honey-blond hair, then hurried out the backroom door.

Jen looked at Shay and shrugged. "I guess I'll leave you to it then." She ushered the serving trolley out into the tearoom.

Shay escorted Lilly and the three other students upstairs to the greenhouse, pointed out the plants on the table in question, gave a short explanation and an apology regarding the current condition of the rosary bean plant, and hurried back down to give Jen a hand. She made a dash through the back room and quickly scanned the tearoom from the doorway.

Jen was at the counter, and it appeared all that was required from Shay was to clear the tables as the customers lined up like schoolchildren to pay their tabs. She'd have to hand it to her sister for creating order in a chaotic situation. After all, Shay and Jen's husband, Dean, hadn't dubbed her the queen of efficiency and organization for nothing.

Shay replaced the tiered cake plates on the trolley with a large gray bin, and pushed it from table to table clearing teacups, spoons, and sandwich plates. She spied Gran still seated at the table for two, where Zoey now joined her. "Good," Shay muttered, "just as I thought last night. It seems a truce has been established." Shay smiled and stacked the last of the dirty dishes into the bin.

There was a tug on her shirtsleeve.

Shay jerked and turned. Her chest tightened. "Hello . . . Jasmine," she said, fighting to keep her breathing even. "What can I do for you?"

"Pfft!" Jasmine glanced away, shaking her head, a look of annoyance visible on her face. "It's been nearly a week since you told me you would contact me about a reading, and I'm still waiting to hear from you."

"I know, and I apologize, it's just been—"

"Did I hear that you want a reading?" asked Mayor Cliff Sutton's wife, Cora, as she joined Jasmine.

"Yes," Jasmine said, fixing her steely gaze on Shay, and then glanced at Cora, her entire demeanor softening. "I know she's busy, but you'd think that after a week she could fit little old me in, wouldn't you?" Her earlier haughty look centered back on Shay.

"Well," said Shay, "it's only that—"

"I'd love to have a reading too," chimed in Cora.

"So would I," added the statuesque, gray-haired woman who reminded Shay of the television character Dorothy save for her anxious demeanor.

"What's this I hear?" said Julia Fisher. "You're all booking a reading? I want one too, and I'm sure what's-her-name who joined the group last week, you know, the librarian, will want one."

"Nadine Freeman," added Cora.

"Yes, her," said Julia, "and I know Dot Simpson from the town hall would be interested too. It's only too bad she had to rush back to work, or she'd be here now, and she would be giddy at the idea."

"Oh, and Millie, Doctor Patterson's wife," chimed in the statuesque woman, "told our table just today that she'd love to have her leaves read sometime."

"You're right, Faye, I heard her from our table. She'd be upset if we all booked a reading and she missed out," said Cora, turning to Shay. "So, you see, we can keep you busy for an entire week just with the members from our group alone."

"That's the problem," said Shay, her apologetic gaze darting from one woman to the next. "I only have time in the day to perform one reading because the shop's too busy now, and I'm already completely booked in the afternoons for the next two weeks. Then with the festival coming up, I just don't have the time to fit any of you in, let alone all of you."

"Then do us as a group," piped up the imposing woman Cora had called Faye.

"Yes," added Julia. "We could come in the evening if your afternoons are booked. Tassi works then and she can help in the front while you do a reading in that back room for us. It will be perfect. The evening is probably better for most of us anyway, or at least those of us who have a career." She gave a cutting side glance directed toward Jasmine.

Jasmine flashed Julia a look of utter disdain. "Some of us are lucky enough to not *have* to work for a living."

"Yeah, by latching onto a rich man," mumbled Julia under her breath.

"Now, ladies, remember the code of our group," said Cora, flashing the two women a smile that smacked of a warning.

"You see," cried Faye, stepping between Julia and Jasmine, "it's settled. Just give a date, and we'll all be here."

"The problem is I have never—"

"I'd like to sign up too," said Zoey from over Shay's shoulder. "That is, if you'll let an outsider into the reading." She glanced at Cora.

"You're hardly an outsider, Dr. Laine. Yes, the more the merrier, I say." Cora fixed her hopeful gaze on Shay. "What do you say, Shay?"

"She'd love to," said a soft, singsong voice, and a warm, craggy hand rested on Shay's arm.

Shay looked down at Gran and shook her head. "But I've never done a group reading before."

"I'll help ye, m'dear. That's what Gran's here for," she said, patting Shay's arm reassuringly.

"It's settled then." Jasmine beamed. "Is Friday at say . . . six-thirty-ish okay?" She glanced at the small group congregated around Shay and Gran, and they all nodded in agreement. "Then Friday it is." She shouldered her handbag, sauntered toward the door, glanced back, and gave Shay a self-satisfied smile as she pushed it open. Then she shimmied across the sidewalk and hopped into Peter's waiting car.

Chapter 7

Shay studied the fine lines running through her palm and compared them with the image Gran had placed in front of her as part of today's lesson. "Okay," she said, frowning, "I can see clearly where the heart line is. There's my head line and my life line"—she pointed to her hand—"but it's all these references the image makes to the mounts of Apollo, Luna, Mercury, and so on that are throwing me off. I don't know the first thing about astrology and don't think I can learn about it by tonight."

"Focus on the basics. For example, take a good look at Tassi's hand." Gran smiled at the young woman seated across the table in the back room, gently reached over and turned Tassi's palm upward. "Here, look, ye can see her life line. See how bold it is, and her head line, here, running through the center of her palm, shows her to be highly intellectual."

Tassi sat a little taller in her chair, and Shay didn't miss the flush that appeared on her usually pale cheeks.

"The angle of it also speaks to her way of thinking. See, hers is on an angle. It's curved a wee bit, which means she's open and intuitive. But if her head line was straight, it would tell ye that she's more rigid in her thinking." Gran set Tassi's hand back on the table and looked at Shay. "That's all the basics ye need to know for tonight because all the details of palmistry isn't where yer strength lay anyway."

"Then why do you think I need to know even this?"

"Because it gives ye an opening to do what ye do best, dear."

"Which is?"

"Reading people and their energy, of course. Here, let's pretend ye are reading Tassi tonight, and ye've just told her everything about her head line and her life line that I did. Now take her hand in both of yers, close yer eyes, and draw in a deep breath. Keep yer eyes closed. That's right, feel her energy running between yer two hands. Can ye feel her?"

Shay nodded.

"Good, now what do ye sense from her?"

"Fear . . . sadness . . . loneliness, but"—Shay let Tassi's hand slip from her fingers—"I know all those things about her because I know what she's going through with her father and her fear of having to go live with him."

Gran smiled at Tassi and placed her hand between Shay's again. "Now, take another breath and go beyond the veil of what ye know. What do ye see or feel?"

Shay took not one but two deep cleansing breaths and allowed the energy from Tassi's hand to flow freely with hers. "Darkness . . . I see darkness around her.

She's trapped," Shay cried, then opened her eyes and looked at Gran. "What was that?"

Tassi shifted in her seat, looked questioningly at Shay, and shrugged. "Maybe it's because I feel so helpless now that Dad's filed the custody papers."

What was the first lesson Gran taught Shay that week? No matter what Shay sees when doing a tea leaf or any other kind of reading, she is to always keep it positive when interpreting her findings to the client. That advice rang true to her now, and she smiled reassuringly at Tassi. "Yes, that must be what I saw."

Her gentle smile hid what she knew. The darkness surrounding Tassi went farther than having to go live with her father until her eighteenth birthday next year. It was more like a shadow that consumed her very being and snuffed all light out of the young woman's soul. Shay involuntarily shivered and abruptly got up from the table. "I think we'd better get set up now. The group will be here soon," she said, avoiding both Gran's and Tassi's puzzled looks as she began to clear the table of the teapot and cups.

"Aye, 'tis time I get back to the pub anyway. The evening rush will be starting soon."

"What?" Shay spun around as a swell of panic raced through her. "You're not staying? But what if—" Shay stopped midsentence when she saw the look on Gran's face as she gazed over at Tassi. Had Gran seen the same darkness surrounding the girl that she had?

"No, ye'll be fine. Trust yer instincts." Gran flashed her a reassuring smile. "Remember to count on yer sister to do the brewing and pouring so ye can focus on the readings."

Tassi's eyes widened. "But Jen's never helped with a reading before. It's usually me who assists Shay."

Gran turned her faded blue eyes on Tassi and warmly smiled. "'Tis best she learns then, 'tisn't it?"

Tassi opened her mouth, but Shay flashed her a warning headshake. "Are we finished with our lesson then?" asked Shay as Gran made her way toward the door.

"Only this week. Next week we have much work to do," she said with a chuckle, then ambled through the tearoom and out the front door.

Shay shrugged, then flipped out a clean white tablecloth and eyed Tassi as it fluttered over the table and set itself right. "I agree with Gran on this one, I'm afraid. I think tonight it's best if Jen assists."

"But she's never helped with the readings before, and she thinks it's all phooey anyway. You know she'll have nothing to add except a few sarcastic comments pointed at Julia or Jasmine, and it'll spoil everything. Then how are you going to feel when that group up and finds another tea shop to meet at?"

"It's because of Jasmine coming that I think it's best you don't assist tonight. I can't help but think that she's going to push your buttons worse than she would Jen's, and perhaps the darkness I saw was you and she getting into an altercation." She shook her head. "Jen's helping tonight, and that's my final word on the matter. I'll talk to her first and make sure she behaves herself."

"I can behave myself too."

"I know you can," Shay said, retrieving two pots from the overhead kitchen cupboard, "but . . . no, I think her being here is going to be harder on you than you think. It's best you look after the front of the shop while Jen and I look after the ladies back here."

"Fine," scoffed Tassi, setting the cups from the cupboard on the counter with a clatter.

"Tassi, please. I know you want to help but—"

"You aren't going to believe this," Jen huffed as she marched into the back room. "Cora from the Little White Glove Society just called. It seems they're running late. They can't get here until a quarter to eight."

"But they know we close at eight."

"I know," said Jen, "and I reminded her of that, but it didn't seem to matter." Jen shook her head. "If we'd known ahead of time, we could have planned for it, but tonight I have to pick Maddie up from the library when they close at eight because Dean has Hunter at his swimming lessons until eight-thirty. So, I can't stay." She glanced over at Tassi. "How about you, can you stay a little bit longer tonight?"

Tassi's face lit up, but Shay's heart sank to the soles of her booted feet.

She knew when she hired her sister that Jen's family took precedence over everything else, as they should. After all, Maddie was only thirteen and Hunter eleven. It would be a few more years until they both didn't require the mom-and-dad taxi service, and judging by the way Hunter rode his bike now, it was probably a good thing he wasn't driving a car.

"Okay, we'll make it work." Shay glanced at Tassi and nodded while mentally crossing her fingers that Tassi could turn on her internal filters for the evening. Still, she had an unsettled feeling about it. She took a deep breath, trying to flush it away, focused on the fact that Tassi was growing up, and crossed her fingers for real this time.

In spite of Shay's misgivings, Tassi played the part of the perfect hostess as she cordially ushered the women into the back room. She then returned to the tearoom, hung the CLOSED sign on the door, turned off the front lights, and set about preparing the pots of tea for the reading. All of which was achieved without so much as a second look at or even a word beyond her initial greeting to the woman who was part of the plan to tear her from everything she loved most in her life.

Eased by her young assistant's positive response to what could clearly be an awkward if not a potentially explosive situation, Shay breathed a sigh of relief. She took her seat between Zoey on her right and Julia on her left as Tassi deposited plates of goodies on the table for them to nibble on at their leisure. Shay instructed them to help themselves, to relax and chat freely as they drank their tea. She then proceeded to explain how the evening would work and reminded them to leave about a teaspoon of tea at the bottom of their cups for their reading.

Tassi, teapot in hand, began with Julia, then made her way clockwise around the table, filling the teacups. However, when she got around to Jasmine, the woman thrust her hand over the rim of her cup.

"Don't we get a choice as to what kind of tea we want?" She pinned Tassi with an accusatory look. "I don't want any of that weird witch stuff like eye of newt or something creepy like that."

"Oh," said Tassi, her voice steady. "Then you definitely won't want any of this. However, I could make you a nice, tasty cup of hemlock tea if you'd like."

"Ahh," gasped Jasmine. "Well, I—"

"She's joking." Shay flashed Tassi a cautioning glance. "Aren't you, Tassi?"

"Right, I forgot it's been such a busy week that we're all out of hemlock," she scoffed and held the steaming teapot over Jasmine's hand.

"I assure you, Jasmine," said Shay, "the teapot contains nothing more than chamomile and regular black oolong tea. It's a blend I've found easiest to work with because of the uniform leaf sizes."

Jasmine's hand quivered as it continued to cover her cup.

"Everyone here is drinking the same tea tonight," added Shay, "because it's easier than making individual pots for a group this size. However, if you'd really prefer something different, I'm sure Tassi wouldn't have a problem making you a special pot."

"No!" She took a quick look at Tassi hovering over her with the teapot in hand. "I mean, it's just regular tea and chamomile, you say, and everyone is drinking it?" She withdrew her hand from over her cup. "That should be okay then. It's just that—" a rosy hue spread across her cheeks as Tassi poured her tea—"I've had a bit of a queasy tummy and . . ." She glanced around the table while Tassi moved on to pour the next cup. "Sorry, I know I was the reason we were late tonight. It's just that . . ."

"Pfft, don't you worry about it," said Cora from her seat across the table. Her amused smile faded, and she took on a more serious tone. "We're all women here, and if there's one thing we all know about, it's tummy troubles, right?"

Her words garnered murmurs of agreement except from Julia, who leaned into Shay and shielded her mouth behind her hand. "I wouldn't put it past that one to have gotten herself pregnant just so she had a better hold on that rich guy she's got her claws into," she whispered.

A sharp gasp came from over Shay's shoulder. She turned to see Tassi directly behind them. Tassi's face drained of all color as she glowered at Jasmine. *Oh dear.* This was the moment Shay dreaded, but she certainly hadn't seen it occurring because of Julia making some off-the-cuff remark.

Shay started to rise to her feet, but Tassi shot her a look and shook her head, then set the teapot on the counter with a thud. Her shoulders quivered, but then she straightened her back and turned back around toward Shay.

"You okay?" Shay mouthed. At Tassi's nod, which was accompanied by a weak smile, Shay whispered, "Good."

Shay retook her seat and scanned the white-gloved ladies, trying to determine how far along each was in consuming her tea. As usual, Faye appeared distracted with her continual spoon-wiping and readjusting of her cup and saucer. Shay hoped the woman would be finished with her tea by the time the others were ready for the next steps.

"Now what?" asked Zoey, gently pushing her cup and saucer closer to Shay.

"Now, we can start." She smiled at her and glanced around the table to make sure everyone, including Faye, was paying attention. "The rest of you can watch the demonstration while you finish your tea, and it's important that during these steps no one, not even me, touches your cup." Shay proceeded to demonstrate with her own cup and saucer. "First, with your left hand, take your cup by the handle and silently ask the question you want answered tonight. Then swirl your cup three times from left to right."

Everyone was following along with her instructions except Faye, who'd finally decided her place setting was adequate and was busy gulping down her tea.

"Now," Shay continued, "with your left hand take your paper napkin and place it over the saucer."

The ever vigilant Tassi quickly handed Faye a fresh napkin to replace the crumpled, well-worn one she clutched in her hand.

Shay fleetingly smiled at Tassi and nodded her approval. "Then, again with your left hand, slowly and carefully invert the cup over the saucer, allowing the small amount of tea to drain out."

"How long does it take?" asked Julia, lifting the edge of her cup.

Shay smiled at her. "You can't rush it, and it's best to leave it upside down for about a minute."

Julia shrugged and removed her hand.

"After a minute, again with your left hand, rotate the cup three times on the saucer and then turn it upright. Make sure the handle is pointing south." Shay gestured to the opposite wall from her as a reference. "You'll see that most of the tea leaves are stuck to the sides and bottom of the cup in a variety of shapes and clusters, and that's where I come in." Shay smiled and reached for Zoey's cup.

"Wait," Jasmine said, pushing her cup and saucer away from her. "Since I'm done too, and Peter and I are leaving town tomorrow and this reading was *my* idea in the first place—she glanced at each person around the table with a smile that dripped of saccharine—"it's only fitting that I go first, don't you think?"

Cora let out an exasperated sigh. "Jasmine, Dr. Laine is our guest. She was the first done preparing her tea cup, so let her be the first to have her leaves read."

"It's fine, Cora," said Zoey. "I'm in no rush. Jasmine can go first."

Shay glanced at Zoey, knowing she had been waiting all week for her reading, and was a bit unconvinced that it was fine with her.

When Jasmine edged her cup and saucer closer to Shay, Zoey just smiled and sat back in her chair.

"Tell me, tell me, tell me what it says. I can't wait, and I need to know tonight before I go back to the hotel," squealed Jasmine excitedly. "I did just as you said to do and thought about my question the whole time I was turning and swirling the cup. Now tell me what you see."

Shay glanced around the table to get a reading from them on Jasmine's pushy behavior, and all she got back was a shrug of resignation from Cora.

Shay blew out a deep breath, pulled Jasmine's cup closer, and peered into it. On first glance, it was the usual lines and squiggles. Then she refocused and cleared her mind of any further thoughts of Jasmine and focused on what she saw inside the cup, recalling the instructions Bridget gave in her journals and the same ones Gran enforced this week. *Trust your first impressions. Don't second-guess yourself. Let the process guide you and let it come naturally.*

Shay calmly examined the shapes of the tea leaves and how and where in the cup they were distributed and tried to recognize the various shapes and figures of the leaves that had clumped together. She blinked to refocus when her mind wandered back to Bridget's instructions. *Do not try to force the answer. Let it naturally appear.*

She lifted her head and smiled at Jasmine.

"What? What do they say?"

"I'm not sure what it means, but I'm guessing you might. The first thing I see is an object that looks sort of like a kettle?"

"That makes sense since we're having our leaves read, doesn't it?" chuckled Dot from the far side of the table.

"Yes, I suppose it does," said Shay, racking her brain, trying to remember what the kettle image meant.

"Is that all you see?" sniped Jasmine. "You mean I went through all this for you to tell me I was getting my tea leaves read?"

"No . . . there's more," said Shay, peering back into the cup, all too aware of the amulet growing warm against her skin. "I see the letter *P* but it's—"

"That's it!" cried Jasmine, leaping to her feet. "See, I knew it. *P* must stand for Peter, and proposal! He *is* going to ask me to marry him."

"Or . . . P for pregnant," whispered Julia under her breath.

"Let me see, let me see!" Jasmine reached across Zoey and snatched the cup from Shay, giggling as she peered down into it. "Yes, it's right there. I see the *P*. . . ." Her words were broken by a bout of raspy coughing. "I . . . I can see it. . . ." She coughed again, but this time her voice was strangled when she tried to speak. "There's the . . ." Her face turned bright scarlet. She clawed at her throat and let out a sharp gasp. Her eyes rolled back. Then she fell forward, hitting the table with enough force to rattle the teacups and send spoons flying.

Chapter 8

Shay wrapped her arms around her knees and curled into a ball in the corner of her sofa. Never in her life had she actually witnessed a person die. The image replayed over and over in her mind, and she feared she'd never be able to erase it.

Repeated soft knocks on her back door roused her from her thoughts. She slowly eased herself from her cocoon position, then forced her legs to behave as she stumbled through the living room and kitchen. When she opened the door, a pair of electric-blue eyes and an uncertain half smile greeted her.

"I just wanted to make sure yer doing okay."

"I guess," she said, leaning on the frame of the open door. "You know, at least as well as can be expected." She glanced over Liam's shoulder. "Where's Zoey? How's she doing?"

"She came home, threw back a couple of whiskeys, and went to bed."

"Maybe that's what I need to do too."

"How about I fix ye a cup of tea instead?" A sheepish smile tickled the corners of his mouth.

"Sure. Why not," she said, stepping back. "If you're making it, then I'm drinking it because I don't think I have the energy to do it myself."

"It sounded like it was a rough one for everybody," Liam said, filling the kettle and retrieving the teapot and a tin of chamomile tea from the floating shelf over the stove. "I heard there's going to be a big investigation too."

"I hope so," said Shay, taking a seat at the small kitchen table. "I wasn't Jasmine's biggest fan, but it's weird how she died out of the blue like she did, being so young and all. I wonder if it was an ulcer that burst or her appendix? She had been complaining about her stomach earlier. I just hope they can find out what it is because I'm sure Tassi's dad is beside himself with questions, not to mention grief, especially if the *P* that I saw in her cup did mean proposal."

"Actually, that's something I wanted to talk to ye about." Liam turned his back on the gurgling kettle and fixed his gaze on Shay. "I was talking to Dean, and the coroner's initial examination at the scene suggests she was probably poisoned."

"Poisoned? How? When?" Shay unfolded her knees from where she'd drawn them up on the chair to her chest and edged to the front of her seat.

Liam winced and refocused on the steaming kettle and began filling the teapot.

"You aren't saying Dean thinks she was poisoned at the tea leaf reading, are you?"

Liam, without turning around, shrugged.

"Oh no! I hope it wasn't the plate of sandwiches we put out. They were left over from the day's service, but they'd been kept refrigerated . . . unless . . . they were accidentally left out too long, and it was the egg salad ones that went off." Shay groaned, replaying in her mind how many times the trays of sandwiches had been taken out during the day and then put back in the fridge. "No," she shook her head. "I know the sandwiches were only out long enough to fill the serving plates, and they were then put right back in the refrigerator. We're always so careful about the food."

"I guess we'll find out after the toxicology report comes back." Liam set her cup on the table in front of her. "Do ye want to do the honors or should I?"

"I don't even want tea now," she said, pushing her cup away. "I'm just sick with the thought that we could be responsible for that poor woman's death."

"Now, now, don't go getting yer knickers in a knot. Remember, she was a tourist in town, and I'm sure she and Tassi's dad ate at every meal. If it was food poisoning, it could have come from anywhere."

"You're right." Shay absently tapped her fingers on the table. "She did mention she was feeling queasy before the reading, which was why the group was so late in arriving, and just because she died in my shop doesn't mean I'm to blame." The vise grip around her chest eased, but then her gut tightened. "Except . . ." Shay's eyes widened. "The Little White Glove Society was in this morning for their usual tea and scones. So, it still could have been something she ate in my shop. Oh no! What if I *am* to blame?"

"Now yer going down rabbit holes. Drink yer tea

and take a deep breath. As Gran says, don't go borrowing trouble. Wait and see what comes out in the report, then worry if ye need to. Until then no amount of worrying will change the outcome."

"You're right," said Shay, dragging her steaming cup closer. "I just think—"

"Don't trip on that rabbit hole."

"Okay, you win. I'll change the subject until we know for sure."

"That's my girl." Liam grinned at her over the rim of his cup.

The cup slipped in her fingers. Had he just called her *his* girl? No. She grabbed a napkin from the holder on the table to wipe up the bit that had sloshed, and reminded herself that her daydream bubble had burst when he had asked Zoey to move in with him. But she did have to admit that him sitting across the table and the soothing tone of his singsong Irish accent, which had morphed nearly into a full brogue since he'd spent the last two months back in Ireland, was something she could easily get used to again, and something she had missed while he was away.

"How's Gran settling in?"

A wry smile crossed his face. "It depends on who ye ask."

"What do you mean?"

"According to her, it's just grand, but if ye ask Zoey, not so well."

"Oh dear, I thought that when I saw them one day in the tea shop together maybe they had reached an understanding and things were going better."

Liam pressed his lips tight, slightly shrugged, and

glanced around the kitchen. "Aren't we missing some-one?"

His abrupt change in the topic told Shay that things at home might not be going as well as she had hoped, but clearly the subject wasn't something he wanted to discuss. She shifted her focus and tried to recall what he had just asked her. "You mean Spirit?"

"Aye. It's not like him to be away especially after ye've had such a shock tonight, is it? Or has something changed these past months I don't know about?"

"No, nothing's changed. He's the same free spirit he's always been. He seems to go where he's needed most, and I guess tonight he decided that he was needed elsewhere. When the deputies finished taking all of our statements and released us, he bolted as soon as the door was opened," Shay said as she set her cup on the table. "But," she added wistfully, "I will admit it would have been nice to have him here with me when I came home after . . . well, you know."

"Hmm. It does seem odd then since me Gran thinks he's yer familiar."

"My what?"

"Yer familiar. Ye know, the companion animal as-signed to attend and guard ye."

"I've never heard of that before." She looked at Liam. "Are you saying Spirit is actually a spirit and not a real dog? Because he sure feels like he's real."

"Nah, he's real all right. He's just got these un-canny—"

A dog's bark echoed through the cottage.

Shay's eyes widened, and she laughed.

Liam chuckled. "As I was saying, he has this uncanny ability to appear when his assistance is needed."

"Or . . ." said Shay with a soft laugh as she rose to her feet, "whenever we talk about him, it seems. But I'd better go let my wandering friend in now. He must be starving to carry on barking like that."

"Maybe he's protecting ye from a rabid raccoon."

"Yeah, that must be it," she laughed as she opened the front door. "It's about time, mister, although I should have known you'd come home when you got hungry enough. Okay, get in here."

Spirit sat back on his haunches and whined.

"What is it, boy?" Maybe Liam was right about the raccoon after all, but then she heard soft sobs coming from the far porch chair, and she flipped on the outside light. "Tassi? What are you doing here?"

Spirit groaned and went over to the girl and laid his large head on her lap.

"I just can't be at my auntie's tonight. My father and mother and Aunt Jo are screaming at each other, and it got to be . . ." Her words got lost when her sobs came harder and faster.

"Oh no!" Shay darted over to her and sat on the side table, taking her hands in hers. "I'm sorry to hear you were put in the middle again. But death, especially an unexpected one, is hard on everybody, and sometimes people's first reaction is to lash out at everyone around them."

"It's not just that." She turned her tear-filled eyes on Shay. "My father filed an official police complaint against me. Can you believe my *own* father did that?"

"What in the world for?" asked a bewildered Shay.

"Someone from the reading told him later about the jokes I made." She glanced at Shay. "You know about the eye of newt and then the hemlock. So, he filed a report, accusing me of practicing *witchcraft* of all things and making a direct threat to kill Jasmine."

"That's ridiculous. Everyone there knew you were joking. In hindsight it probably wasn't the most appropriate thing to say, but, nevertheless, it was meant in jest, right?"

"Yeah, I don't even know what eye of newt is," Tassi croaked between renewed sobs.

"Your father's a lawyer, right?" asked Liam from the doorway.

Tassi nodded.

"Did he file this accusation with the courts?"

"He must have because he was there at the bottom of the porch steps with a deputy." She glanced at Shay. "Dean was the one at the door though with some official-looking piece of paper."

"Did you see what was on the paper?" asked Liam, pulling over the other chair.

She shook her head. "My mom read it. She said it was a formality because I was a minor, but the sheriff was within his legal rights to question me about it as long as an adult accompanied me during questioning."

"What kind of questions did Dean ask?" Shay said, squeezing Tassi's hand reassuringly.

"He was great and apologized. He said my dad had made sure that in his filing he had covered all the bases, and although Dean knew there was no *witch-*

craft being practiced at the shop, he was still forced to ask me about what I had said."

"And?"

"And I told him I was joking. We don't even have any eye of newt in the shop."

"And we certainly don't have any hemlock either," added Shay, a hint of hopefulness in her voice. "He can verify that with Mia if he needs to since she went through all the plants in the greenhouse."

"What did Dean say then?" asked Liam.

"Nothing. He just repeated how sorry he was, but since there was an official complaint made, he had to follow up on it."

Liam nodded in agreement.

"See, then it's okay," said Shay. "Dean doesn't suspect you of causing her death, and your dad's just in shock and lashing out. He wants to blame someone for it. After he sleeps on it, and the autopsy is complete, he'll settle down, you'll see."

"Yeah, but that wasn't the end of it. After Dean talked to me, he and dad left, and I thought it was over. Then a while later, my dad came back."

"With a deputy?" asked Liam.

She shook her head. "No, and that's when it all broke loose and the fighting started."

"You mean," said Liam, "your father still thought you had somehow killed Jasmine with witchcraft?"

"Yeah. He said he knew I hated her and blamed her for him leaving Mom, combined with the fact that the coroner suspected poisoning to be the cause of death. That didn't mean I still didn't do it with another poison. After all, I worked for a witch who was probably the leader of that silly ladies' group Jasmine had joined, which was probably one of those witches' covens he's read about, and I was forced to kill her as part of some initiation ritual."

"What?" Shay gasped.

"Was he talking about the Little White Glove Society?" asked Liam.

"Yeah, I told him that was crazy talk. They were only a ladies' tea group and came in during the day when I was in school anyway. Then he pointed his spiky finger in my face and said it didn't matter. One way or another, he'd make sure that *witch's* store was closed down permanently." She drew in a deep, shaky breath. "That's when I left."

Chapter 9

Shay cupped her fresh-brewed coffee between her hands, rested her feet on the old trunk she used as a coffee table, and took a long, much-needed sip to allow her morning elixir to work its magic. She had to admit there was a certain sense of accomplishment in getting a precocious teenager up and out the door on time for school without all the theatrics—ones she vividly remembered she and her sister partaking in when they were Tassi's age. To her astonishment, the girl was almost human at the breakfast table. A morning behavior Shay didn't recall from her own high school days and something she had to give Tassi big props for especially given what occurred last night.

However, what really left Shay speechless was when Tassi actually left for school early. That was something Shay didn't ever remember doing, unless she was rushing off hoping to catch a glimpse of her latest crush before classes started. She nestled into the deep back cushions of the sofa and took another sip of her morning brew and wondered if the change in Tassi's demeanor today was because of a boy. Oh well, whatever it took to get her young friend's mind off the drama of the previous night was a blessing, and it made Shay wish she had someplace to run off to in order to escape all the questions about last night circling her mind.

"It's going to be a long day, boy," she said, glancing over at Spirit, asleep in his bed bedside the fireplace. His only reaction was a groan as he shifted, curled up, and tucked his nose farther under his tail.

"Some company you're going to be today," she mocked, then reached over, retrieving her phone from the coffee table, and began scrolling through her text messages. When she found no recent updates from Dean or Liam, she tossed her phone on the sofa beside her. "Yup, a long, boring day."

She took another sip, got up, walked over to the bay window, and stared out toward the beach. Normally, a day off from the shop would have entailed a morning swim, a run with Spirit on the beach, perhaps some shopping on the boardwalk or eating some of the yummy food from the assortment of vendor stalls that popped up during tourist season, but today, nothing appealed to her. Her mind was too focused on what was happening at the tea shop, and whether the suspected poisoning was going to be traced back to the egg salad sandwiches.

Ever since the night before when her brother-in-law, Dean, had called to inform her that the tea shop would have to remain closed while they finished processing it because it was the scene of a sudden death, she couldn't think about anything else. No matter how many times she replayed Liam's wise words in her mind, what-ifs still crept back in. Not to mention the fact that the amulet's warming became increasingly annoying, which sent her senses spiraling right along with her thoughts.

She glanced down at her empty cup. "Hmm . . ." She looked over at Spirit again. "It seems I need another cup of coffee . . . a very large one . . . in a paper cup."

Spirit's ears perked forward and like a shot he was at the front door before she could grab her backpack and bike helmet.

She slipped on her helmet, clipped the chin strap, and coasted her vintage red bike along the wooden sidewalk in front of the other four original fisherman's cottages along the beachfront row that led her to the terraced stairway and up to the back row of five more cottages, and then on up to the main road toward town.

Once at the top, Shay pushed down hard on the pedals, launching the bike on a brisk pace, and followed Spirit hightailing it down High Street. She reveled in the swoosh of the light morning breezes tickling her cheeks. If she wasn't on her way to check on the status of her shop being closed until the actual cause of death was determined, life would be pretty perfect in this artsy little town she had grown up in and had fallen in love with all over again.

When she reached her destination, she hopped off, leaned her bike against the short wall that surrounded the Cuppa-Jo outdoor patio area, dropped into a faux-wicker chair, and adjusted it so she had an unobstructed view across the road of Crystals & CuriosiTEAS.

Even though Dean had warned her about the tea

shop having to remain closed, the all-too-familiar yellow police tape cordoning off the entrance made the tea-reading nightmare too real in her mind, and her chest constricted with uneasiness at the similarities. Unlike last year though, there was no body on the roof. No, this was far worse than that. This time the body was taken right out the front door of *her* shop.

"How's my favorite redhead doing today?" Joanne asked from over Shay's shoulder.

"Your favorite redhead? I'm the only redhead you know."

"There's Jimmy Carver."

"Yes, but he's five, and he eats bugs."

"Which is why you're my favorite redhead," Joanne said with a laugh, then placed a steaming cup on the table in front of Shay.

Shay glanced at the cup, then up at Joanne.

"The look on your face when you rode up and saw the yellow police tape told me you'd need this. Also..." She flashed Shay a good-natured wink. "I promise, not a single bug was harmed during the brewing process either."

Shay shook her head and chuckled as she took a sip. "Mm, thank you." She smiled. "But given the choice between *that*"—Shay gestured toward Crystals & CuriosiTEAS—"and bugs, I think I'll take the bugs."

"I guess the tape's necessary since there was a sudden death on the site."

"I know, but I sure hope that after Dean checks out all the other restaurants and sees I'm not the only place Jasmine ate, it can come down soon." Shay glanced down the street to the hotel entrance. "I don't see any yellow tape around the hotel, but Jasmine told me that's where they were staying, so I assume they also had a meal or two in their dining room."

"Just because there's no tape up doesn't mean they haven't been investigated. There's no tape around my place either, and they came in this morning to check out my kitchen because you told him the sandwiches you serve come from Cuppa-Jo."

"I wasn't pointing a finger."

"I know, it's just procedure. They have to cover all their bases to try to track down the source."

"What did Dean say when he was in here?"

"He didn't come in. He just called to make sure I was here, and then a minute later in walked a couple of deputies to take food samples. They had a look around, took the samples, and left." Joanne sighed and sat on the chair next to Shay.

Shay glanced at her. "That means they'll be testing the treats from the Muffin Top Bakery too, I suppose. I'd better give Muriel a call to warn her."

"They were already there first thing this morning since she opens so early."

"Ooh," Shay moaned and sat back, fixing her gaze on the fluttering yellow tape across the road. "This is a nightmare, isn't it?"

"Yup, and Peter breathing down Dean's neck every step of the way probably isn't making it any easier on any of us."

"I imagine he is. Her death was so unexpected, I'm sure he wants answers as bad as the rest of us."

"I think it goes deeper than that."

"What do you mean?"

"Hmm," Joanne said with a wince. "I'm guessing when Tassi stayed at your place last night she told you about Peter's threat to shut down your shop?"

"Yeah?"

"And, as you know, he's a prominent lawyer in the county."

"What are you saying? It sounds like Dean's following procedure and doing exactly as he should to establish where the food poisoning came from, right?"

"I guess." Joanne shrugged.

"Do you know something I don't?"

"No, it's just that . . ."

"What?"

"I get the feeling that no matter what any of the investigations of other restaurants show, Peter will still be convinced it was something in your tea shop."

"But that's ridiculous if the facts point to something else."

"When Dean called, he kind of told me that Peter was watching this investigation pretty closely and had let him and everyone else, including Mayor Sutton, know that he has friends in *very* high places. So, Dean's not taking any chances, and he's making sure nothing's missed while they try to determine Jasmine's cause of death."

"That's good, isn't it?" said Shay. "I know I'll sleep better once we find out what happened."

Jo's head jerked back. "Hi Jen, want a coffee?"

Jen waved her off. "Joanne," she panted breathlessly as she took a seat in one of empty chairs at the table. "I've been calling and calling you for the last half hour and so has Dean. Why didn't you answer?"

Jo's hand shot to her apron pocket. "Sorry, I guess my phone's still in my jacket pocket inside. Why? What's wrong?"

"Where's Karen?"

"She had to go to Monterey to meet with her lawyer about the custody hearing. Why?"

"Because . . . Dean's just gone to the school and picked up Tassi, and she needs a parent or guardian with her."

"What on earth for?" asked Jo.

Jen's face paled, and she swallowed hard. "He needs to question her about Jasmine's murder."

"Murder?" Shay gasped. "It wasn't food poisoning? I mean, that's what I assumed when he said it looked like poison."

"I guess not. Dean told me the preliminary toxicology report came back, and it showed a high level of some toxic substance in her system, and it wasn't one of the standard foodborne toxins."

"Do they know what it was?" asked Joanne.

"He's not saying much to me at this point. He only said he needs someone to be with Tassi while they question her because whatever it is that they found wasn't something common, so it's highly unlikely to have been an accidental poisoning."

Joanne pinned a stunned look on Shay. "Could it have come from one of the plants in your greenhouse?"

"Ahhh . . . I . . . I don't know. I got rid of all the plants that were poisonous, so—"

"Then why did they pick up Tassi?" asked Joanne, rising to her feet. "She's just a kid, and if Shay says she got rid of the poisonous plants she had, how would Tassi have had anything to do with them?"

Shay shook her head. "She wouldn't, but I'll check with Mia to make sure there's nothing else up there that's toxic that we might have missed."

"You'd better," said Jen. "Dean will probably want to question you again later, especially if it's traced back to a plant, so find out for sure before you talk to him. But Dean's interested in Tassi right now because of what she said during the reading, so, we'd better hurry up and get to the station, Jo," Jen said grabbing her handbag from under the table.

"But from what I understood last night, whatever she said at the tea leaf reading was a joke, right?"

"Yeah," said Jen rising, "but I guess her comments are now being considered a threat because of what they found in the preliminary autopsy. But I don't really know since I wasn't there. That's just what Dean told me."

"That's ridiculous." said Shay. "We don't even have eye of newt and especially not hemlock in the shop. That I am one hundred percent . . . well, at least ninety-nine percent sure about."

"Let's hope you're one hundred percent right, because if you're wrong, they'll find it." At the sound of screeching tires, Jen gestured across the street as three sheriff's department cars pulled up in front of Crystals & CuriosiTEAS. "But we really have to go, Jo. Come on. I'll give you a ride, and you can be with Tassi as her guardian until Karen can get here."

Chapter 10

Shay's shoulders slumped. What a nightmare. Poor Tassi. The girl already suffered from anxiety and felt as though she didn't fit in with her peers. Now to have been dragged out of school and driven away in a sheriff's car, of all things, must have been devastating. Shay tried to focus as she tapped Mia's number into her phone, but her call went directly to voice mail. She then tried calling Adam's number, in the hope Mia was with him, but got voice mail again.

Shay clicked off without leaving a message for him either and tried to figure out what to do next. When she glanced up at her tea shop, it was now a hub of commotion. She counted five, no six, deputies coming and going as they loaded clear plastic bags of what appeared to be every cup and teapot in the shop plus all the jars of dried teas and herbs she had on hand in the kitchen and storefront.

This wasn't only a nightmare. It was one of hers coming to life right before her eyes. Had this been

what she and Spirit had sensed last week about the poison plant table? Shay wished now she had listened
closer to Mia's explanations of which plants contained
what. She had shut down when she heard "deadly poison" and hadn't heard much after that. Her biggest fear
was inadvertently poisoning her customers, and even
though she had taken precautions and had the plants in
question removed, there must have been something
else growing in the greenhouse that had escaped them
all and made its way into her tea blends. Then a
thought caused her to gasp for breath. Tassi had done
the last collection and drying, and all the what ifs surrounding that raced through Shay's mind.

Liam!

Her thumb hit his number. "Liam? Hi, um . . . is
Gran at the cottage with you, by chance?" She struggled to keep her voice steady. Liam had a habit of running to her rescue, but in this case, it was Gran who
needed to rescue her. "Monthly inventory? Right, it's
the end of the month. I forgot. Okay . . . yeah, I'll be
right over." She clicked off, stuffed a five-dollar bill
under her coffee cup, and dashed across the road to
Madigan's Pub.

Shay pushed the heavy door open and stumbled
blindly into the dimly lit pub. She blinked repeatedly,
willing her eyes to adjust from the bright sunshine before she took another step. "Liam, are you here?"

"Yeah, by the bar. That was fast. I only just unlocked
the door. Ye must have been close by."

"Yeah, I was. Is Gran with you?" she called, tentatively taking a couple of steps toward his disembodied
voice.

"No, she's up in the office, doing the final tally before we open for lunch. What in the world has ye in such a state this time of the morning?"

His voice had drawn closer as he'd spoken, and as soon as her eyes adjusted, she found herself staring into his eyes, the same ones that generally calmed her or made her legs like jelly, but today they weren't powerful enough to remove the dread lodged in her chest. "I just need to talk to her." Shay darted across the bar, weaving around tables and chairs; dashed up the stairs; hung a sharp left on the top landing; rushed over to the office door and knocked. "Gran, are you in there?"

"Out here, me dear," Gran called from behind her in the outdoor patio area. "I'm just taking a break and having a nice cuppa tea. Come and join me."

Shay dashed back across the landing and out into the morning sun again. She shielded her eyes. Gran sat at a table in the shade of the brick wall that connected to Crystals and CuriosiTEAS' second-floor greenhouse. "I don't have time for tea, but can we talk for a minute?"

"Of course, me dear." The old woman rose to her feet. "But what in the world has ye in such a dither?"

"Oh, Gran, it's horrible," said Shay, shaking as she sat down hard on the chair next to Gran's. "Tassi was taken in for questioning about a woman's death. They think she might have poisoned her."

"Tassi? Poison someone?" Gran sank back down into her chair. "No. Never. Not that girl."

"I know, it's crazy, but you've poked around in my greenhouse. Have you ever seen poison hemlock growing in there?"

"Poison hemlock? No, and I know me hemlocks. I know some people confuse it with parsley or even baby's breath because of the white flowers, but I also know Bridget was no fool, and she would never have grown something as deadly as that in her greenhouse."

"What about eye of newt? Is there any of that in the greenhouse?"

Gran's face screwed up in a smile. "Eye of newt, ye say?"

"I don't know what it is, and I think I've only ever heard about it way back in school, and the witches in *Macbeth* used it in a spell. So it must be pretty deadly, right?"

"Oh, me dear." Gran let out a hearty laugh. "Eye of newt is the old-world term for mustard seed. That's all." Shay sat there stunned, staring blankly at her. "Back in the day, the healers that some called witches used different names for the plants and herbs they used in their potions and healing treatments. It was a sort of code word. Ye know, ta keep their secrets so people wouldn't treat themselves and would come to them instead for healing and spells."

"It's just mustard seed?"

"Aye, and toe of frog is buttercup, wool of bat is holly leaves, but why de ye ask?"

Shay took a deep breath and delved into the events of last night and this morning. "So, you see, Tassi made a joke, not an appropriate one in hindsight, but a joke nevertheless, and now she's being questioned about a murder."

"But I thought it was food poisoning?" Liam's voice boomed from the doorway behind Shay.

She pivoted in her chair and stared at him. "According to Jen, it was a toxin and not one generally found in food, so most likely it was given on purpose and not accidentally."

"Did she say what the toxin was?" asked Gran. "Scores of foods we eat every day can be highly toxic. Like almonds and fiddleheads. Apple seeds contain cyanide, so you have to be careful not to eat them, and rice can contain arsenic. Nutmeg in high enough doses and even potatoes with a smidge of green on them can kill ye."

"No, Dean didn't tell Jen. He only told her that the preliminary report was back, and it wasn't a common food poisoning."

"Poor Tassi," said Liam, pulling out the chair beside Shay's.

"I know, that's what I said. But if it was something from my greenhouse that accidentally got in with the herbs we dried, I don't think I can deal with the fact that my stupidity caused a death and Tassi is taking the blame for it."

"Hold on," said Liam. "Let's not get ahead of the facts here. Take a deep breath. We just have to wait and see what the final report says before ye run off all willy-nilly."

"You're right." Shay's hand tugged at the amulet pouch and lifted it away from where it burned against her skin. "I've done nothing but jump to conclusions since you told me last night that Dean said it looked like poisoning, because somehow I feel responsible since Jasmine died in my shop."

"Did anyone else at the reading get sick or show any

signs of possible poisoning?" asked Gran calmly from over the rim of her teacup.

Shay shook her head. "I guess that's a good thing. At least I didn't wipe out half the Little White Glove Society in one sitting."

"There ye go again," Liam said with a tsk. "Yer taking the blame, and ye don't even know what the facts are."

"You're right, you're right," Shay said, scolding herself by softly slapping both her cheeks. "I need to turn my mind off. It's just that I've never had anyone die in front of me before."

"'Tis hard, isn't it?" said Gran softly as she laid her warm hand on Shay's arm.

Tears welled up in Shay's eyes, and she nodded.

"I hope I'm not interrupting," Dean called out from the patio entrance. "But, Shay, I'm going to need to ask you a few more questions about last night."

"Is she going to need a lawyer?" asked Liam, rising to his full six-foot-three height.

"No," said Dean. "No one is being charged at this point. I just need a few minutes with Shay to clear up a few things."

Liam eyed Dean skeptically and then looked down at Shay. "I can stay if ye want."

"That's okay. I can talk to Dean. I have a few questions of my own."

"All right, if yer sure. Remember, Gran and I are just downstairs if you need us." Liam smiled reassuringly at her and then helped his Gran to her feet.

He ushered the woman across the patio but paused

in front of Dean and opened his mouth to speak. However, he snapped it shut when Gran flashed him a warning glare and jerked his arm. He shook his head in resignation and looked helplessly over at Shay, but Gran tugged him toward the stairs. "*A Stór,* yer not Garda any longer, remember," Gran harshly whispered. "Let the man do his job."

"But—"

"No buts! Ye shush now, da ye hear!"

The next sounds were the thumping of their footsteps as they descended the stairway.

"Wise woman, that one," Dean said with a chuckle as he jerked his thumb toward the hallway behind him. "Sometimes I think our friend forgets he retired from the police force." He motioned to a chair at Shay's table, and she nodded. He removed his sheriff's cap, laid it on the table, and took a seat. "I'm sorry about this, but I have a couple of more questions about last night."

"I don't know what else I can tell you that I haven't already, but can you tell me what kind of poison killed Jasmine?"

He shook his head.

"Why not? This is me, Shay, your sister in-law, and the one whose shop Jasmine died in. I have a right to know."

"That's not information we're prepared to release yet."

"But that's crazy. How am I supposed to know if something growing in my shop resulted in that woman's death?"

"That's why I can't tell you what's in the autopsy report. We have to find a link to the source first, but I can tell you it's not looking good for Tassi right now."

"Which is ridiculous," Shay huffed. "Tassi is no more capable of killing someone than I am."

"Maybe not, but so far all the evidence points to her."

"What evidence?"

"She had motive and opportunity, and we're still working on the means and how it's connected."

"To her?"

"It's looking that way, Shay. I know you think the world of her, but her feelings about why her parents divorced are well known, and she's just admitted at the station that she held a grudge toward Jasmine."

"Of course she did. She sees her as the reason her parents split up, but Tassi has a grudge against the whole world right now. She's seventeen, and you don't see her going all helter-skelter out there on everyone else she feels upset with, do you?"

"No, but she made a verbal threat directly to the victim before she fell over dead."

"She made a joke, that's all. We don't have poison hemlock in the tea shop and eye of newt is nothing but mustard." Shay sat back, crossed her arms, and stared at Dean. "I don't think either of those are enough to hold her on, do you? So, unless you have something else, *sheriff*, I suggest you look elsewhere for the means and a suspect."

Dean sat back, stretched out his long legs, and returned Shay's defiant stare. "That's the thing, Shay, the poison found in her system could have come from only one place in town, and so far we only have one seventeen-year-old girl who was upset enough to have given it to her."

He grabbed his cap from the table, stood up, and pushed his chair in with a screech on the cement flooring. "Does the fact that she overheard Julia telling you that Jasmine might have been pregnant ring any bells from last night?" he asked, leaning on the table. "That's not something you mentioned before to me, is it?"

"No," Shay said, toying with Gran's cup on the table. "I didn't think it was important. It was just an off-the-cuff remark by Julia, who, by the way, wasn't fond of Jasmine."

"Yes, but it was shortly after the girl discovered she might be replaced in her father's life with a new baby that perhaps she saw her only way out was to end the life of the woman she blamed for her parents' divorce in the first place."

"That's a lot of speculation."

"We have witnesses." He shoved his cap on his head and pushed strands of light brown hair up under the brim. "Look, I know we're like brother and sister, but can we stop sniping at each other? I think we're both after the same thing. I don't like the idea that Tassi could be a murderer, but so far, the only evidence I have points to her, and you just confirmed another piece of it."

"But I got the feeling that no one in that group liked Jasmine. I have no idea how she wormed her way in with them in the first place but—"

"How many of them would have had access to je-quirity beans?"

Shay recalled that Mia said the pods on the rosary

bean plant were also called jequirity beans. She swallowed hard. "Is that what poisoned her?"

"Yes. As much as I don't want that information getting out, you've left me no choice because I understand that until a week ago you had the plant in your greenhouse. Is that right?"

Shay hesitantly nodded.

"At any time would Tassi have had access to it?"

"Of course, she would have. She was always up there helping with the collection of flowers, leaves, and stems for drying and brewing."

"I don't care about mint leaves or lemongrass. What I'm asking is would she have had access to the jequirity bean plant?"

"I suppose, but she wouldn't have had a reason to even touch it. We work from a tea recipe list of Bridget's, and I assure you that none of the teas have . . ."

"What?"

Shay reeled. Tiny beads of perspiration formed on her brow as she struggled to get her breath.

"Is there something you're not telling me, Shay?"

The plant that had killed Jasmine was the same plant that had gotten knocked off the table, the one Tassi had cleaned up after, including collecting the beans that had scattered across the floor.

"Shay, what is it?" Dean leaned forward on the table, pinning his unyielding gaze on her. "You can be charged as an accessory if I find out you've been withholding information in a murder investigation."

Chapter 11

Shay perched on the edge of a bar stool with a cup of tea Gran had insisted she have to help put color back into her cheeks, and glanced around the room, which was quickly filling up with the lunch-hour rush. All the smiling, happy faces surrounding her did nothing to alleviate the growing knot in the pit of her stomach. Had she just given Dean the proverbial smoking gun that would seal Tassi's fate? Her stomach pitched, and a cold shiver snaked up her spine. She leapt up, darted to the door, flung it open, stepped out and sucked in a deep, cleansing breath of sea air.

From the sidewalk, she studied the gold lettering across her store windows: TEACUP READINGS, PALM READINGS, AND PROTECTIVE AND HEALING STONE TREATMENTS. If that was true, why hadn't she seen this coming and changed things so that it wouldn't happen? This was all her fault, not Tassi's. "What have I done?"

"Shay? Are ye all right?" a familiar sweet singsong voice asked from behind her.

"No, Gran, I'm not." She spun around, stifling a sob. "I have no business messing with things I don't understand, and because of that, a woman died."

"Did ye poison her?"

"No!"

"Then come sit and tell me what it 'tis ye don't understand."

With total disregard, Gran flipped up the police tape and led Shay to the bench under the tea shop window. "Now tell Gran what makes ye think this is yer fault," she said, taking Shay's hand comfortingly in hers.

"I saw it."

"What do ye mean ye saw it?"

"It was there in Jasmine's cup. The *P* I saw didn't stand for Peter or proposal or pregnancy. Now I know it stood for poison. It was as clear as day, so why didn't I see the sign sooner when I could have done something about it?"

"Aye," Gran said, nodding in agreement. "Hindsight makes us all *seers*, doesn't it?"

"But you don't understand. I saw the sign *before* she died."

"I see, and now ye blame yerself and think ye could have changed what the universe had already set in motion." She patted Shay's hand reassuringly. "Tell me, had this woman drunk her tea when ye saw the *P*?"

"Of course. I was reading her leaves after she drank it, just like Bridget's instructions state."

"Then if this poison was in her tea, she had already consumed it, right?"

"Yes, I suppose. But why didn't I have a sign *before*

this happened so I could have stopped her from drinking the tea?"

"Didn't ye?" Gran quirked a shaggy white brow. "Think."

Shay closed her eyes and considered all the events leading up to the fateful reading. "There is the fact that I didn't want to do the reading in the first place."

"Aye, there's that. So, if yer logic is right, then 'tis me that's to blame because I convinced ye that ye were ready."

"Yes, but if it was truly a sign not to go ahead with it, I should have known and stood my ground and stopped it, but I just thought my feeling about it came out of nervousness."

She nodded. "Not trusting yer instincts, I see. What else did ye sense leading up to last night?"

Shay racked her brain, trying to unravel all the thoughts that were tied up in knots. "There was the incident with Spirit last week. He knew something was going to happen and tried to protect Tassi from going near the poison plant table."

"And?"

"And she ignored his warning and set her gloves and shears down on it. He pushed her away, but in doing so, the poison plant that killed Jasmine dumped on the floor."

"Did ye tell Tassi to ignore yer warning about the table?"

"No, and I had it clearly marked. Then later, I foolishly allowed Tassi to clean up the mess and dispose of the spilled rosary beans, and now she's going to be charged with murder."

"I see, and ye blame yerself?"

"Yes, I should never have let her clean it up because now it's the one thing that connects her to the poison used."

"There's that hindsight again." She nodded. "And where are the plants now?"

"I . . . um . . . had them removed last week but not until it was too late, it seems."

"And do ye think Tassi kept some beans to kill this Jasmine on the off chance ye might do a group reading and she would be there?"

"No." Shay emphatically shook her head. "She couldn't have known then about a group reading because I didn't know there would be one at the time. Besides, when it was booked, I had a bad feeling about her assisting with it." Shay looked at Gran. "You did too, and even said as much."

"But you let her anyway?"

"No! Circumstances made it inevitable that she would. I had no control over it, and I was only afraid of an altercation, so I relented. I never dreamed it would turn out like this."

"And do ye still think ye didn't see the signs that something wicked was going to happen?"

"No." Shay shook her head. "Not when I piece it all together now. I guess I did, but then why didn't I make more of an effort to stop it?"

"Because ye did everything ye could. Remember, seeing and knowing are different from being able to change what's already in motion because there's still free will, me dear. Sometimes what ye see can only help ye deal with what's to follow."

"Then what's the point?" Shay glanced over her shoulder at the golden lettering across her tea shop windows. "Bridget was supposed to have been a seer, yet she didn't see her death and change the outcome, did she?"

"But she did make certain she took care of ye before her sight was shadowed, didn't she?"

"Yeah."

"Me dear, remember that the biggest lesson ye must learn is that a seer is only a guide. Ye might be able to see what's ahead and advise, but ye can't change what is to be. There are too many other forces at work that ye can't control. Like Tassi having to be the one to assist ye with the reading. Ye might have stopped the reading, but who's to say this woman wouldn't have met her end in another way and in another time?"

"So, what you're saying is that even though I knew something bad was going to happen, I couldn't have changed it. I could have only warned her to be careful if I had followed my instincts."

"Exactly, trust what you feel and don't second-guess yerself because that's what ye've done all along, isn't it?"

Shay sat back and stared unseeingly across the road toward Cuppa-Jo. "That's exactly what Bridget writes over and over in her journals, and something I keep questioning in myself."

"What else did Bridget give ye?"

Shay's hand immediately went to the bulge under her blouse.

"Do ye listen to the telling of the blue bottle?"

Shay gasped and pivoted toward her. "You know about the blue bottle?"

Gran's eyes sparkled.

"Did Liam tell you about it?"

"No, me dear. I knew yer gran and her mam, and I know that Bridget didn't only give ye this." She gestured to the tea shop behind them. "She would have made certain that bottle stayed in the family."

"Wait. You knew my grandmother and great-grandmother?"

"Aye, and ye have their same fairy eyes, ye do."

"Fairy eyes?"

"I believe ye have a picture—"

"Excuse me, ladies."

Shay turned toward the booming voice from the doorway of the tea shop and was met by a glare from a sheriff's department deputy. "I'm afraid you can't be on this side of the yellow police tape," he said. "This is an active crime scene, so I'm going to have to ask you to step back, please."

Gran groaned as she used the backrest on the bench as support to hike herself to her feet. "'Tis my fault, Officer. These old bones needed a nice sit-down for a minute. We'll be on our way now, won't we, deary?"

Shay nodded at the officer and gave him an apologetic smile.

"Liam, the love of my life, had me up far too early this morning for the counting, and now it's time for this old lady to walk home so I might work out some of the creases in these old bones. Then I think a nice nap is called for." She glanced down at Shay, who was still processing the fact that Gran didn't just come from the same county as her family in Ireland, but actually knew them.

The same family that she knew nothing about and had desperately tried to find a connection to. In the past year, she had lost every truth she thought she knew about herself, and she needed this woman to help her put together all the new pieces of the jigsaw puzzle that had been thrust into her life. *Open the door and let Gran in.*

"Wait." Shay glanced at the deputy. "I want to walk with you because I need to know about my gran and my great-gran."

"Not now, me dear. There'll be plenty of time for that later," she said, glancing over at Spirit, sitting at the curbside. "Ye have someplace else to be now."

"No, honest, I have no place else to be now that they've closed my shop."

"Aye, ye do."

"Where?" Shay glanced over at Spirit, who'd started his dancy-prancy thing he did when he wanted her to follow him.

"Ye'll know when ye get there," Gran said with an impish twinkle in her eyes. She turned and set off on a brisk pace that would have rivaled that of a power walker half her age.

"Those old bones move pretty good, if you ask me," the deputy said with a chuckle.

Shay watched Gran hightailing it down the street, glanced over at him, and shrugged. Spirit barked a demand for her to follow while continuing to dance at the curb in front of Lillie's by Design, the dress shop on the corner, right next door to Shay's. There was no doubt by his performance that he was on a mission. Gran had said Shay would know where she was going when she got there, but a surprise expedition to an unknown destination wasn't what she needed now. She needed answers.

Gran had just shown her the tip of what she felt in her gut was an iceberg when Gran mentioned something about a picture before they were interrupted. Shay gazed back up the street as any glimpse of the answers she needed right now from Gran vanished along with her in the heavy foot traffic.

Chapter 12

All Shay wanted to do was go home and sort through the old photo albums of Bridget's to see if she could spot the similarities in the eyes that Gran mentioned, then press her for more information on her family she knew nothing about. However, it appeared Spirit had different ideas.

He turned his large head toward her and loudly barked his impatience before she'd even finished clipping her chinstrap. "I'm coming. I'm coming," she called and hopped on her bike. When he turned a sharp left at the corner and raced up First Street away from the direction of the beach and her cottage, she saw that going home clearly wasn't part of his plan and he had something else in mind for the day.

Since she apparently wasn't in charge of this excursion, she hoped Spirit's plan had something to do with Tassi and how she could get her out of jail, because none of what happened the night before made sense. Tassi wasn't a killer, no matter what the police thought or what evidence they had proving otherwise. As she pushed down hard and drew in a deep breath to help propel her up the incline of First Street, Shay vowed to prove her young friend's innocence if it was the last thing she did.

When they shot past the corner of Fifth Avenue, Shay was disappointed. If the destination wasn't Julia Fisher's real estate office, as she'd hoped because the woman knew everyone in town and might have had some insight into who would have wanted Jasmine dead, then where was her guide leading her?

When Spirit dashed across First and bolted south on Fourth Avenue a block later, Shay was baffled. This road led to the municipal buildings, hospital, and the business district in the town center.

As she sailed around the corner and pumped her legs hard to keep up with Spirit, she crossed her fingers that he was leading her to see her old friend Dr. Adam Ward. Perhaps Spirit sensed he had information Dean hadn't shared with her and she could use it to prove Tassi's innocence. She could only hope. When Spirit made a sharp left and darted up the stairs leading into the adobe-styled sheriff's department building, she knew Spirit had led her here not to help her solve the case, but to give comfort to their young friend, who no doubt was scared to death, sitting in a cell with a murder charge hanging over her head.

"You're a good friend, Spirit," she said, hopping off her bike and patting the dog's large head. "You wait here, and I'll see if they'll let you in with me for a quick visit with our girl. I know seeing you will boost her spirits. Back in a minute." She edged past him and into the station, tucking her helmet under her arm.

"Good afternoon," said a deputy as he rose to his feet from a desk beyond the front counter. "May I help you?"

"Hi, my name is Shay Myers, and I'd like to know if—"

"Shay?" called Dean, walking out of an office in the back corner of the communal office space. "What brings you in?" he asked, tossing a file folder on a desk as he passed on his way over to the front counter.

"Hi, Dean." She glanced awkwardly at the deputy. "Um, I mean Sheriff Philips. I came in to see Tassi, and I was wondering if Spirit might go back with me. I know she'd love to see him, and it would perk her up," Shay said hopefully.

"Hmm," said Dean, crossing his arms, "that might be a bit of a problem."

"Spirit doesn't have to go in. I thought I'd ask is all, but can I see her?"

"Okay, let her back, Deputy Kramer."

"But, Sheriff?"

"Just let her back."

"Okay." The deputy pressed a buzzer at the end of the front counter that released the lock on the gate.

Shay scooted through, smiled at the young deputy, and followed Dean to his office in the back corner of the large room as he'd gestured her to do.

"Why are we in here?" she asked, taking a seat in the chair he motioned to as he closed the door behind her.

Dean went behind his large desk and pulled a file

folder from the top of a pile in his basket marked Open Cases but left the folder closed on his desk. "There might be a bit of an issue with you visiting Tassi here today."

"Why, have you moved her to the juvenile detention center in Monterey already?"

"No." He shook his head.

"That's good." She let out a sigh of relief. "I don't know if she'd be able to deal with that. You know, because of her anxiety issues and all."

"Well, she's safe and sound at home."

"Oh . . . really? I . . . I wasn't expecting that. I mean since I told you this morning about her cleaning up the jequirity bean plant and all."

He pursed his lips and blew out a deep breath as he flipped open the file folder in front of him. "There've been a few developments since I last saw you."

"Developments?" Shay said excitedly and leaned forward in her chair. "Does that mean you found the real killer and Tassi's free?"

"No . . . it means . . ." He scanned over the notes in the file. "It means the coroner's office has sent over the final report of the autopsy and the crime scene."

"And it *was* food poisoning?" she asked optimistically.

"No, the cause of death is just what they initially thought." He read aloud from the report, "'A lethal dose of abrin, a toxin commonly found in *Abrus precatorius*, also called rosary bean or Indian licorice. It's a plant of the pea family Fabaceae and generally found in tropical regions. However, the jequirity plant is an invasive species, which has been showing up in various

regions of the United States, including California.'"
He closed the file. "So, it seems your greenhouse
might not be the only place this plant was growing in
the area."

"You mean that beautiful but deadly plant is growing wild out there?" She waved her arm widely in a circular motion. "If people find it, they might think they
can take it home to plant in their own gardens because
it's so pretty, but the consequences could be lethal."

"Yup, and according to the consulting botanist, the
head doctor at California State University, Monterey
Bay's Agricultural Plant and Soil Sciences department,
Mia Harper, that seems to be the number one reason
it's now showing up in every region of the country.
Pretty but deadly to the untrained eye."

Shay sat back in her chair. "Except the person who
gave it to Jasmine knew it was deadly, didn't they?"

"So it seems, which brings us to the rest of this report. The tea in the teapot tested negative for abrin.
There was none found in any of the dried plant containers that were tested and there was no residue on the
counters or on any of the utensils. In other words, there
was no trace of abrin found in the shop except upstairs
where you'd indicated the plant fell to the floor and the
beans were scattered, which is logical. Traces would
have been evident in that case, and because of the dis-
bursement pattern, it seems to corroborate your claim
of an accidental mishap."

"Does that mean you can take down the yellow
crime scene tape, and I can get back to work?"

"Not so fast, I wasn't finished. According to this report, the only other place in your entire shop where

abrin was found other than the conservatory and on the gardening gloves and the shears, which is where you said it would be found, was in Jasmine Massey's teacup."

"But how can that be? If it was nowhere else, how would it end up in her cup?"

"This is why I had to release Tassi on house arrest. I don't have enough evidence to keep her here or officially charge her at this time. However, because of this in the report, her release is pending further investigation of the shop, which might take another day or two. It also means your shop has to remain closed while we make sure we didn't miss something, because you're right, it doesn't make sense."

Shay sat back and her mind raced with everything Dean had just shared. "I don't get it. If there was no poison in the teapot or anywhere else, then how in the world did the poison get into her cup? It had to have come from someplace, right?"

"Now you see my latest dilemma. This went from what should have been an easy case to one that's probably going to end my career."

"How so?"

"In two words: Peter Graham."

"Well, I can see that he wants this resolved. Jasmine and he had been together a couple of years, and I can only imagine that it's come as a big shock to him. I'm sure he's just lashing out as he's trying to make sense of this and wants answers as bad as the rest of us."

"You'd think so, but it seems to go deeper than that for some reason. I'm sure you know he's an influential lawyer in the county, if not the state, and he's made us aware that he has friends in high places including the state capital. So, I have the mayor breathing down my neck to get this closed ASAP to get Peter off his back before it goes any higher."

"Hmm, deeper you say?" Shay frowned and looked at Dean. "One thing I do know about abrin poisoning is while it's deadly in high enough doses, in lower doses it can also take a day or two to actually kill the person who ingested it. Jasmine was complaining about tummy issues that night. Could she have been given some crushed up poison beans over a few days leading up to the day of her death? Perhaps it was in something . . . say, like her lipstick, meaning it would have then transferred into the cup when she drank her tea."

Dean's eyes widened. "Look at you go all police detective on me. That's exactly the angle I'm looking at now. The problem is, I just got word from the district attorney, and Peter's not going to hand over any of her personal belongings for analysis without a warrant."

"But I thought he wanted answers?"

Dean raised his brows.

"Oooh . . . I bet we're thinking the same thing."

Dean weakly smiled and shrugged his shoulders, a gesture that suggested noncommittal agreement. Of course, that could only be her guess.

They sat in silence as Dean's fingers fidgeted with the folder in front of him, and Shay's mind buzzed with a million questions, but she took her cue from his narrowed lips. Family or not, he certainly wasn't going to offer up anything more to her, not with his career on the line and with a high-ranking official for a suspect breathing down his neck.

She thanked him for what he had shared, wished the deputy at the counter a good day, and scurried out onto the sidewalk, gasping for air with the realization of where her thoughts were leading.

Could Peter be Jasmine's killer, and if he was . . . why was he so willing to point the finger at his own daughter? Nothing about this made sense. No wonder Spirit had tried to protect Tassi from Peter last week when he showed up at the school and later had guarded her so vigilantly until her mother came from Carmel. Shay's senses spiraled, and she couldn't make sense of any of it. There was more going on than anyone suspected, and until she figured out what that was, Tassi might be in danger from the man who had just filed for full custody of her.

Chapter 13

Spirit was nowhere in sight, but Shay had a hunch where he'd gone. The same place she was headed now. Tassi needed them and most likely a large steaming cup of her favorite stress-reducing tea blend too. However, since Shay didn't have access to her shop, Tassi would have to settle for a mug of her once preferred mocha cappuccino.

She powered down hard on the pedals, flew down the incline of First Street, and sailed around the corner onto High Street. Panting, she leapt off her bike, released the kickstand, and hurried toward the entrance to Cuppa-Jo. Before she could open the door, it bounced open with the help of a hip check by Joanne as she edged out, balancing a tray of steaming coffees.

"Have a seat. I'll be right with you," she said to Shay as she scooted past her to a nearby table of six.

Shay peered through the glass door but couldn't spot an empty seat inside, and then scanned the patio area, which appeared to be just as full. "Okay . . ." She sighed and leaned against the brick wall beside the door. She glared at the yellow police tape still fluttering in the breeze around her shop entrance, and it broke her heart. The kickoff to the annual Fall Harvest Wine and Artisan Festival, one that rivaled even the biggest ones in the state, was fast approaching. Judging by the crowds at the coffee shop and up High Street, the participating wine growers and artisans were already converging on their little town. Add to that the tourists who wanted to make sure they had their choice of the best hotels or bed-and-breakfasts, and Shay saw potential profits swirl mercilessly down her business's drain.

"Stay positive," she mumbled to herself. "With any luck this will be over soon, and then it's back to business as usual."

"Sorry about that," huffed Joanne breathlessly, surveying the patio. "I think that couple over there"—she gestured as they gathered their packages from under the table—"are nearly done. If you can hang on a minute, you can have their table."

"Actually, I'm not staying. I heard Tassi was home, so I wanted to pick up a cup of her favorite mocha cappuccino. I thought it might help lift her spirits."

Jo's eyes darkened. "You haven't been home this afternoon?"

"No, why?"

"Then you don't know?"

"Know what? Come on, you're scaring me. What's happened?"

"I'll be right back," she said, then disappeared inside the coffee shop and returned with a large brown envelope. She slid the contents out and with a shaking hand gave it to Shay.

"What's this?" Shay stared at her and then glanced down at the paper. "A restraining order! What? From whom?"

"Read it. It was issued by none other than Peter Graham on behalf of the minor Tassi Graham."

"Does Tassi know about this?"

"Yeah, a copy was just delivered to Karen at my house, and I assumed one was also delivered to you, but if you haven't been home—"

"This is ridiculous," said Shay, reading the court order. "It says I'm not allowed to go within one hundred feet of her for any reason, and she isn't allowed to be within a hundred feet of me or Crystals & CuriosiTEAS." She looked anxiously at Joanne. "But I don't understand. What have I done?" Shay frowned, rereading the last paragraph. "Wait." She glanced across the cobblestone road to the door of her shop. "One hundred feet? That means she can't even come here to the coffee shop?"

"Yup, that's what it means, and why I also received a copy. So, if she shows up here and might on the off chance come in contact with you, I could put an end to it and send her on her way."

"I know Peter's grieving and probably blames me, but—"

"Did you miss the part where he says you're a bad influence on a young impressionable mind who has caused undue harm and stress to the minor, Tassi Elizabeth Graham?"

"No, I read it, but that's crazy."

"I know, and it kind of makes you wonder what other tricks he has up his sleeve."

"And why he's doing this." Shay reread the document again trying to comprehend what it all really meant, and shook her head. "I can't believe he actually got a judge to sign off on this, and so fast."

"Well, like I told you this morning, Peter Graham is a powerful, influential man with friends in high places."

Shay's eyes burned with tears. "What could his reason for this be? Does he think I somehow manipulated Tassi into killing Jasmine?"

"It kind of looks that way, doesn't it?"

"Which means he does really think Tassi poisoned her."

"Yeah, he made that clear last night, and I know Tassi's really upset. I think this might be enough to send her over the edge. Working for you has been the best thing that ever happened to her. It's really turned her around and given her a sense of purpose, and she loves you and Jen like the sisters she never had. This has devastated her."

The queasy feeling that hit Shay's stomach when a court deputy shoved a brown envelope into her hands while she was leaving Jo's followed her all the way down the crowded boardwalk as she pushed her bike toward home. Not even the aroma of deep-fried cinnamon and sugar–sprinkled churros—her guilty little pleasure—filling the evening air could tempt her. She was too busy mentally speculating on all the possible reasons for Tassi's dad's behavior. She knew from experience that grief wore many different faces and went through several phases, but something about his knee-jerk reaction didn't settle well with her. It wasn't just the sense that a piece of her heart had been ripped away because she had become so fond of Tassi and saw her as a little sister. There was something else triggering the man's actions and Shay shivered over the prospects.

Perhaps Peter Graham did murder his girlfriend. If she was pregnant, the news might not have sat well with him, and getting rid of her was the only way out that he could see. But . . . why would he set his own daughter up for the murder? What could he possibly have to gain by doing that? Those questions paled in comparison to the one eating away at her gut: What did he have to gain by cutting Tassi off from Shay and keeping her away from her and the tea shop?

After she got home and started brewing a pot of honey lavender tea—one mentioned in Bridget's journals to help relieve stress—it hit her. Peter was launching a defense for his daughter. This meant he was most likely attempting to create reasonable doubt in the minds of the jury by implicating Shay, the tea leaf reader and owner of the shop where his daughter was only an employee. If that line of defense resulted in a not guilty verdict for his daughter, he would get away with murder, create a solid case that Tassi was an unwilling victim of the crazy shop owner's influence, and bolster his side of the custody battle.

Shay turned off the kettle, rummaged through the drawer beside the pantry cupboard, and dug out a notepad and pen. She sat down at the small kitchen table and divided the blank page in front of her into three columns, labeling one Peter, one Tassi, and one Murder Evidence. If there was any way she could show evidence linking Peter instead of Tassi to the murder, Dean might have enough to question him and take all suspicion off Tassi, putting an end to this restraining order.

Crossing her fingers with her left hand, Shay scribbled away with her right, and after several minutes of writing and grumbling to herself, she read over what she'd written. Her chest heaved.

Abrin poisoning from a jequirity bean plant
None found in tea shop except in Jasmine's cup
    and traces in greenhouse on Tassi's work
    gloves, shears, and the floor where the plant
    landed
Tea brewed and served by Tassi (who had access
    to plant and beans earlier in the week)
Tassi held resentment toward Jasmine

None of this gave Shay any links to Peter, but it did make it clear why Dean considered Tassi the prime suspect in the murder. The only evidence Shay had that might link Peter to the murder was that Jasmine was feeling unwell before the reading. Of course, she could have been pregnant and suffering from morning sickness. However, if she wasn't, then Peter might have poisoned her over a couple of days, which brought her back to the lipstick theory. How else would the poison have ended up only in Jasmine's cup and no one else's?

A knock on the kitchen door made her jump, and

she shoved the notepad away. Patting her chest to put her heart back where it belonged and not in her toes, she opened the door. "Liam?" A rush of well-being washed over her. "What brings you by tonight?" she asked with a quick glance over his shoulder.

"If yer looking for Zoey, she's not with me. She and Gran are . . . well . . . let's just say they're trying to come to an understanding about certain things. I was heading out for a walk to clear me head and saw yer light on and thought . . ." He shrugged and glanced at her with a flicker of uncertainty in his eyes.

"Sure, come on in." She studied his face as he edged past her and took a seat at the table, and she inwardly winced. Either he was dog-tired after a long day or things at home were worse than he'd let on. "Want a cup of honey lavender tea?"

"What did ye say to me last night . . . oh yeah, if yer making it, then I'm drinking it." He chuckled weakly and pulled the notepad closer. "What's this?" He glanced over the page.

"You're the ex-detective. You tell me," she said with a wry laugh as she filled his cup.

"It looks to me like yer playing detective yerself."

"No, I'm just trying to make sense out of everything." She set the pot down and took a seat. "I got a restraining order today from Peter Graham, Tassi's dad."

"For what?"

"That's what I'm trying to figure out. For some reason I'm not to be within a hundred feet of her or her me, which also means she can't be at Cuppa-Jo with her aunt."

"Did it give a reason?"

"Apparently, I'm a bad influence on a young, impressionable mind."

"Ye gotta be kidding."

"Nope, that's what is says."

"So"—he glanced down at the page—"what did this tell ye?"

"Not what I was hoping it would."

"What do ye mean?"

"It seems Peter has it in his head that I'm running a witch's store or something. At least, that's what Jasmine said the first day she came in."

"Has he ever come into the teahouse himself?"

"Not that I know of, and if he'd come in when Tassi or Jen was working, I would have heard about it. Tassi told us this is the first time he's even been to Bray Harbor since her parents divorced."

"Then he could have been in when Bridget ran it?"

"I suppose. Maybe that's why he thinks it's a witch's store. She did have a lot of weird stuff in there before Tassi and I cleaned most of it out to make it more of a welcoming teahouse." Shay glanced at the pad and shook her head. "But sadly, everything I've come up with still leads to Tassi being the one with a motive and also access to the poison that killed Jasmine."

"What did Dean say?"

She relayed their afternoon conversation, including the part about the poisonous plant now being found in the wilds of California, and sat back. "But at this point, Dean doesn't have a link to Peter having access to a jequirity bean plant, and since he won't give up any of Jasmine's personal belongings for analysis until a warrant is issued, there's no way to prove that he did come across one and could have tampered with her belongings."

"Then we have to find a link between Peter and a jequirity bean plant."

"How are we going to do that?"

"I don't know, 'tis a catch-22 situation, isn't it?"

"What do you mean?"

"I mean, since Dean can't get a warrant to test Peter and Jasmine's belongings based on suspicion, and has to show some proof to get one issued, but one of the only ways he's going to get proof is to test their belongings, right? So . . . we'll just have to find another way to get him some proof. Now, ye say it's growing wild in the hills?"

"That's what Mia told Dean, but I was thinking. Perhaps the reason Dean hasn't got a warrant yet is because he's waiting to see if Jasmine was pregnant. If she was that could have been the cause of her nausea and not long-term exposure to abrin."

"Meaning," added Liam, "Peter might not have had anything to do with her death, which would save Dean from starting a career-ending investigation into the high-and-mighty Mr. Peter Graham."

"And all those *what-ifs* still only leave us with all the actual evidence pointing to Tassi as the prime suspect."

"Not necessarily." Liam tapped his finger on a line in her notes. "Dean might just be having a hard time finding a judge to sign off on a warrant for their hotel room and belongings. Especially if this Peter fellow is as connected as ye say he is in yer notes."

"Yeah, there's that too, I suppose. We can only hope

they find something there . . ." Absentmindedly, Shay circled the rim of her teacup with her fingers. "Because it still doesn't make sense as to how the abrin ended up in Jasmine's cup when it's nowhere else in the shop."

"Except upstairs."

"Yeah, where it should have been, given that's where it was growing for years."

Liam sat back, his gaze focused on the list Shay had written. "Who else at that reading besides Tassi wanted Jasmine dead?"

Stunned, Shay looked at him. "I don't think most of the group particularly liked her, but no one seemed to dislike her enough to kill her. At least, that's not the impression I got. There was bad blood between her and Julia, but to kill her"—Shay shook her head—"no, I never felt that."

"Well, someone wanted her dead, and until we figure out who that someone is, it looks like Tassi might stand trial for murder." He gestured to the notepad. "Because I agree with you. Everything you have on *here* points to her."

Shay grabbed the pad and wrote, *Find out more about Peter Graham, Tassi's past before her parents divorced, and when she came to live with her aunt, Jo, in Bray Harbor.* "What about that?"

"It's a good start, but if we want the answer, we have to ask the right question."

"What would that be?"

Liam slipped the pen from Shay's hand and wrote, *Find out more about Jasmine's past.* "Someone wanted her dead, so there must be a reason, and I don't think rubbing everyone the wrong way was enough to get her killed."

"Yeah, probably not, so there has to be something else."

"Then we have to dig. Who was Jasmine? It has to be someone from her past."

"What about my theory about Peter wanting her dead for some reason like her being pregnant?"

"If she was, then yes. It might be a good theory, but in cases like this, I always looked at the victim to see if there was someone in their past who might have wanted them out of the way. Sometimes it's not the obvious choice like Tassi or even Peter, but something or someone seemingly totally unrelated."

"Where do we start? Because if we start asking too many questions about Peter and Jasmine's past and Peter gets wind of us nosing around, it'll cause nothing but trouble, and I'll never be able to see Tassi again."

"Ye know me, I have a few contacts left in law enforcement and can make inquiries, but ye, *a chara*. Stay out of it."

Chapter 14

"**O**ut damned spot! Out, I say!" Lady Macbeth's famous line from Shakespeare's *Macbeth* rolled off Shay's tongue as she scrubbed a stubborn spot on her front step. It was no use. For all she knew that darkened area had been there since John O'Toole, a fisherman from Howth, Ireland, built the cottage after he founded Bray Harbor in 1854.

She tossed her scrub brush into the soapy water–filled bucket, sat back, and smiled with satisfaction at the results of her past two days of hard labor. Every inch of her cottage, inside and out, including the weathered whitewash on the outside, looked ten years newer. Even though she knew the wash down with a hose was only a quick fix, it would do until she could apply a fresh coat of paint. If her shop remained closed much longer, she saw a paint sprayer and buckets of white paint in her near future. "And that prediction"— she turned to Spirit, lying on the beach behind her, basking in the noon sun—"has nothing to do with reading my tea leaves or being a seer." She laughed.

He raised his head, glanced at her, moaned, yawned, and settled back down in the warm sand.

"And, by the way, thanks for all your help."

He let out a little *woof*, which sounded to her much like *whatever* as he didn't even open his eyes.

She shook her head, stretched out her neck, and gathered up her cleaning supplies.

Spirit raised his head, barked, and leapt to his feet, his tail wagging excitedly.

"Now what?" Shay scanned the porch.

"Allo, Shay, are ye here?" called a sweet, singsong voice from the side of the cottage.

"Out front, Gran," Shay called, then set down the bucket and wiped her hands on the knees of her cropped jeans as Gran toddled around the corner of the porch, carrying a basket nearly as big as she was. "Whoa, let me help you with that." Shay bolted off the porch to Gran's side and slipped the basket handle from her. "What's all this?" Shay peered into the basket. "Are you going on a picnic?"

"'Tis just a couple of small Irish stew pies made from last night's dinner. Liam just can't seem to get enough of me Irish stew." She pointed to a plate inside the basket. "There's a few boxty cakes and—"

"They look like potato pancakes."

"Aye, call 'em what ye will but boxty cakes it is. And, of course, some sweet breads, clotted cream, jams, and butter for after."

"It all looks *soooo* good. My mouth's watering just smelling it all."

"Then why don't ye put on a pot of tea, and we'll have a nice cup while we eat these before it all gets cold."

"Any preferences for the tea?"

"Strong and dark, just the way we Irish like it." She gave her a sly wink as Shay headed for the cottage door. "And I think ye'd better bring out three cups and an extra chair when ye come back."

"Is Liam joining us?" Shay's heart did a little flutter that she hoped didn't resonate in her cheeks, bringing out the mottled monster her alabaster skin could never hide.

"Liam?" Gran shook her head. "No, he's working at the pub today, but I can feel it on the wind. Company's a-coming, it is."

Shay eyed Gran suspiciously as she backed through the door. She knew through Liam that his gran was known as a seer back home, but to sense that they would be joined for an impromptu lunch seemed too far-fetched even for Shay. She shrugged. Only time would tell. Shay set about preparing the dark, rich black tea Gran had requested and hesitantly laid out three cups as instructed.

As she finished, she heard Gran laugh, and she wondered if the woman was chatting away with Spirit. However, when a male voice rumbled indistinctly through the closed door, Shay's shoulder blades tensed. How had the old woman forecasted such a thing? Gran's laughter broke Shay out of her questioning reverie, and a shiver coiled through her.

"Of course Gran must have invited someone to join us. Impromptu lunch, my foot," she mumbled as she set the tray on the front hall bench. Then she grabbed a folding chair from the small hall closet, tucked it under her arm, and balanced the tray with teapot, cups, and plates, which rattled as she slowly edged the screen door open with her hip.

"Dean?" she cried when she saw to whom the male voice belonged. "I didn't know you were joining us today."

"I . . . um, hadn't planned on it," he said sheepishly, rising to his feet from a wicker porch chair and taking the tray from Shay's hands. "I stopped by to give you some news and . . . well . . . it seems Gran has plenty of food and invited me to stay for a bite, if you don't mind."

"No, of course not." Shay opened the folding chair and took a seat between the two of them. "So, you just *happened* to stop by?" She looked skeptically at Gran, then at him.

"Yeah, I wanted to tell you that your shop's been cleared so you can reopen anytime now."

She shot an incredulous glance at Gran, who was sipping innocently on her tea, and then at Dean, her unexpected guest, and she swallowed hard. "That's . . . that's great news. Thank you."

Shay peered over at Gran again but there was no telltale look of "I told you so." Shay's mind skipped between what had just occurred with Gran's seer abilities, and with what Dean was saying about her shop finally being cleared to reopen, but when her thoughts finally settled she frowned. "That's great news," she said.

"Except Jen has an appointment this afternoon, and I don't think she'll be able to change it. And I suspect after your deputies have gone through everything, the shop will need a good cleaning before I can reopen." The thought of more cleaning made her inwardly cringe. "But I can do that after we eat I suppose, then I can open tomorrow." She tentatively smiled. "Yes, I can make it work," she confidently whispered to herself, her smile broadening.

"Good, then let's eat." Gran reached into the basket, removed the three individual-size Irish stew pies she'd brought, and set them on the plates.

Dean popped the last crumbs of his sweet bread into his mouth, sat back, rubbed his belly, and grinned. "I must say, Gran that lunch was the best surprise I've had in weeks. If they're not secret family recipes, I'd love to get them for Jen to try at home."

"Tosh." Giggling, she waved him off and deposited her dishes back into the basket. "I'd be happy to share them with ye."

"Good," he said, rising to his feet. "I hate to eat and run, but I do have a murder to solve." He picked up his sheriff's cap, stroked the brim between his fingers, looked hesitantly from Gran to Shay, and smiled. "Thanks again, this was great." He started down the porch steps but gripped the handrail and turned to Shay. "I wasn't going to do this because nothing has been initiated yet, but just in case, I probably should give you a heads-up on something that might be coming down."

"What's that?" asked Shay.

Dean's cheeks flushed as he drew in an uneven breath. "Peter Graham has been making noise about filing a civil lawsuit against you."

"You mean the restraining order against Tassi wasn't enough? He wants to sue me now too?"

"Yeah, so it seems." Dean's gaze dropped while he played with the brim of his cap again.

"What's he going to sue me for?"

"He wanted me to charge you for practicing without a fortune-telling license."

"What? Is there such a thing?"

"In some areas, yes, however, not in Bray Harbor, and I told him as much."

"But let me guess. He's not one to take no for an answer so a personal lawsuit is his next move?"

"Yup, after I told him a license wasn't required in Bray Harbor, he went to the DA's office to see if he could have you arrested for practicing witchcraft."

"What!" Shay shot to her feet and stared in disbelief at him. "Witchcraft?"

"Yeah, he's going back to the Witchcraft Act of 1735 passed in England, of which we were a colony at the time. It made it illegal to declare that a person was practicing witchcraft. The act ended witch-hunting in England and the colonies, but it also made being a witch illegal because the act made it illegal for anyone to claim they had magical powers."

"I've never claimed to be anything like that."

"I know, and the DA's office informed him that the act was repealed in England in 1951."

"Okay?" She crossed her arms over her heaving

chest as she struggled to fill her lungs. "So, the DA has no legal grounds to follow through, right?"

"Unfortunately, it was never superseded by an act of Congress. Someone wanting to persecute a person who claims to have magical power in the U.S. could invoke the ancient statute in a lawsuit."

"You're kidding?"

"Nope, the only thing the DA said was that it wasn't likely to go anywhere because of the First Amendment's guarantee of freedom of religion, which protects religious beliefs, including beliefs in magical powers and practicing them as long as they do no harm to others."

"There you have it. The tea leaf readings don't harm anyone because he can't possibly prove that's what killed Jasmine since no poison was found in the tea used during the group reading."

"This . . . is why the DA isn't keen to issue any charges even though he has state officials breathing down his neck. However . . ."

"However, what?"

"Peter is now seeking to file the civil lawsuit against you, using the same line of defense he did with securing the restraining order, which argued that your continued practice of witchcraft and forcing the minor Tassi Elizabeth Graham to participate in rituals of magic and witchcraft had a detrimental effect on a young, impressionable mind and caused undue harm and stress to the aforenamed minor."

"But I'm not a witch, so how exactly is he going to prove that I am?"

Gran placed her gnarled hand on Shay's arm and gave it a squeeze, telegraphing for her to keep quiet.

Dean shrugged. "I can only tell you the charges he told the DA's office he was going to file when they wouldn't charge you. If he follows through with his threats, I guess the rest is up to him to prove in court."

"So, I'm to be tried as a witch?"

"Sorry, Shay, I'm only giving you a heads-up. Nothing has been filed yet, but be prepared in case he does. Then any outcomes are for the courts to decide." He shoved his cap on his head and strutted down the wooden-plank sidewalk toward the terraced stairs.

Shay turned to Gran, who'd only just removed her hand from Shay's arm. "This is crazy. I'm not a witch. How in the world can he prove I am?"

"Perhaps yer not, but yer fourtime great-gran was also accused of being just that."

"What are you talking about?"

"Do ye know nothing about yer family legacy and the Early name?"

Shay shook her head.

"Sit, child. I think it's time we had a talk."

The fine hairs on the back of Shay's neck prickled. She suspected the iceberg she'd been avoiding since Gran had arrived was now directly in her path and there was no going around it or turning back.

Chapter 15

Shay shivered when a cold wind wrapped her in its arms. "You're saying that this great-great-great-great-grandmother of mine, this woman named Biddy Early, was a witch?" She sat down hard on the wicker chair beside Gran.

"Let's just say she was a healer and a seer, a follower of the old ways. Da term *witch* was used by the church folk to explain the dealings of those who work with elements they fear and don't understand." She turned to Shay and fixed her faded blue eyes on hers. "Remember, me dear, for as long as people have been people and getting sick and dying, herbal medicines have been used as cures. The people who concocted them were only seeking out remedies in nature to create medicines from herbs, plants, seeds, berries, bark, roots, and flowers. Much like the natives here in America did for millennia before the settlers came."

"Are you saying there are no such thing as witches, then?"

"Not like ye see in the storybooks about a black-cloaked hag stirring a boiling caldron under a full moon, at least. Aye, there are those who use their knowledge for bad or to bring harm to others, but most are just simple folk who have learned the ways of the natural world and use their gifts and talents to do good and help ease other people's troubles." Gran tsked and shook her head. "Ireland has had its fair share of troubles through the ages, ye know. Many a folk dying and suffering. At one time, it was one of the poorest countries in all of Europe, they said." Tears formed in Gran's eyes. "Aye, me country has had its share of grief, ye be sure of that. 'Tis no wonder why a woman like Biddy was sought out far and wide for her gifts. People actually called her the 'wise woman of Clare.' Even some of the priests did, they say."

"Interesting." Shay glanced at the cottage door and drummed her fingers on the knees of her cropped jeans. "If she was my great-great-great-great-grandmother, she was alive during the great potato famine, right?"

"Aye, she was that."

"I've read about the potato famine. Over a million people died during those times. The founder of Bray Harbor and the man who built this very cottage and lived in it, John O'Toole, a fisherman from Howth, came over after he lost his wife and two sons."

"It was hard times. Me own grandmam and Dadaí said food and money were scarce, and doctors, if there were any, were too expensive for most. The sick had no choice but to turn to herbalists and healers like Biddy during those dark years in Ireland."

Shay shook her head. "I can't even imagine what those poor people went through."

"The Irish are a resilient folk, though, me dear. They have followed the ways of the little people, ye know, de leprechauns, fairies and such, for so long that it's part of the culture. Could be why way back when the witch trials started over in England and Scotland it never took hold in Ireland. It was and is in our blood to look to nature and the fairies for answers. So, when a woman like Biddy came around, she was revered and sought out as a mystic and healer, which is why when she was charged with being a witch, it was dropped. The people loved her. She could give them hope, and if not, at least help them through their suffering."

"Is that how she became known as the 'wise woman of Clare'?"

"I think it had more to do with the fact that she was a woman ahead of her time. Until recently, the medical people dismissed and were suspicious of healing with plants and such. Now, those same treatments she used are recommended by doctors for ailments, and herbal extracts, tinctures, oils, and teas are found in chemists' shops, markets, and even on the internet, or so I'm told."

Gran refilled their teacups and stared off over the shoreline. A soft smile formed on her age-creased lips. "Biddy's gifts were so extraordinary that legends grew and spread about her. There was some that thought she was a descendent of the goddess Danu, ye know." She nodded and tenderly smiled. "Danu, like

Biddy"—she glanced at Shay—"and you, had a head of vibrant red hair that could be seen from far, far away. Ye see, Danu was known as the mother of the Tuatha de Danann. Dey were a tribe steeped in magic and healing and ruled Ireland four thousand years ago." Gran's voice drifted off into a singsong brogue as she recalled the ancient legend. "Over time, da Danann became the sidhe, the fairy folk or the Good People who lived in a parallel but invisible universe. The Good People taught Biddy's mother, Ellen, their language and skills, which she passed on to her daughter. Dey say the child then spent seven years away with the fairies. Fairy folk, Biddy was reported to have said when she returned, have a need to share their secrets and wisdom, and they did with her."

Shay shifted in her chair. "But aside from the myths and legends, what can you tell me about the woman herself and how my mother fits into the picture?"

Gran took a sip of her tea and set her cup on the small round side table. "Well, Biddy was born in lower Faha near Kilanena, County Clare, in 1798 to a man named John Thomas Connors, a poor farmer, and his wife, Ellen, who had learned the old ways of healers and who baptized their wee girl as Bridget Ellen Connors. However, her mam's family name had been Early, and later Biddy, as she became known as, took on and kept the Early name even though she was married four times. She always kept her mam's family name, believing her gifts were inherited through the women in the family. After all, her mother had taught her all about herbs and how to make potions, just as her own mother had taught her and her mother before that."

"So, this Biddy's mother was a healer too?"

"Aye, and well known in the county too for her herbal cures. She started teaching her little girl her family recipes from a young age. As a matter of fact, dese recipes were regarded as family secrets and were to be guarded no matter what, which was common for the time. Like I said before, if everyone had them, then no one would seek out the healers, right?" Gran chuckled. "Sadly, though, when Biddy was sixteen years old, her mother died, leaving her in charge of the household. Den just six months after, her father died too. Such a young girl herself, she couldn't pay the landlord's rent and had to leave her home."

"Did she make a living selling her teas and cures?"

"It's hard to say. Not much is known about those years in her life. Most think she wandered the county roads working wherever she could along the way and learning more about herbal cures. As time went on, she started to make a name for herself as a healer and seer, and, of course, as her reputation grew, so did the legends and stories about her." Gran glanced over at Shay with sparkling eyes. "They say Biddy's powers came from a mysterious blue bottle she used to conjure her potions and help her see things no one else could. How this bottle came to her no one knows for certain, but it's said it was gifted to her by none other than Titania, Queen of the Fairies."

Shay's mind flashed with an image of the picture hanging in the back room of the tea shop. "Really?"

"Aye," Gran eyed her, smiling, "and her blue bottle was never found after her death." Her gaze remained focused on Shay. "Some said it was because the fairies came back to collect what was theirs. Others say they took it to make sure it went to the next Early daughter in line. But who knows for certain?" Gran gave her an impish wink.

Shay reflected on what Gran had just told her as her fingers played with the tether on the leather pouch she wore under her shirt. "It's said that in every legend there is a basis of truth."

"Aye, dey do dat," said Gran, rising to her feet, "but I'm afraid I have to take me leave now."

"Wait. The other day you said something about a picture. Did you mean the one of my birth mother, Bridget, holding me when I was a baby?"

"Nah, it's one of yer gran and great-gran."

"My gran and great-gran?" Shay glanced down at the bulge under her blouse, and her eyes widened. "The bottle didn't disappear, did it? After Biddy died, it was passed down in the family and eventually went to my mother Bridget, and now me, right?"

"Aye, I expect that's how it went," said Gran, rearranging the containers in the basket.

"Then I'm not just any Early, but a descendant of Biddy Early, the famous Irish witch?"

"Der's no doubt about dat." Gran grinned at her over the basket.

Shay sat straight up and let out a soft gasp. "But that also means, since I don't have a daughter, the Early legacy will die with me, right?"

"Who's to say ye won't?" Gran playfully winked as she looped her arm through the basket's handles, then turned toward the steps. "Der's more at play here than ye know," she softly chuckled.

An image of electric-blue eyes highlighted by a boyish grin filled her mind, and her heart rate quickened, but she quickly brushed it off when an equally strong one of a pair of bewitching forest-green eyes followed, leaving her cold and empty inside. "I wouldn't hold your breath," she muttered and stared at Gran when she started to descend the steps. "Please wait. There's so much I need to ask you. What can you tell me about the Earlys? I need to know about Biddy's children. Her descendants are relatives of mine, and I'd like to track some of them down. Maybe I'm not the last Early daughter."

"'Tis said Biddy had many children, being married four times and all, but most were laddies. Other than yer great-grans, gran, and yer mam, any other lassies born from de lads wouldn't have had a pure bloodline to the Early women's magic and all that holds. So, me dear, for now, at least, ye are the last of the genuine Early women."

"Can you tell me about the others, my uncles, cousins, any of them? At least the ones you know of, and if there's anyone left I could get in touch with. Since I discovered Bridget was my mother, I've been so lost and feeling unconnected to family."

"I know it must have come as a shock ta ye, and I will, me dear, but right now, I think there's just time for a wee nap before I get Liam's supper cooking." Gran smiled and shifted the basket onto her other arm.

Shay leaned forward in her chair. "But there must be more you can tell me about Biddy and her magic before you go."

Gran waved her free hand dismissively. "I could, but it's hard to know truth from legend anymore. If ye want to learn more about what others said of Biddy and her gifts, I think ye can read some of those tales on that internet thingy. Then ye can make up yer own mind about her from there." She studied Shay's face intently and grinned. "Ye might even put yer mind at rest about yer family and find there's great magic in that family line of women and that ye've inherited many of her qualities. Not to mention de hair." She chuckled as she stepped down onto the wooden sidewalk.

"Okay, I'll check it out." Disappointment settled into Shay's chest, and she sat back. The rolling waves crashing onto the beach momentarily lulled Shay into a mental place where she could try to digest everything Gran had told her, but then beads of perspiration formed on her brow. "Oh no!" She shot upright in the chair. "Did you just say her life is documented on the internet?"

"I did. De facts as well as de legends," Gran said from the side of the porch.

"That's not good." Shay's voice teetered on hysteria, as she leapt to her feet.

"But ye wanted to know more about her. Aside from a library, it's da best place, I guess."

"But don't you see? If Peter Graham makes good on his threat to sue me for practicing witchcraft and gets hold of that information, it will prove his case."

"Hmm . . . dat it would, wouldn't it? I guess we'll just have to see what can be done. Don't worry, child. Trust in de fae and in all de gifts ye've inherited." She paused at the end of the railing where it attached to the cottage and gazed up at Shay on the porch. "Even those ye have chosen to ignore." She smiled and disappeared down the side path to the back gate.

Chapter 16

Shay's eyes widened as she flipped from one article to the next in her search on her laptop for information about the famous Irish witch Biddy Early. It was all here just as Gran said it would be. Article after article established the notoriety surrounding Biddy, especially after 1903, when her life story was first published. Articles illustrated how she would gather herbs and plants before sunrise to ensure the morning dew was still present on them, believing that the secret to her cures was the dew, which represented the secretion of the light of dawn and the key element in eternal life.

A multitude of articles discussed the blue bottle Biddy had mysteriously acquired and elaborated on how it had become as famous as she was. Researchers and writers seemed to agree that all Biddy had to do was look into the dark mixture within the blue bottle, and she would know the correct cure for her visitor.

Then Shay's breath stuck in the back of her throat when she read the following:

> *In 1865 Biddy was accused of witchcraft under the Witchcraft Act of 1586 and was brought before a court in Ennis. This would have been unusual in Ireland in the 1860s since most witchcraft trials had stopped. However, when the few who agreed to testify against her later backed out, she was released for lack of sufficient evidence. Many local people including the county priests supported her healing practices.*

Shay tossed her laptop on the sofa beside her. It was all there on the internet in black and white for everyone to see, including the fact that Biddy Early was arrested and stood trial for practicing witchcraft. This information would be a gold mine in Peter Graham's hands, and there was nothing she could do to stop him from finding it.

Her phone pinged out a text alert. She snatched it from the trunk-style table and glanced at the message.

I'm free now for a few hours. I can meet you at the shop to help clean. See you soon! xxx

Shay smiled. Jen always seemed to know exactly when Shay needed her help most, and it made Shay wonder which one of them actually had the inky feelings. She laughed, and by the time she got to the door, Spirit, tail wagging, was already sitting there, the strap for her bike helmet between his teeth.

"You and Jen are both something else." She laughed

and off they went. Spirit led the way up High Street, as usual, and Shay pedaled like a madwoman in an attempt to keep up. When they arrived at Crystals and CuriosiTEAS, the cold hand of dread gripped her chest as she scanned the front of her shop. Thoughts of Tassi's dad making good on his threat to have her teahouse closed down, one way or another, brought the tears that had been burning behind her eyes to her cheeks. It seemed no matter the outcome of the murder investigation, Peter, by way of threatening to sue her for practicing witchcraft and endangering Tassi, was more determined than ever to end the legacy of Bridget's lifelong work.

The fading red banner over the shop entrance fluttered in the sea breezes, and the two rustic wooden benches that sat in front of the bay windows still invited passersby to sit and rest their weary feet. Shay recalled the delight Tassi had in planting the wildflowers in the two large ceramic pots that bookended the benches and now spilled over with blooms. The thought that the legacy that Bridget had entrusted to Shay by way of her bequeathment could soon be gone forever caused the ghostly hand that gripped her chest to spread its cold fingers to the pit of her stomach.

She pushed the glass door open and took a deep breath in the hopes that the mixed aromas of pungent, earthy smells and seductive spices lingering in the air would invoke the much-needed calm over her as it had in the past. "Jen, are you here?"

"In the back," her sister called from the back room. She opened the door with one hand, and with the other she patted the coiled blond braid piled on top of her head. "I brought coffee. I thought two hours of cleaning required something with a bit more kick than tea."

"You'd be right about that." Shay scanned the disheveled shop between the front door and the door her sister held open to the back room and feared what she would find behind that door.

"Have you talked to Liam yet?" Jen asked.

"No, I haven't even seen him for the past couple of days, which is really annoying and frustrating. I should be the one out there gathering information to try to clear Tassi's name, not him."

"Except you don't have the contacts he has, and I'm pretty sure he, being an ex-detective, will be able to get information you can't."

"I know, but she worked for me, and I feel so responsible for what happened because it's my tea shop, and I was the one who brought all those people together." Shay sighed. "I just feel so useless."

"Well, you're not useless. From what you told me, you've acquired some pretty good housekeeping skills the past two days, so grab a rag and let's get this shop sparkling again so we can open for business tomorrow morning."

Shay frowned. "Yeah, I guess, but even the thought of that right now makes me feel inadequate."

"How so?"

"Because without Tassi picking up the evenings and you having family obligations, I'll be putting in twelve-hour days, and I'm not sure with all this murder stuff and Peter's threats of a lawsuit that I have the heart for that right now. Plus, I have to get all the inventory back up before the festival."

"Do I sense a pity party coming on?"

"No, I'm just being realistic."

Jen looked at her with sparkling blue eyes. "Then you're going to want to hear what I have to tell you."

"What? You can work evenings now?"

"No, that hasn't changed, and it won't. Family first, remember?"

"I'm family too." Shay put on her best little-girl pouty lip.

"You are, but you know what I mean. Dean and I finally have some quality time together since he got the promotion to sheriff and works mostly days, and with the kids and their schedules, I need to be home in the evenings, but . . ."

"But what?"

"You aren't going to believe who I ran into today at the library when I was there volunteering for Hunter's class field trip."

"Who?"

"Faye Cranston."

"Who?"

"Faye, the woman who's a member of the Little White Glove Society. The lady you said reminded you of Dorothy from that old television show."

"Right, the one with the cleaning disorder."

"Yes, her. She was there working as a volunteer in the library, and we got to talking."

"Okay . . ." Shay eyed Jen suspiciously.

"It seems her husband died a few years back, and she's really been struggling with that. So, she's been seeing a therapist who advised her to go back to work at least part-time, which was why she was helping out at the library."

"That makes sense. The only way I managed to make it through the last couple of days was to stay busy and not think about everything that was going on."

"Exactly what he told her. Anyway, she then asked about Tassi, wondering how she was holding up after that horrible evening. I told her—"

"You didn't tell her about the restraining order, did you?"

"Of course not. I only told her that Tassi was taking it pretty hard and would be taking some time off."

"Good."

"Then she told me"—Jen grinned—"that she and her late husband used to own a chain of restaurants in San Diego."

"And?"

"And although it's been years since she waited tables that's how she started out with their first restaurant. He cooked, and she ran the front of the house, and then she asked if maybe she could work a couple of Tassi's evening shifts."

"Isn't she afraid of what the Little White Glove Society ladies might say about her working here?" Shay stuck her nose in the air and pretended to sip from a teacup with her pinky sticking straight out. "Waiting tables isn't a very prestigious job." She giggled at her failed attempt at sounding posh.

Jen quirked an eyebrow at Shay's antics. "That's why she offered to work evenings, I guess. They aren't around then, and they'd probably never know. She said it would help with her therapy immensely while also helping us out now that we're in a staffing crunch."

"Hmm . . ." Shay fixed her gaze on the floor, hoping that the wooden planks would give her an answer. "I don't know, but we're desperate, aren't we? The problem is, I wouldn't be able to leave her here alone, at least to start."

"I know it's not a perfect plan, but if she works out, maybe you could get at least a few hours' break in the evenings to harvest and dry the herbs that we're going to need to refill all those." Jen waved her hand toward the empty jars and bottles that were once filled with dried teas and herbs before Dean and his deputies had confiscated them for lab analysis.

"Yeah," said Shay. "At least I'd still be here to lock up at closing."

"That's what I was thinking, so yes? You think we should take her up on her offer?"

"Well . . . we have no choice, do we?" Shay said hesitantly as she continued to struggle with the idea of bringing in an outsider. The tightness across her chest extended to her tummy, settling like a rock in the pit of her stomach, and just when everything had been working so well with Tassi. Over the past year, they had created a nice, cozy family type of group here. It worked out so well, for all of them, but . . . she was going to have to face facts. That had all changed.

Her mind raced with thoughts and she conveyed each one to her sister as they popped into her head. "I mean, I could post the position, and we could hold interviews . . . but we wouldn't have anyone in place immediately. With the festival coming up, I'm going to be busy enough replenishing our shelf stock. If we hire her, she could start soon, and with any luck, Tassi will be back by festival time. By then, Faye would be into the full swing of how we do things and could help out with that too." Shay drew in a deep breath. "So . . . yes, why not? Let's give it a shot."

"Good, because I already told her she could start tomorrow."

"You did what?" Shay threw the soggy cleaning rag at Jen, who ducked it with the lithe motion of a cat on a hot stove.

The next morning Shay was busy with the revolving door of hordes of visitors and customers. A sense of crushing panic niggled in her stomach as she kept an eye on the dwindling supply of tea blends disappearing off the shelves. *Some seer I am,* Shay thought. If she had been worried that being closed down for almost a week was going to hurt her business, her crowded shop proved her wrong . . . again.

However, it didn't take her long to figure out that not everyone dropped in for tea and goodies, and she excused herself from a few tables of nosy guests clearly there for gossip about the murder instead of tea. In her mind, if the tea drinkers also happened to get a free side dish of gossip, it appeared that none of them were complaining. Maybe that should be her new sales pitch. She glanced at the gold lettering on the windows and grinned as she refilled another guest's teapot with water. Yeah, clearly her instincts were off when it came to tea leaf and other readings, so she should just forget about that and offer tea and local gossip as the shop's main draw. That appeared to be what a lot of patrons were after today anyway.

She smiled at Cora as she rang up her bill for her share of the Little White Glove Society's table and drew in a deep breath of relief as she waved the last straggling members of the group off.

"Jen, are you okay to clean up on your own before the lunch-hour rush starts?" Shay asked when her sister flew by with the gray bussing bins. "I really should get upstairs and start harvesting, or we're not going to have anything to sell."

"Sure," Jen called back over her shoulder as she started dumping napkins and plates into the top bin. "I'll give you a shout when things get too busy for me on my own."

"Perfect." Shay ascended the spiral staircase to the greenhouse and came to a halt. The same sense that had overcome her the day Spirit had stood guard by the poison table rushed through her now. Some of her instincts might be lacking lately, but this sensation of foreboding didn't appear to be one of them. Something was wrong, but what?

She scanned the rows of raised plant tables, but everything looked as it should. She even got down on the floor to inspect under the now empty poison plant table, hoping there might be a rosary bean the police had missed and that was what was causing her feelings of uneasiness, but there was nothing. It was clear they had been thorough in their crime scene investigation. She stood up, grabbed her pruning shears from the pot-

ting table, and headed to the herbs she needed. However, the sense that something was off still gnawed at
her gut, and the warmth from the pouch around her
neck grew increasingly uncomfortable and stung her
skin.

"Shay, are you up here?"

She swung around. Faye Cranston's salt-and-pepper
head of hair came into view as she climbed to the top
of the wrought iron staircase.

"Hi, yes, out here in the greenhouse."

"Jen told me it would be okay if I came up. I hope
you don't mind." Faye made her way past the stairwell
and joined Shay.

"Not at all. I was just going to start harvesting. What's
up?" Shay set her shears back on the potting table.

"I was hoping that you'd let me start orientation for
my new job this afternoon."

"But don't you and the other society members generally go shopping or something in the afternoons? I
heard Cora say this morning that Martins in Monterey
has a big fall sale. I assumed you were all taking a
drive to go to that."

"No, she's going there. Her husband, the mayor, has
some meeting he has to attend, and the others had er-
rands or work, and . . ." Her gaze dropped. "I suddenly
felt lost. I had nowhere else to go. Afternoons are
tough on me, you see. I was so used to being busy with
the restaurants and arranging food orders and deliver-
ies for our five locations that I'm really struggling now
that it's all gone." Tears formed in her eyes. "Being part
of the Little White Glove Society since moving here
last year has been a big help in filling my mornings,

but . . ." Her fingers played aimlessly over the leaves of a thyme plant beside her. "The afternoons and evenings are still empty since my George passed."

The dark hand of sadness waved over Shay. Being empathic she could feel others' sadness as well as their joy, and from what flushed through her now, Faye needed relief from her deep-seated sorrows. "I can't see why not. There should be a clean apron hanging on the hook by the food dehydrators in the kitchen. If you want to put one of those on and follow Jen around, she can show you where everything is. I'll be down in a while, and we can see what else you need to get started."

"Thank you." Faye poised her hands in a prayer pose, and her face beamed.

When Faye walked away, Shay smiled at the bounce to her step that hadn't been there when she had arrived. She picked up her shears and clipped rosemary sprigs, which were good for relieving stress; thyme; and mint leaves. These three ingredients helped build the variety of bedtime tea blends, which were some of her biggest sellers.

After she had collected what she needed from one table to help temporarily replenish her supplies, she moved on to harvesting stalks of lemongrass, a deliciously green, citrusy-scented tall grass that helped reduce inflammation, lower cholesterol, and relieve anxiety. She'd also discovered that it was a great additive to most of her other tea blends too, not only because of its healing properties, but because lemongrass's fragrant aroma and flavor added a little zing to other blander or bitter-tasting herbs, such as valerian root, which, in Shay's mind, tasted like dirt.

Speaking of dirt, she rubbed her gloved hands together in anticipation of harvesting her favorite root, dandelion. Digging them up from the fresh soil with her trowel always took her back to the days when she and Jen were little girls digging out the dandelions from their parents' lawns. Her mother would actually pay them one cent for each plant they dug out. Little did Shay know then about the health benefits of this so-called weed.

She held the root ball up and smiled. It was a perfect detoxifying herb with mild diuretic properties, and very popular with many of her customers because it could also be used as a coffee substitute.

She glanced down into the large divided wicker tray she used to sort the cuttings and mentally calculated that she had more than enough for the first batch of drying. She glanced at her phone, checked the time, and hurried downstairs. As she balanced the tray in one hand and gripped the iron railing with the other, she reminded herself to add to the top of her current to-do list that she needed to install an elevator, or at least a pulley system for the trays. The thought of spiraling down the stairs and landing on top of her produce had her wincing in imagined pain.

After filling the small food dehydrator that Bridget had left and the larger one she had purchased, she washed up, put on a clean apron, and went into the front, fully expecting to find chaos since it was approaching afternoon teatime, even though Jen hadn't sent out a call for help. She hoped her sister hadn't made a mistake in hiring Faye on the spot and wasn't trying to save face and suffer silently through the consequences.

She stepped through the backroom door and froze. "What happened?" Shay muttered as she scanned the room, buzzing with customers. She blinked and rubbed her eyes. Faye was serving and chatting with customers. Jen, once again, had managed to bring what should have been a chaotic service to order and had customers lined up like schoolchildren at the counter to pay their tabs.

"Need some help?" Shay whispered in Jen's ear.

"Nope, all under control. You'll just throw our rhythm off. Feel free to go back to what you were doing." Jen smiled and thanked the customer she was serving and turned to Shay. "Seriously, everything is working out great. Faye really knows what she's doing and has this place running like a machine. So scoot, we're fine out here." She waved Shay away and smiled at the next two women in line.

"Okay then." After watching Faye explain the goodie cart and how the pricing worked, Shay went over to the open shelving units of packaged tea blends, made a mental note on which flavors she needed to start packaging first, and headed into the back room.

"Hi, Miss Myers."

Shay turned to see Mia's student Lilly Sullivan at the door. "Hi, Lilly, but please call me Shay," she said, walking over to her.

"Okay, Shay. We have your empty plant pots outside in the van. Did you want us to bring them in the back door?"

"Don't you need them?"

"No, Professor Harper likes to use the ones the college has. It keeps everything uniform for watering, and growing. You know, for the research and the tests we have to conduct."

"I see. Sure, if you want to drive around back, I'll open the door."

"That's what I thought." She looked around the full tearoom and chuckled. "I'd guessed that hauling them through here wouldn't be a great idea."

"Not really." Shay smiled. "Have the plants been beneficial to your studies?"

"Yes, it's amazing the collection you had. Some of them we could only read about since we never had the real specimens to work with, and it's so cool. Others, like that rosary bean plant you gave us?"

Shay nodded.

"We had one that we found at the side of the road just growing there. Professor Harper thought perhaps someone had found it growing in the wild, taken it home, and then found out how deadly the beans were and just dumped it."

"I hope they didn't find out after an incident with a child or a pet."

"That's what she said. But the coolest thing is your plant must be the real deal and directly from India because after running some lab tests we discovered that genetically it's even more toxic than the one we had."

"Even more poisonous?"

"Yeah, something must have been genetically changed with the other one. It still maintained its poisonous qualities, but not like the one that had been cultivated in a closed environment."

"I still can't figure out why Bridget, the woman who left me the shop and greenhouse, would have had that plant or any of the poisonous ones."

"A friend of mine, Jennifer, has a necklace that was her mom's, and she said her mom had bought it from the woman who used to run this store. I was looking at it one day, and it had rosary beans on it. I know that the beans were used for centuries in jewelry making. So maybe that woman used the beans to make jewelry as a side hustle."

"Yes, but you also must have read that thousands of workers died over the years after pricking their fingers while stringing the beans because they are highly toxic." Shay shivered. "So, be careful with it, but I'm really happy to hear the plants have been so useful to your studies."

"Oh, they are. Even my lab partner, Stephen, the guy with the glasses who was driving that day, found them useful. For his literature class, he wrote about Agatha Christie's poison garden, the one she had in Torquay, England. Did you know she was a pharmacy assistant back in World War One, and in most of her books, poison is the murder weapon? She had a garden where she grew a lot of the plants she used in her books. How cool is that? Talk about doing research for books. Anyway, he did his paper on her poison plant garden and got an A."

"So, Agatha Christie used a lot of the same plants in her stories?"

"I don't know if they were the same ones as yours, but Stephen said she did use the same plants she grew in her garden as murder weapons in a lot of her books."

"Did she ever use rosary or jequirity beans as the murder weapon?"

"I don't know. English lit isn't my thing, but he's driving the van today, so when we bring in the empty pots, you can ask him."

"I will, thank you. Okay, see you around back in a minute."

Lilly hurried off, and their words left Shay thinking. What if the killer didn't have actual knowledge of abrin poisoning but had read about it being used in one of Agatha Christie's stories, or some other book, and it just happened to be the same murder weapon that had been growing in her greenhouse? The question now was, how would Dean take her latest theory? It would certainly open up a whole new pool of suspects.

Chapter 17

Stephen was little help when Shay posed the question to him about rosary beans being used in a murder mystery novel. He couldn't recall for certain but didn't think Agatha Christie had used that particular plant in any of her stories. Although, he did say when he and Lilly finished the latest lab project they were working on for Ms. Harper's class, he would double-check to make sure he was right, and also do some research to see if any other novelists had.

Shay had a sinking feeling that she was back to square one. If the killer hadn't learned about using the plant as a murder weapon from a novel, did that make the rosary bean plant a weapon of convenience? After all, it had been growing in her greenhouse, it was her tea shop that had brought all those people together, and clearly one of them had been a killer. That meant, in some respects, she was responsible for a woman dying right in front of them.

She knew in her heart, and as Gran had pointed out,

it wasn't her fault *directly*. However, the fact of the matter was, it did happen in her shop, making it her duty to find out why and how it happened. Stephen's news only left Shay bubbling up with even more resentment over the situation as she waved him and Lilly off when they'd finished taking the empty pots upstairs.

She should be the one trying to find out what led to Jasmine's death instead of cleaning and scrubbing her cottage and tea shop just to take her mind off what Liam was working on behind the scenes. To make it worse, there hadn't been a word from him in two days. No text, no calls, and no drop-in visits.

Shay whipped off her apron. "Jen, since you and Faye seem to have everything under control, I'm going out for a few minutes, okay?" Her voice held the commanding tone of a decree rather than a question.

"Um, sure . . ." Jen looked curiously at her, then returned to scooping out some dried thyme into a small bag for a customer.

Shay dashed next door to Madigan's Pub, gave her eyes a moment to adjust to the abrupt change in lighting, and eased her way to the bar through a group by the door waiting for a table. She stood there a moment, then cleared her throat.

"Be with you in a moment," called the silver-haired bartender Carmen over her shoulder as she was filling the second of two jugs of beer from a large keg on the back counter. She swung around and set them down with a thud. "Jugs up," she called to one of the servers, who whisked them away for a thirsty group off in the back corner.

Carmen's face, deeply etched by too many years spent in the sun, broke into a wide-mouthed grin. "Well, if it isn't my favorite psychic lady. How you doing today, hon?"

Shay shook herself from her internal guessing game of how Carmen managed to spike her silver hair into such deadly looking points. "I'm okay, but judging by how busy it is in here, I should be asking you how you're doing."

"I'm great, but I sure don't remember it being this busy before the fall festival last year. Not sure what's up. Maybe it's the weather. Seems more like summer than fall, yeah?"

"I heard the wineries had their best growing season in years, so maybe everyone's started celebrating their good fortune early."

Carmen leaned across the bar and whispered with a chuckle, "As long as all their so-called wine groupies still come in here for craft beer, I'm happy." Then she added, "Now, what can I do for you? Since it's teatime, I know you didn't come in for a jug of our new craft beer, so what's up?"

"I was looking for Liam. Is he up in the office?"

"No, sorry. He and Zoey went to Monterey yesterday."

"Monterey? Yesterday?"

"Yeah, I think he had a meeting with one of our distributors, and Zoey had something she had to do, so they decided to make a little vacation out of it."

"A vacation?" Shay's eyes narrowed. *How could he do that now? He knows how important it is to clear Tassi.* It was no wonder she hadn't heard from him. He was probably lounging poolside at some fancy hotel. The thought made her dig her nails into her palms to keep from screaming.

"Um, yeah." Carmen eyed her uncertainly. "He said they'd be back later today, tomorrow at the latest, though, if that helps?"

"Thanks." Shay tried to paste a smile of gratitude on her face, but she sensed it came off more like a snarl when she saw the look on Carmen's face.

"I'll tell him you were looking for him," she said meekly as Shay spun on her heel toward the door.

"Nah, that's okay. It's not important." Shay stopped and looked back. "Is Gran here today?"

Carmen shook her head as she grabbed another jug. "She said she had something to do, so she wouldn't be in."

"Okay, thanks." Shay shielded her eyes as she stepped into the afternoon sunlight and dashed back into the tea shop. Her earlier resentment shot from bubbling to a rapid boil when she glanced over at Faye chatting freely with two of Shay's regular afternoon customers. In her current mood, the sight didn't settle well on her already unsettled stomach. She gritted her teeth at the nerve of the woman carrying on with so much ease like Faye and the customers were old friends and this was *her* shop.

Liam's face popped in her thoughts, and she bit her inner cheek. How dare Liam take off when he promised her he would investigate Peter's and Jasmine's pasts. He couldn't possibly leave everything hanging in limbo. Didn't he know that it was tearing her and Tassi apart and . . .

She glanced over at Faye again as she casually but professionally explained the sandwich and goodie options to a foursome who had just sat down. Liam and Zoey had probably stayed at some five-star hotel last night, and here she was cleaning and scrubbing and . . . She gasped and clasped her hand over her mouth as her mind ricocheted between erratic emotions. *Whoa!* Was this the green-eyed monster of jealousy rearing its ugly head?

Shay couldn't believe where she'd let her thoughts take her. This wasn't her. Faye was a great addition to the team and had slipped into her new role effortlessly. Shay should be grateful. As for Liam and Zoey, any feelings she had for him were in the past, and she and Zoey had become friends. She should be happy for all these people. *So, why am I not?*

"Faye's a dream, isn't she?" whispered Jen after she slid up to Shay's side. "Even after Tassi comes back, I hope we can find a way to keep her on. With her experience in the industry, it took her all of two minutes to streamline the service, the trolley, and organize the kitchen."

"She seems efficient," said Shay, studying Faye's serving skills. "But let's not get ahead of ourselves here. It's her first day. Let's see how it works out, okay?"

"Yeah, for sure, but . . ." Jen took off her apron. "Now that you're back, Faye said she had everything under control, and I should take off early. She said it would be a nice change for the kids if I was there when they got home from school."

"She did, did she?"

"I agree. It's been a while since I was there after school. I think it would be a nice treat for us all."

How could Shay argue with that? If she did, she would come across as the ogre in this scenario, but the idea that Faye was now in charge—her first day on the job— was enough to take Shay's resentment from simmering to boiling over—again. "I need a cup of lemon balm and chamomile tea." If she didn't relax immediately, she *would* say something she'd regret.

"Enjoy your evening," she called out to Jen as she darted into the back room and frantically filled the kettle.

She gripped the edge of the counter while she waited for it to boil, and counted . . . one . . . two . . . three . . . Then she drew in a deep, slow breath in hope of easing the pressure building inside her head. This was not her. This person she'd become was a stranger. Tears leaked from the corners of her eyes as she prepared the tea, and poured out a cup, then slid onto a chair. She pulled her knees up and cradled the warm cup in her hands. *Breathe, just breathe.* She repeated as a mantra while she took in the heavenly natural aromas of the delicate flowery scent of chamomile with its hint of the minty citrus notes of the lemon balm, and then sighed with relief when the elixir finally began to work its magic.

In that moment it seemed that for the first time since the tea leaf reading, her head stopped spinning. She took another sip and let the comfort in her cup pour through her. It was as though the entire week the world had gone sideways, and she wasn't in charge of her own thoughts or emotions. She'd been in reaction mode, not action mode, and the sense of losing control had overwhelmed her.

She sat up straight with the realization that it had nothing to do with Faye, Liam, or Zoey. It all came back to staring death in the face and not being able to do anything about it, but that was about to change. *Bridget*. She needed Bridget's help if she was going to figure any of this out. She needed to talk to her mother, and that's something she hadn't done since that night.

She leapt up and started toward the spiral staircase. Her foot slipped on the bottom rung. To catch herself before she hit the wall, she grabbed at the black curtain that was draped around the perimeter of the back room. The curtain slipped, revealing the corner of the painting that hung at the bottom of the stairs. She purposely kept the painting hidden from curious onlookers who might raise too many questions about her resemblance to the red-haired woman portrayed as the fairy princess receiving the blue bottle from Titania, Queen of the Fairies. That bottle and the properties it contained had been the reason two people had died the previous year. It would only take one person who was familiar with the Irish legends to put two and two together and figure out Shay was now in possession of that legendary amulet.

She lived in fear every day that someone would discover her secret. Not even her own sister knew she had it in the rare blue diamond around her neck. The possibility that someone else could lose his or her life over it was too much for Shay to imagine. As Shay glanced at the picture in passing, a sense of urgency rushed through her. "*Use your gifts*," said a gentle whispered voice as it brushed across her ear. *"Don't second-guess. Trust your gifts. . . ."*

"Bridget." She grabbed the wrought iron railing to steady her wobbling legs. "You're right. I have been ignoring them," Shay whispered back at the painting. "Reacting, not acting. I need to find Gran. She can help me refocus."

She dashed over to the backroom door, flung it open, and came face-to-face with Faye. "Hi . . ." Startled, Shay feigned a smile and took a step back. "Ah, perfect timing. I was just coming to find you to let you know I had to—"

"Good, because I wanted to talk to you too."

"Sure," Shay said hesitantly. She studied the woman's flustered face and then guilt set in about her earlier reaction to Faye's very existence, it seemed, borne out of what? Shay wasn't certain, but right now she had a sinking feeling that Faye had picked up on it and was about to quit. Just when Shay had come to terms with having her around as an extra set of hands in Tassi's absence, too. "Look, if it's something I said . . ."

"You said? No, I only wanted to thank you for giving me this opportunity, and let you know that I haven't enjoyed myself this much since George and I used to have our first restaurant." The woman's eyes filled with tears.

"Oh . . . I see. Well . . . I'm glad everything is working out. Jen had nothing but great things to say about you and your work. So, I guess it's me who should be thanking you."

"You don't have to do that." A blush crept up Faye's neck. "It's been a great day, and I can't wait until tomorrow. I'm so excited about working for you. I'm just bursting inside."

Shay smiled at her, and this time she meant it. It wasn't Faye's fault Shay had felt inferior. It wasn't Faye she was mad at. It wasn't Liam's or Zoey's fault either. It was the whole situation, and if she wasn't careful, she would drive away everyone in her life. The woman clearly knew what she was doing, and if Shay would quit being stubborn, she'd know she could learn a lot about running a restaurant-type business from this woman. "Tomorrow at four, then?"

Faye's face dropped. "Not till four? But I thought if I was here to help out with lunch, it would free you up." She gestured to the dwindling packaged tea supply on the shelves.

"I don't want to burn you out, and when Jen offered you the position, I thought it was clear you'd be covering Tassi's shifts, four to eight."

"She did, but after today, I can see my help is needed beyond that. As I told your sister, you're doing me a favor. My therapist said the last thing I should be doing is moping around on my own, and this"—she gazed around the shop—"is the perfect medicine, not to mention the scents in here." She looked at Shay. "Do you find that whenever you walk through the door something washes over you that takes away all your stress? It's like a free aromatherapy session, and I love it."

What to do, what to do? It was clear that Faye was benefiting from the same external forces that made Shay fall in love with the shop right from the beginning too, but . . . she still couldn't shake her earlier feelings of resentment. *Or is it inferiority and jealousy?* Her thoughts spun with everything that had happened, and she took a deep breath. All she knew was that Gran could help her, and she needed to find her.

Bringing her twirling thoughts back around to Faye, Shay glanced at the empty shelves. "Well, the festival starts in just over a week, and I guess until it's over you can work full-time, and then hopefully Tassi will be back, and we can work something else out then. How does that sound?"

"That sounds perfect." Faye beamed as she headed for newly arrived customers and greeted them as though she were a maître d' at a fine-dining restaurant.

At least the woman was bringing some class to Crystals and CuriosiTEAS. Shay began clearing empty tables and resetting them for service. She shook off the strange feeling of bussing tables for a woman who had just started working for her. As owner and boss, she should be rubbing elbows with her customers, not scraping off food bits with a rubber spatula. She shook her head and studied Faye as she floated around the room, chatting, refilling teapots with one hand and holding out a plate of goodies for customers to choose from with the other without even skipping a beat. Shay shoved the green-eyed monster back into its dark, dank corner in her mind and let Faye have her moment. Shay was a bigger girl than she had been behaving, and when the day was finished, she'd take care of the business that had played into her erratic emotions as of late.

When a lull in business came as dinnertime approached, Shay took Faye aside and explained that she had some things to take care of in the evening and that they were closing early. Although the woman showed her disappointment, Shay suspected that her feet could use the break too. As much as Faye had the heart for the work, it was clear her advancing age was not as keen as her heart was.

Shay hopped on her bike, clipped her helmet, glanced around for Spirit, and shrugged as she set off. She hadn't seen him all day. Struck with a sense of nagging uncertainty about her senses lately, she needed to find out if her hunch was right. Instead of heading straight up High Street to Crystal Beach Cottages, she hung a right at the first corner and pushed down hard on the pedals as she flew past Fifth Avenue, Sixth Avenue, and Seventh Avenue, where she took a sharp turn to the left.

She sailed past the first block of various-styled adobe homes that had been the first residential community built away from the coastline in Bray Harbor. When she came to a charming Spanish colonial house with a front courtyard that was across the street on her left, she eased off the pedals and glided to a full stop. She mentally judged the distance she was from the house and crossed her fingers it was one hundred feet, as stipulated in the restraining order. She scanned the entranceway and front garden for signs of life and, more importantly, any signs of an elusive white German shepherd.

A spiked rainbow-colored head of hair appeared at the top of the stucco fence that encircled the back yard and laughter rang out from across the street.

"Go get it, Spirit!" Tassi yelled with delight. "I'm not chasing the ball for you." There was a yip and a bark of excitement, and Tassi laughed again.

Shay's heart swelled. Even though she couldn't check on Tassi, it seemed Spirit had made it his mission to keep her company through her house arrest. Shay smiled and then glanced around. Peter was a resourceful man. She wouldn't put it past him to have installed cameras outside to make sure Shay didn't try to get close to Tassi. She pushed down hard and labored down the street. All she had to do was be seen across the road and he'd probably hit her with a stalking charge next.

Now on to find Gran. She sailed down the hill toward the cottages and turned up the back lane between her row and the back row of cottages. When she saw Liam's car in the driveway beside his cottage, she stopped and went through her back gate instead of stopping in to see Gran. Now probably wasn't the right time to ask her for her help. The resentment toward Liam from earlier built up inside her again, proving that she still had to sort out her mixed emotions about him taking off when he told her he'd be investigating both Jasmine and Peter.

She put her bike in the garden shed, went inside to make some supper, and tried not to be furious with him, with herself, and with the world. *Trust your gifts*, she mentally repeated as she shuffled through her pantry, trying to find something appealing for dinner.

Chapter 18

Poached eggs on toast consumed and a hot cup of lavender and honey tea in hand, Shay headed out to the beach to try to collect her thoughts and sort through her crazy emotions. She sat on a log, stared at the crimson water reflecting the setting sun's colors, and spotted a piece of driftwood bobbing up and down in the rolling waves.

It reminded her of how many times in her life she had felt like that piece of wood with no clear direction, dependent on the wave of life, completely at the mercy of the rolling waves and whatever path was thrust upon it. She visualized pushing the small floating log so it would take a different path to the shore. It twisted and turned with the waves and rolled sideways, fighting to upright itself only to return to the same path the waves had led it.

She drew in a deep, slow breath; refocused; and mentally tried to force it to take a different path than the one it was being guided on by the waves just as she had wanted to do with her own life for years. But just as it had been with her, the log continued to bob along the path of least resistance as it made its way toward the shore. She bore down, and a rush of energy surged through her. The log jumped and rode to the shore in the wave's curl instead of being pushed by it. She raised her brow as the wood tumbled onto the shore. *Same end but a different path taken.*

She hugged her warm teacup to her chest and shivered in the cooling evening air. Behind her Spirit barked, and she turned to see him sitting at the bottom of the porch steps, wagging his tail.

"You finally decided to come home, did you?" She laughed and walked across the sand and pebbles to the wooden sidewalk. He barked a greeting again and then whined and darted up onto the porch.

"Shay? Are you home?" Zoey's all-too-familiar voice called, accompanied by a banging on the kitchen door.

Spirit let out a yip, wagged his tail, and looked back at Shay as she hurriedly ascended the steps and joined him.

"Hi, Zoey," Shay said, leaning over the side railing. "I'm here. Come on around." Her eyes widened when Zoey grabbed the handles of two oversized suitcases and proceeded to puff and groan, while maneuvering one bag then the other across the uneven boards of the planked sidewalk to the porch steps.

"Um . . ." Shay tried to formulate the words to express her confusion when Zoey left them at the bottom and climbed up the stairs. "Are you going on another trip?" Shay asked, mystified by what she'd just witnessed.

"Nope, but I've done it." Zoey huffed and sat down hard on a porch chair. "I've told Liam that the cottage just isn't big enough for the three of us, and I've moved out."

Shay uncertainly eyed the two large suitcases and then Zoey. "And?" Shay glanced at the luggage again and swallowed hard.

Zoey looked at Shay then at the suitcases and chuckled. "Don't worry. I'm not moving in with you."

Shay hoped the sigh of relief she let out went unnoticed.

"I've called that real estate agent I was using, Julia Fisher, to take my condo off the market, which she'll do first thing tomorrow, and then I can move back in."

"I guess it was a good thing it hasn't sold. It must have been fate or something."

"Now you're sounding like Gran," retorted Zoey, who then winced and apologetically eyed Shay. "Anyway, tonight, I'll stay at my assistant Sheila's. As a matter of fact, she's coming to pick me up in a minute since my car is still at the clinic." Shay looked questioningly at her. "Yesterday Liam picked me up from there, and we headed directly out to Monterey." Zoey shifted in her chair. "I saw your lights on and thought I'd let you know what was going on. I hope you don't mind."

"No, of course not. I'm glad you did." Shay pulled the other porch chair over and took a seat. "But did you and Liam talk this through? Are you sure you have to move out? Is there no way the three of you can make this work?"

"Yes, we talked and argued, but I'm afraid he's . . . not going to go against family in this one." Zoey fiddled with the handle of the red handbag on her lap. "Don't get me wrong. Gran is a lovely person, she really is, and she cares so much for Liam. They're really very close. But . . . two alpha females in the same house just doesn't work." She looked up at Shay. "I tried and bit my tongue as best I could."

"Then what happened tonight?"

"When we got home from Monterey, I was stunned to see that she had packed up all my Rex Brandt watercolor paintings that I'd hung up in the living room. I couldn't believe it. I've been collecting those for years, and Liam knows how much they mean to me. Anyway, then she had the nerve to say that they didn't have the right *energy* for the room, and if I insisted on hanging them, I could add them to all the other ones in our bedroom."

"What did Liam say?"

"He said adding them to the ones I'd already hung up in the bedroom while he was away was fine. Then he took me aside and told me he just wants his Gran to feel at home. That she's been having a hard time since his granddad passed, and it's going to take her time to settle down and feel comfortable, so I should just be patient."

Shay smiled weakly.

"And he's right. I know this has been hard on her.

I'm not heartless, you know. But it's what he said after that that made me decide the cottage wasn't big enough for the three of us."

Shay winced inside. She'd come to know Zoey well enough these past few months to know she didn't beat around the bush when making her likes and dislikes known and wasn't one to sugarcoat anything.

"He told me that Gran was here to stay so I might want to think about boxing up some of the decorations and the few pieces of my furniture I had moved in so they could make room for her belongings because it would help her immensely through her grieving process."

"So, this isn't just an extended visit for her?"

Zoey shook her head. "Apparently she told him she's not ready to retire and living with his mom, who is retired now, would be a fate worse than death for her. She loves helping at the pub every day and . . ."

"And what?"

"She's taken a shine to you and your shop. That's why she's always dropping by the tea shop."

"I thought it was because she's Irish, and aside from their beer, they do enjoy their tea too," Shay said with a soft chuckle, trying to dispel the tension emanating from Zoey.

"She couldn't give a hoot about the tea. She's been studying you when she stops by. Why do you think she's always so willing to help you with the readings and all that other stuff?"

"I think that's just because she's familiar with that

world, and she knows I'm interested. She only wants to feel needed and, well—"

"Pfft," huffed Zoey. "I think she's been watching and waiting."

"For what?"

Zoey shrugged. "Who knows? I know Liam thinks the world of you, which is why when we became neighbors I sought you out too. It helped make me miss him less. The two of you seem to have such a strong connection—"

"Whoa." Shay put up her hands. "I think that's just because of what we went through last year, nothing more. Don't worry that there's something going on between us."

"I never thought there was. I know Liam cares for me, or he would never have asked me to move in with him. It's Gran I think who wishes there were something more going on between the two of you. Remember, they did spend the last two months together, and she knows a lot about your past and what happened . . ."

"Yeah, but—"

"But I get the feeling that when I left tonight, she saw it as an opening for . . . well, you and him to get together. As a matter of fact, when I think about it, I think that's what she's been trying to force since she arrived."

"Do you really think she would resort to sabotaging her grandson's relationship with you based on nothing but stories she's heard about me?" Shay shook her head. "No, Liam told me she is a very wise woman. I think there's something else going on with her and

with her interest in me." She recalled the familiar feeling she sensed from Gran when they met and some of
the things she had told her about Biddy Early and the
fact that Gran knew her grandmother. She reached over
and patted Zoey's hand. "Don't worry, you and Liam
will sort this out and everything will turn out as it's
supposed to."

"Is that one of your feelings or are you just trying to
placate a friend?"

"I just know he cares for you. Like you said, he
wouldn't have asked you to move into the cottage if he
didn't."

"Except he doesn't care enough to try to lay down
some ground rules and set boundaries with Gran so we
can all coexist. It seems I'm the one who is supposed
to do all the giving in." Tears filled Zoey's eyes. "Then
she said something really strange when I was leaving."

"What?"

"She said, 'This is for the best. It's not good for
fairies to mix with others not of their kind.' What in the
world does that mean?"

Shay shrugged.

"I know she's into all that psychic stuff and the Irish
legends are important to her, but is she losing her
mind? Does she think Liam and I are fairies but different kinds? I'm worried about her."

"What did Liam say?"

"He never heard her, but I'm afraid she's got dementia or something."

A car horn honked from the direction of the rear
lane.

"That'll be Sheila. I told her I'd be waiting outside and to honk when she got here." Zoey dashed down the steps and grabbed the handles of her bags. "Thanks for letting me unload. I'll drop by the tea shop and let you know any developments." She trudged around the side of the porch and disappeared into the dark.

Shay looked at Spirit. He looked up at her, ears up, head slightly cocked, then whimpered as he looked in the direction Zoey had gone. It was clear that he was just as confused by what had happened as she was.

Shay wondered if the whole world had gone crazy. She wished she knew more about astrology because something definitely wasn't right with the planets and stars. Was it one of those planetary retrogrades people blamed bad events on? If it was, it must be a doozie because everyone's worlds, including hers, were falling apart simultaneously.

She shook her head as she tidied the porch, called for Spirit to come, then flipped off the light and made her way into the kitchen. She knew Liam and Zoey loved each other—that had been clear to her for some time now—and she hoped they could make their relationship work out, with Gran included. But she also knew Gran was a strong-willed person, and if what Zoey had said was even remotely true and Gran had set about splitting her and Liam up from the get-go, any reconciliation was out of the question.

"What's that saying? Not my monkey, not my circus." She shrugged and chuckled as she filled the sink to wash the dishes. She drew in a slow, even breath, allowing the hot soapy water flowing over her hands to

wash away all the negative energy that had been building up inside her. When the dinner dishes were cleaned
up, she looped the kitchen towel over the handle of the
oven door but froze when a shadow moved across the
small window of her back door. She grabbed the frying
pan from the drying rack, wheeled it high, and flung
the door open. A scream caught in the back of her throat.

Chapter 19

"Liam?" she cried and lowered the pan to her side. "What are you doing skulking around my back door?" She glanced down at Spirit, who yipped, wagged his tail, and watched them both with hopeful eyes. "Some watchdog you are, buddy." She shook her head and looked back at Liam. "So . . . did you want to come in, or are you going to camp out on my back step all night? If that's the case I can at least give you a blanket."

"Nah, I'm good."

Somehow she didn't believe him. Her flippant words hadn't even garnered a glimmer of a smile. Who was this stranger on her step? It sure wasn't the Liam she knew.

"I . . . I . . ." He averted his gaze from hers as he shuffled from one foot to the other. "I went for a walk on the beach and saw yer light on and . . . but . . . I don't want to impose."

"Since when, given that you generally come through the door like a SWAT team." She looked down at Spirit, who was panting, his tongue lolling out. "But, I think our friend here is hoping you'll come in. So you'd better get in here, mister, or you'll be answering to him." She tugged at Liam's shirt collar and guided him to a chair. "Much better, but you sure look like you need a cup of tea."

"Whiskey is more like it." He sat down and raked his hand through his ebony hair.

"Sorry, all out, but I do have some wine. One of the winegrowers dropped off a couple of bottles at the tea shop in the hope I'd give out samples of his wine before the festival."

"Ye don't serve wine there."

"I know, I told him too," she said, riffling around in the pantry cupboard. "But he told me to keep it anyway and share them with friends. I guess there's a people's choice award given out, and he's hoping that by spreading the word early, it will give his wine a leg up or something." She produced one wine bottle, a corkscrew, and two juice-size glasses and set them on the table in front of Liam. "Want to do the honors?"

Liam uncorked the bottle, filled the two small glasses to the brim, took a sip of his, and then downed the entire glass in a continuous gulp. He started to pour himself another as Shay sat eyeing the dwindling supply in the bottle. "Take it easy. I only have one more bottle if you're trying to tie on a big one tonight," she said, toying with her untouched glass.

"Sorry, I'm just trying to clear my head." He pulled the bottle closer, filled his glass to the rim, and shrugged.

"I don't think a wine-fogged head is exactly a clear head, but I do have something that *will* clear it." She got up and put the kettle on.

"Tea, really? After the night I've had? Pfft." He downed another glass.

"Not just any tea," she said, scooping out tea leaves from a canister. "One that's meant for this exact situation and it's served with what you need most."

"What's that?" he said, reaching for the bottle again.

"Someone for you to talk to about what's got you into this state to begin with."

"Nah, ye don't want to hear my problems."

"You hear mine all the time. So tonight it's my turn to listen." She set the teapot and two cups on the table, slipped the wine bottle from his fingers, and removed their glasses.

Reluctantly at first, but then with more animation, Liam proceeded to relay what had occurred between him and Zoey, not only that evening but about the tension that had been building since he came back from Ireland and how it all had come to a head. When he finished, he looked at the wine bottle over on the counter and started to get up. Shay grabbed his shirtsleeve and pointed to the cup of tea she had poured him.

"Yer worse than Gran," he jeered and grudgingly took a sip. "Ye know, that's not half bad for tea. What's in it?"

"It's from a recipe of Bridget's to help calm and clear the head. A little marshmallow root, a sprinkle of rosebuds, some basil, and a dash of cinnamon chips." Shay took a sip of hers and smiled at him over the rim. "I'm glad you like it."

"Believe it or not, I do." He took another sip but then pushed his cup away.

"Are you hungry?" she asked, eyeing his haggard face.

"Nah, just trying to make sense out of tonight." He looked over at her. "All week I've asked for a sign that Zoey and I were meant to be, that things would work out, but then this happened. Am I crazy for not backing her and letting her leave like that? Or was it something not meant to be because I won't . . . I can't choose her over me own kin?"

"Maybe you and Zoey are just star-crossed lovers?"

"What does that mean?"

"It's just something I read in one of Bridget's journals. Sometimes the universe answers our questions by not giving us what we want but what we need at the time. Maybe it's trying to tell you that this isn't the time for you and Zoey. After all, Gran just lost the love of her life, her soul mate or life mate, whatever you want to call your grandfather, and she's going through her own soul searching. Perhaps the universe is telling you it's time to take a step back in your life and focus on Gran and what she needs and wants right now. After that's looked after, it will be the right time for you and Zoey." Shay shrugged and took another sip of her tea.

"I don't know. Maybe I'm babbling, but it made sense in my head before I said it."

"No, I think yer right. This isn't the time for me and Zoey because deep down I'm not even certain she is the right one for me at all." He glanced over at Shay. "I was engaged once before, ye know."

"No, I didn't know." Shay sat upright in her chair. "What happened?"

"I got this same feeling and called it off a month before the wedding."

"Hmm, maybe it's commitment you're afraid of?"

"No, I think it has more to do with something Gran's always said."

"What's that?"

"It's not good for fairies to mix with others not of their kind."

"You said that's something Gran's always said?" Shay poured more tea into her cup. She wished now that she hadn't removed the wine bottle from the table because after Liam's statement she needed a real drink too.

"Aye, me whole life. She raised me cousin Conor, after my auntie and uncle were killed in a car accident, and he got the same warnings as I did."

Shay eyed Liam's downturned gaze and hesitantly edged to the front of her seat. "Do, do you know what Gran means by that? Does she think . . ." She gulped. "Does she think you're all fairies?"

Liam tossed his head back and belted out a chesty laugh. When he'd caught his breath, he wiped the tears from his eyes and looked at Shay. "No," he said, still chuckling. "It's her way of saying that ye boys need to find a nice Irish girl that understands the old ways or ye'll never be truly happy like her and Granddad were."

"Oh." Shay let out a sigh of relief. *So much for Zoey's dementia theory.*

"I'm sure if things had been different, she would have made me stay in Ireland just so she could set me up with every lassie in the county." He chuckled. "But after she heard about ye, she was chomping to get back here."

"Then she never had any intention of going to live in San Francisco with your mom."

"No, she said she needed to meet the fairy princess because she had a message for her."

Shay dropped her teaspoon midstir in her tea. "What message?"

He shrugged. "I don't question her. I just follow."

She recalled the familiar sensation she had the first evening she'd met Gran. Was it possible they were in fact kin, like true-blooded kin and not just kin by way of their Irish roots?

"Liam," she said, cradling her cup between her hands as she shifted in her chair, "the first night you brought your gran into the tearoom, I had the queerest feeling that we knew each other. Is it possible that she and my Irish family are related?"

He sat back and eyed her suspiciously. "Are ye asking if yer my sister, then?"

"Not your sister." At least she hoped not. "Maybe a first or second cousin?"

His eyes sparkled mischievously in the overhead

kitchen light. "No." He took a sip. "No redheads in my family. We don't allow it."

"What do you mean, you don't allow it?"

"If a red-haired babe is born, the elder of the family takes the wee bairn out into the woods and leaves it for the fairies to raise. She did tell ye about the red-headed Biddy Early and how she went to live with the fairies when she was a wee lassie, didn't she?" He winked playfully.

Shay picked up the tea leaf ball from the saucer she'd set it on and tossed it at him. He ducked, and it clattered on the brick floor behind him. "You're incorrigible," she said, laughing.

"Did ye just try to kill me? Yer own kin?"

"You said we weren't kin," she mocked, taking another sip and glaring at him over the rim of her cup.

"Aye, and that's a good thing, I'd say. We also don't take to murders in the family either." He dropped his gaze and played with the spoon on his saucer.

"But speaking of Biddy Early, Gran did tell me about her."

"Really? Then ye know."

"Know what?"

"Nothing, it's her story to tell. Go on, what were ye going to say?"

Shay looked skeptically at him but went on. "While you were in Monterey, Dean dropped by and told me that Peter Graham is planning on filing a civil lawsuit against me."

"For what?"

"Practicing witchcraft."

"Ye've got to be kidding."

"No, that's why Gran told me about Biddy. Apparently, she was charged with witchcraft too, and . . . well, that means it's all over the internet—"

"And that means that Peter can find the proof for his case."

"Exactly."

"Then we make sure he can't prove it."

"How do we do that?"

"I know the tale, and now ye know the tale, but does Peter know yer related to Biddy Early?"

"I . . . I don't know. I guess I just assumed with my birth mother, Bridget, having the Early name and then her leaving everything to me, he would have figured it out, and that's why he was filing the lawsuit, besides, of course, wanting to keep me away from Tassi, for some reason."

"That's yet to be figured out, but right now I think ye can rest easy about the lawsuit. It's not common knowledge that yer in any way related to a nineteenth-century Irish witch. So, he hasn't any grounds to stand on. But"—his eyes sparkled—"I forgot in all the commotion of tonight to tell you what I found out in Monterey about Mr. Peter Graham."

"Do tell." Shay edged closer to him.

"First, it's as Dean said, he's a very powerful and influential man in the county and the state, it seems. His father is a California State Supreme Court judge."

"Oh . . ."

"Aye, and he has learned to use that family connection to help bolster his career too, it seems."

"No wonder Dean is getting pressure from the mayor about this case."

"Yup, and the mayor is getting pressure from the state legislation. It seems Peter has told everyone he knows about what happened and what he thinks is going on here, and the mayor's worried because all levels of government seem to have their eyes on little old Bray Harbor right now."

"But that also means if he's that well connected and determined that I'm at fault here, he has an army of private detectives at his disposal, and he will eventually turn up information about my connection to the Early family, and then I will have to go to court to prove I'm not a witch, of all things."

"Then ask yerself why he is so bent on making ye the bad guy here."

"That's exactly what I've been trying to figure out. One theory I came up with is that he's afraid I have too much influence over Tassi and he's losing control of her. Out of jealousy and spite, I don't know, he's trying to separate her from everyone who really cares for her, her own mother included." She fixed her gaze on Liam's. "Think about it. He's not fighting the fact that she's the number one suspect in Jasmine's murder, which you'd think would be the first thing a father and a lawyer of his standing would do, right?"

Liam nodded.

"So, my theory is that he can play the superhero and swoop in and save her from those he has already set up in the eyes of the law as being a bad influence on her. After all, with his influence, it probably wouldn't take much to have her murder conviction, if it came to that, overturned or, at least, have her released into his custody for the duration of her sentence."

"That makes sense if you combine it along with something else my contact discovered. . . ."

Shay waited for Liam to continue, but he only sat there, stroking his teacup handle with his fingers. "Which was?" She wanted to shout but restrained her voice and asked quietly.

"Do ye know if Tassi gets some kind of inheritance when she turns eighteen?"

"I don't know. I never thought of that. I know her mother's family comes from money, and her grandfather passed away a couple of years ago, so maybe."

"Did you know money is one of the top reasons people commit murder?" He glanced over at her.

She shook her head.

"Ask yerself this." Liam leaned forward on his elbows. "Her parents divorced over a year ago, and until recently, Peter Graham has had no interest in his daughter. Then suddenly he wants her to come and live with him. When she makes it clear she has no intention of doing that, Jasmine dies, and he's launching a reasonable doubt case in her defense by going after ye. Given his reputation of being a top-notch defense lawyer, it will probably succeed. Then Tassi has no choice but to live with him because he has also discredited ye and her life here in Bray Harbor. After proving her mother can't be trusted with making good decisions for her, bam, she's under his control. She turns eighteen, and he becomes the executor of her estate until she turns twenty-one, which makes him the sole recipient of trust or inheritance by being her legal guardian."

"Phew." Shay took a breath. "That's some theory, and one I hadn't thought of."

"It's not a theory."

"Then when Tassi turns eighteen, she'll be rich?"

"Yes and no. Apparently, the money is then transferred to her legal guardian in trust, which when her granddad set it up, he assumed would be her mother when Tassi turned twenty-one. She's worth millions."

"Millions?"

Liam sat back in his chair, crossed his arms over his chest, and nodded.

"Does Tassi know about the money?"

"No, according to what my source dug up, her granddad wanted it kept that way until she turned eighteen and graduated high school. He also made a stipulation that when she turned twenty-one, she had to have at least two years of college behind her. If not, she doesn't get the money until she turns twenty-five. He didn't want it to go to her head and for her not to do anything with her life because she would never have to work again unless she wanted to."

"But if Peter's the estate holder until she does receive the money, he has access to it, right?"

"At least the interest from it, but I'm not really sure how a case like this would work. Although with him being the lawyer he is, I'm pretty sure he has it all figured out."

Shay shook her head and laughed.

"What's so funny?" He leaned forward and pinned her with a questioning look.

"It's not funny. It's all so sad. I could never figure out why he was the first to point his finger at Tassi as the murderer and then try to blame it all on me, but it all makes sense now."

Gran had been right in response to Shay's previous guilt over doing nothing to stop Jasmine from dying. There *were* powers she had no control over at play here. Who'd have known what Peter Graham was really up to and what—she shivered—he was capable of.

Chapter 20

Shay waved the last group of the Little White Glove Society ladies off and started to clear their table. She looked up, grinned, and slid over beside Jen, who was clearing the table beside hers, and gestured with her head toward the window. "It looks like someone is about to get a morning visit from her hubby. Kissy, kissy." Shay laughed as she playfully elbowed her sister in the ribs.

"Oh, stop it!" Jen giggled, her cheeks taking on a rosy hue as she looked out, but then her face paled. "I don't think so . . . the look on his face tells me this isn't an I-was-missing-you-and-had-to-see-you visit."

"No, you're right," said Shay, studying Dean's dour expression as he crossed the street from where his patrol car was parked in front of Cuppa-Jo.

Jen softly gasped and glanced at Shay. "That restraining order you got didn't include me, did it?"

"No. Why?"

"Because last night after dinner, I took Maddie and Hunter out for ice cream, and we stopped by and picked up Tassi on our way."

"You saw her? How's she doing?"

Jen shook her head. "Not good, but she put on a brave face for the kids, and I think she enjoyed the outing."

Jen's face lit up in a grin as the overhead doorbells jangled out their greeting. Dean stood imposingly in the doorway. He glanced over at two women sitting at a table by the window, smiled, and then abruptly took on the same stern expression he had had on the street as he strode over to Shay and Jen.

Jen's smile quickly faded. "What's wrong?"

"I just need to talk to Shay for a minute," he said, then wrapped his right arm around Jen, pulled her close, and brushed his lips across her cheek.

She pulled back and looked at him, concern clearly in her eyes. "What's wrong with your left arm? Why is it pressed to your side like that? Did you hurt yourself?" she asked, reaching for his left hand.

"No, I'm fine," he said as he turned his body away from her advances. "I just need a minute with Shay, alone."

"Okay . . ." Jen said, dropping her hand. Her face telegraphed her distrust in his words as she eyed him closely. "But if I find out later that you're walking around with an injury and didn't have it treated today, you'll get no sympathy from me tonight."

"My arm's fine, honest." He smiled reassuringly at Jen, then looked at Shay. "We need to talk."

"Fine, let's go in the back room."

"Perfect." Dean stood back and gestured for her to lead the way.

"Go ahead," Shay said. "I just need to put this bussing bin back on the cart and I'll be there."

Dean strutted toward the back, and Shay studied his body movements to see what her sister had noticed. Yes, she was right, he kept his left arm close and tight to his body. Shay looked at Jen. "I'll see if I can find out what happened. Maybe it was something stupid like tying his boot laces, and he's embarrassed to tell you," she whispered as she handed Jen the bin and went after Dean.

"I take it you came up with some more evidence in the case?" Shay said as she closed the door behind her. "But since you didn't want Jen to hear, it must not be good news."

"It's not about the murder." He reached into the left side of his sheriff's department jacket and pulled out a large brown envelope. "It's about this," he said, extending it toward her.

Shay sighed and shook her head. "I don't even need to see it to know what it is."

"Take it. By law I have to put it in your hands." He gestured, shaking the envelope. "Take it, Shay. The mayor instructed me personally to be the one to issue it to you and—"

"Okay," she snapped, and seized the envelope from his hand. "There, consider it delivered."

"Aren't you going to open it?"

"Is that in the rule book too?"

"No, I just thought you might want to know what

civil charges pertaining to practicing witchcraft Peter has filed against you."

"Did Liam come in and talk to you this morning?"

"He did."

"Then you know this is a joke, right?" She waved the unopened envelope in the air. "It proves what Peter is up to."

"The problem is, we'd have to prove intent, and that's practically impossible."

"What do you mean? This should be proof of intent itself."

"No. It only proves that Peter is after you and wants to keep you out of Tassi's life. It doesn't prove what's going on in his head. Unless we can find some documentation delineating his evil plot against you, we can't prove what's going on inside his mind."

"So, he just gets away with extorting Tassi's inheritance?"

"Unless there's a tape, a video, or some notes he's written that will prove he's going to use her to get his hands on her money, yes, he gets away with it, and you'll have to prove in court you're not a witch or practicing witchcraft."

"That's not fair."

"No, it's not, but it's the law. Intent to commit a crime is the hardest thing to prove because unless there's a trail of some kind, we can't prove what a person is thinking."

"What about the proof being in his actions?"

"He's made sure he's covered all his bases. He's discredited you with the first restraining order, her mom by filing a custody suit on the ground she's an unfit mother, her aunt as an accomplice to the goings-on, and now this to seal the deal. He does this for a living, remember. He knows the law better than most, and he's not afraid to use all the resources at his disposal to get what he wants."

"So now what?"

"Get yourself a good lawyer." Dean opened the door, looked back at her, and smiled weakly. "Just remember, you have a lot of friends, not to mention family, on your side, and we'll get through this together."

Shay nodded and absently slid the edge of the envelope between her fingers as her mind raced replaying the recent events. "Wait, what about the autopsy report? Was Jasmine pregnant?"

"No, she wasn't."

"What about the analysis of her personal belongings in the hotel room? Did you ever get the warrant?"

"Yes, it took a bit of time, but we did, and it turned up nothing."

"Not even in her lipstick?"

Dean shook his head. "Nothing. No trace of abrin in anything she had."

"That just doesn't make sense."

"No, but I suggest you stop trying to play detective and start planning your next steps regarding that." Dean gestured to the envelope.

Shay seethed inside as Dean, left arm swinging freely by his side, stopped, kissed his wife briefly on the cheek, and left.

Jen spun on her heel and bolted into the back room. "Did you use one of your miracle cures on his arm?"

"No, it seems his arm was just fine, like he said. He

had this tucked inside his jacket. I guess he didn't want it falling out before he could serve it." Shay thrust the envelope into Jen's hand. "Go ahead, read it. I can't bear to right now."

"Is this another restraining order?" asked Jen, sliding the documents out of the envelope and glancing over them. "What? This can't be for real. It's some kind of a joke, right?"

"Nope."

"Witchcraft?" Jen gasped out as she read further. "I . . . I . . ." She shook her head. "What are you going to do?"

"Dean told me to get a good lawyer."

"That's it? That's all he said?"

"It's a civil suit, so there's not much he can do about it. It seems you can sue anyone for anything nowadays, and Peter is going to try to prove I'm a witch and a bad influence over Tassi." Shay glanced out the door into the tearoom. "Is Faye coming in today at noon or at four?"

"Um," said Jen, still scanning the court order, "she mentioned on her way out this morning that she'd be back around noon, why?"

"I just need to clear my head, and we still need more bags of tea blends made up."

"Yeah." Jen distractedly waved her hand as she continued reading. "Go upstairs. I'll call you if I need you."

Shay hauled her weary body up the spiral staircase and dropped down on the bench beside the potting table. Her earlier seething rose to a full-blown boil. After all, it was easier to be angry than sad, and angry she was. The imprints her nails left in her palms were a clear testament to that. She seized the shears and wildly snipped off passionflower leaves. When she had decimated the poor plant, she stopped, then looked at the pile of leaves and what was left of the spindly stalk, scarcely covered in foliage. She tossed the shears back onto the table and sat down hard on the bench.

How could any of this be happening? None of it made sense. Jasmine wasn't pregnant so her theory about why Peter might have killed her was proven wrong. Heck, even her theory that Peter had been slowly poisoning her prior to her keeling over dead was wrong because no evidence of abrin was detected in her belongings. There was no evidence of abrin anywhere except Jasmine's cup, so how did it get there if not in her lipstick? She hated where her next thought took her, and she tried to push it from her mind, but it kept rushing back. Had Tassi dropped a crushed seed in her soon-to-be stepmother's tea when she served her?

Shay emphatically shook her head. "No, there's no way."

"That's exactly what I said," Liam's voice boomed from the spiral staircase as he made his way into the greenhouse. "Speak of the devil, and he shows his face."

"What are you talking about?"

"Conor, me cousin. I told you about him last night, and bam, there he is sitting in me pub drinking his face off like I'd be all happy to see him after ten years."

"Aren't you?"

"No, but Gran's fawning all over him like he's the long-lost lamb finally come home. He wants something, and I have to figure out what it is."

"Maybe he just wanted to see Gran. You did say she raised him like a son."

"Yeah, until that changeling got a hold of him," Liam scoffed as he took a seat on the bench beside Shay. "He took off for Dublin and led a wild life. He'd come back and caused Gran nothing but heartache only to up and leave her again without a word of where he was going. Me dad, who was Garda, Irish police, found out he'd gone off to work on the continent for some scumbag he'd met in Dublin and was lost to us. Gran never heard another word from him in these ten years. Until today, of course, when Mr. Fancy-pants comes strolling into the pub. I tell ye, he's up to no good, he is."

Shay shifted uncomfortably on the bench and softly moaned.

"What's wrong, *a chara*," asked Liam, turning toward her. "Yer paler than usual. Are ye sick?"

"No. I'm fine." She winced and lifted the pouch off her chest. *Fine?* If a queasy sensation in the pit of her stomach and the heat from the amulet scorching her chest and fingers equaled fine, then she was just fine and dandy.

Chapter 21

"What's a changeling?" Shay asked Liam as they headed down the spiral staircase.

"Do ye know nothing of the fairy folk?"

"I have read some in the books that were in the shop, and I was shocked that the modern romanticized version we hear about fairies wasn't exactly what the Irish legends are based on." She paused at the bottom of the staircase and pulled back the curtain covering the painting of Titania, the Fairy Queen. "Like this. She's so beautiful and gentle looking, but I've read so much that says not all fairies or their intentions are good. Not like in the movies we watch anyway."

"No, there are good and bad fairies, and a changeling is one of the bad ones." Liam studied the painted image. "But ye don't have to worry. If ye've got fairy blood in ye, it's the good kind." He smiled, and his eyes locked on hers, sending a butterfly sensation racing through her chest.

"Oooh." She involuntarily shivered. "What about you? Are you one of the good ones?"

"In spite of what Gran thinks, I don't think I have a bit of fairy blood in me." He laughed and rubbed his shoulder. "I have the scar to prove it."

Shay recalled how Dean told her last year that Liam had been shot in the line of duty when he worked as a detective. It was the incident that ultimately forced his decision to retire from the San Francisco Police Department a few years ago. His brothers in blue apparently did not take kindly to him narcing on a ring of crooked cops. As Liam pointed out to her later, when your own partner shoots you or steps aside and allows you to be shot, their message has been delivered, and it's probably time to think about making a change.

Shay looked at his shoulder. "Yeah, I don't think fairies can get shot, can they?"

"Not according to any legends I've read."

"Hmm." She let the curtain fall back across the painting. "Does that mean Conor is the bad sort of fairy, since you said he was taken over by a changeling?"

"According to Gran, yeah," Liam said, leaning against the food dehydrator counter. "Ye see, changelings are fairies who've been left in place of a human child or baby. They steal the wee one to work as their servant or because the fairy wishes to receive the same love that a human child gives to a human mam, and they leave an ugly or deformed child in its place. Although, sometimes babies are taken out of spite or revenge on a human they think did the fairies wrong."

"And you think Conor was switched for a bad fairy child?"

"I don't, but Gran does. She said he was the sweetest baby she'd ever seen, but after his parents were killed and he came to live with her and Granddad, he changed."

"How so?"

"I only remember that he and I used to be close. Me parents lived down the road from Gran and Granddad. Me mam and dad worked so Gran looked after me most days, and when Conor came to live with them after the accident, he and I were inseparable the first few years."

"How old were you and he then?"

"He was about eight, and I am a year older. We were more like brothers than cousins." Liam's face darkened, and he dropped his gaze. "Then when I was about twelve, me dad, who was Garda, took an assignment in San Francisco to work with the police there on an Irish mob case they were investigating. It was supposed to be temporary, but it turned out to be permanent. We didn't go back except for some holidays after that." He looked up at Shay. "That's when I saw the changes in Conor too. The Garda were always bringing him home in a drunken state, and Gran was getting him out of jail on charges ranging from petty theft to assault. No matter what me or me dad tried to tell her, she always believed that a changeling took the boy we knew and left a rogue in his place."

"It sounds like Conor might have been lost without you around all the time. You said you were close like brothers. It must have been hard on him. Do you think he was just acting out his heartache over you moving away and the loss of his parents and replaced those he loved and lost with a bad crowd?"

"That's what I tried to tell Gran, but she'd hear none of it. She said the fairies only took the fairest, most beautiful children because they admired those traits, and Conor was one of them, and the changes in him were because of the changeling child of a bad seed they'd left in his place."

"As much as I find the Irish folktales fascinating— and some believable—I think this one sounds more to me like people who needed an excuse for having a child that was less than perfect in their eyes. It was easier to say a changeling replaced their own perfect child."

"I know, but something did change in Conor, and that something took him away from the people who did love him and never stopped trying to turn him around again."

"And you think he came here now because he wants something from Gran?"

"I don't think. I know. Otherwise, why would he just show up after ten years?"

"Could it be part of your granddad's inheritance?"

Liam fixed his gaze on hers. "That's my first thought."

"What are you going to do?"

"Not much I can do until he plays his card. Then I'll fight like a gremlin to protect Gran and what's hers."

"Phew." Shay nodded. "I guess I was right when I thought there must be some planetary retrograde in motion right now."

Liam's forehead crinkled.

"It's just that everything seems to be falling apart for so many people right now. Me included."

"Oh no, *a chara*. I'm so sorry and so selfish. Ye were in the middle of something when I barged in on ye." He placed his hand gently on her shoulder. "What happened?"

Shay glanced over at the envelope lying on the table where Jen must have dropped it when she had to go back into the tearoom. "That's what happened." She pointed.

Liam glanced over at it then back at her. "So, Peter made good on his threat to sue you?"

"He did, but worst of all, the theories we had all came crashing down. Jasmine wasn't pregnant, and there was no trace of abrin in her belongings at the hotel. So, it's unlikely that Peter had been slowly poisoning her and that her dying at the reading was just bad timing."

Liam's eyes glazed over for a flash, and then he looked at Shay. "But that doesn't mean someone else hadn't been poisoning her and finished the job at the reading."

"No, but no one except Tassi touched the tea, and I was the only one other than Jasmine who touched her cup. So how did traces of abrin get into her cup? That's the question no one can answer."

His eyes lit up. "There could have been enough abrin in her saliva to transfer residue into the cup. Let me check with Dean and see what ratio of abrin was found in her teacup."

"What would the ratio prove?"

"A high amount would prove it had been added, and a small amount might show she had been given it prior and it was secreted into the cup with her saliva."

"Well, if it wasn't Peter, who else wanted Jasmine dead, and how did they give her the abrin?"

"Exactly, and when I had a case like this where I hit one dead end after another, I had to sit back and re-group because I realized I wasn't asking the right questions. It's like when you're driving and hit a dead end—you have to go backward."

"I just feel like the longer I stare at this problem, the bigger it gets."

"So," Liam said, "we have to stop staring at it as a problem and look at it as a challenge to overcome because so far we've been focusing on Peter."

"That's because neither of us wants to believe Tassi would kill the woman no matter what the evidence points to."

"Yes, but we haven't been investigating who Jasmine Massey was and any other reasons someone wanted her dead."

"Yeah," said Shay, "but if there was something dark and mysterious in her past, surely Dean would have found it when they started investigating her death, right?"

"Not necessarily. The people she knew here and, of course, Peter Graham all verified her identity. There is no reason to investigate the victim unless they are an unknown and can't be identified. The question we have to ask is was there someone in Jasmine's past that might have wanted to harm her?"

"Then you'd better be the one to approach Dean because when he came to serve the papers, he told me to get a good lawyer and to stop playing detective."

"Yeah, leave it to me." He started for the door.

"Are you going to see him now?" asked Shay, following him.

"Yeah, part of me thinks I should go back to the pub to check on Gran, but another part of me is afraid I'll punch Conor in the face if I do. It's probably best I go see Dean now and cool off a bit before I go back."

She grabbed his shirtsleeve as he reached for the handle. "I hate to bring this up, knowing that you and Zoey are, well . . . on shaky ground right now, but the day Jasmine first came into the tearoom, Zoey was here. After Jasmine left, Zoey said Jasmine looked familiar but she didn't recognize the name."

"But she didn't recall where she might have known her from?"

"No, but I could ask her again. Maybe since the first meeting, something might come back to her. It might be a lead to Jasmine's past?"

He slowly nodded. "Yer right. Ye should be the one to ask Zoey. I don't think she'll take kindly to me asking after what happened, and I don't want to get into it again with her right now with Conor here and all. Got enough on my plate." He flung the door open, growled out some unrecognizable Irish curse words, and slammed it shut again.

Shay looked at him mystified, opened the door, peered out, gasped, and closed the door. "You . . . you have a . . . doppelganger out there," she stammered.

"What?" Liam opened the door a crack, peeked out, and closed it. "Nah, we don't look anything alike."

Shay scowled at him, opened the door, and then quickly closed it again. "You could be twins."

"Do ye really think so?" he asked, opening it again.

This time the door swung freely open. "Aye, so there ye are. Although"—Liam's twin glanced down at Shay with impishly sparkling eyes—"I can see why ye want to spend yer time held up in here with such a beautiful lass."

He bent low at the waist, took Shay's hand, softly kissed the back of it, then stood upright but left her hand lingering in his. "Conor Madigan at your service." His voice purred as he appraised Shay from her head to her toes and back again with his unwavering gaze.

"Take yer roguish hands off her." Liam knocked Conor's hand away from Shay. "This is a lady, not one of yer pub butterflies."

"I know who this is." Conor leaned against the door frame, still holding his unyielding gaze on Shay. "Gran's done nothing but talk about the mysterious lady next door, and I had to come and meet her myself."

"Well, ye've met, and now ye can leave," barked Liam.

"Just a minute, both of you. I'm right here, so stop referring to me like I'm not." She glared up at Liam and then turned a smile on Conor and extended her hand in greeting. "It's nice to finally meet Liam's cousin. I've heard a lot about you." She shot Liam another scathing glance and then turned her smile back on Conor. When she stared back into his startling blue eyes, darkness flashed before her. Even though Conor's eyes were the same color as Liam's, his held none of the warmth and light that Liam's did.

Perhaps Gran isn't off her rocker. Instead of the lovely, jelly feeling in her legs whenever Liam gazed at her, Conor incited her legs to stiffen. Fighting the urge to stretch out her muscles, she wondered why nearly identical good-looking men could induce such different reactions.

Liam stepped between them, breaking whatever spell Conor had over her. "Ye've met. What's keeping ye here?" Liam glared at his cousin.

"I think"—Conor pulled himself up to his full height, coming eye to eye with Liam—"we'd better ask Shayleigh if she wants me to leave."

Fiery sparks seemed to fly between the two as they locked their eyes on each other and never wavered, like two bucks posturing to show their superiority. Shay stepped back.

"Ah, there ye are," called Gran, bustling across the tearoom to the back doorway. " 'Tis a sight for dese old eyes, I must say, to see me two boys together at last again." She grinned a wide, toothy smile as she looked from Liam to Conor and patted them on the back so hard they lurched forward, bumping foreheads. "Now, shall we get back to the pub and have a pint and all get reacquainted again?"

The tone of her voice was more like a command and scolding than a suggestion, and Shay had visions of what it must have been like for Gran raising these two headstrong, determined males all those years ago. Now, as Gran herded them both out of the door, Shay could envision her dragging two little misbehaving boys away by the earlobes. It took all her power not to giggle, especially at the expressions of boyish sheepishness they had on their faces as she led them away.

As entertaining as that fleeting interlude had been between Liam and his look-alike, Conor's aura had been troubling. The sensations emanating from him had sparked a flash in her mind. Despite not seeing anything specific, darkness had clearly surrounded him. She hoped that Liam was wrong about Conor's reasons for showing up like he had and that the shadows she'd sensed weren't because he meant Gran harm or was about to break her heart all over again.

But time would tell, and they'd have to deal with that then. She took a deep breath, refocused her energy on the foil bags of tea blends that weren't going to refill themselves, and climbed the staircase once again to begin harvesting.

Chapter 22

"Pfft," Shay sputtered in exasperation, dropped the pruning shears on the potting table, sat on the bench, and curled her lip at the sight of the half-filled wicker collection tray. It was no use. She couldn't focus on her task today. In her heart she knew if she wanted the answers to all the questions catapulting through her mind, she would have to do what she hadn't done in a very long time. She would have to take the bottle out of the pouch.

She impulsively toyed with the amulet pouch, warm against her skin. Her fingers itched to remove the bottle, but her mind reeled with the memories of what happened the last few times she did, and a shiver raced across her shoulders. "Oh, Bridget, why does the power of this bottle scare me so much?" she murmured and closed her fingers around the unopened pouch.

Gran is a wise woman and will teach what I cannot, a whispered voice caressed her cheek like a mother's reassuring touch.

"Shayleigh lass!" Gran's voice echoed up the stair-well. "Are ye up here?"

Shay jerked and turned as the top of Gran's snow-white head of hair came into view. "Um . . . yeah." She touched her cheek where Bridget's whispered words had left a lingering warm sensation. "I'm, I'm over here by the potting table."

Gran huffed and puffed at the top of the railing and when she spotted Shay, she broke into a toothy grin. "Ah, there ye be." She wheezed in a deep breath and toddled over beside Shay sitting down with a thud.

Wide-eyed, Shay gaped at her and touched her warm cheek again. "But, but I thought you were in the pub with the boys?"

"They're having a pint now, but Gran's getting too old for all those carryings-on." She dabbed her fore-head with a hankie and shoved it inside her blouse sleeve.

Shay's eyes widened as she recalled what Liam had said about punching his cousin in the face. "Do you think it's safe? I mean, to leave the two of them alone, especially if beer is involved?"

"Ah," Gran waved her hand, "they've already had their wee donnybrook up on that patio. Now they'll be as right as rain."

"A donnybrook?"

"Fisticuffs. Ye know how two pigheaded lads can be."

"You mean they actually had a fistfight?"

"Aye, they did that as soon as we got back to the pub." She faced Shay. "I know Liam worries about me. He's not been close to Conor since they were wee lads, but I love the boy, raised him like me own sons, I did, but something was always off. Ye know 'tis like yer plants up here." She waved her hand around the greenhouse. "There can be a bad seed in every bunch. You can nurture it and try to change the direction it grows, but once it takes hold and starts germinating, there's not much ye can do except continue to care for it, prune it, and try to make sure it doesn't affect the other plants around it." She nodded matter-of-factly. "That's what I'm trying to do. I know Conor wants something. What, I'm not sure, but until he shows his colors, I'll keep pruning and nurturing him and hoping for the best. Don't ye worry, though"—she patted Shay's hand—"Liam can take care of himself, and Conor's in good hands with him right now. I know Liam will get to the bottom of what's going on."

Then Gran shifted in her seat. The creases outlining her concern filled eyes deepened when her gaze locked with Shay's. Then she encouragingly smiled, and the wrinkles around her mouth took the place of the deep etchings around her eyes. "Now, why don't ye tell old Gran what's got ye in such a state right now?"

Shay sat back and unblinkingly stared at the woman. She knew Liam had told her Gran had a reputation back home as being a seer, but it was like she and Bridget were of one mind . . . her timing was surreal. "It's . . . it's just that I have so many questions. You've mentioned things about my family but didn't elaborate. Tassi is a suspect in a murder that's seemingly impossible to solve, and . . ."

"And what?"

"And I feel so lost and confused by it all. My feelings aren't my feelings, or are they, and I just don't recognize them. I want to curl up in a ball and hide from it all because I don't know what to do."

"Yes ye do. Ye have all the gifts of the wise ones in your fingertips. Ye only have to decide if yer going to use them."

"I can sense people's feelings, but sometimes that seems like more of a curse than a gift. Other than that"—Shay dropped her gaze—"I don't have the same gifts my ancestors did, it seems."

"People are funny creatures, aren't they?" A dream-like gleam cast over Gran's eyes. "As long as people have been on this planet, they've wanted to know and understand who dey were and where dey were headed, but as soon as someone realizes dey have the power to learn that, they realize dey really didn't want to know in the first place, and many, like ye, turn der backs on the gifts dey've been given. Don't turn yer back on yer gifts, child." Gran gestured to the bulging pouch under the neck of Shay's blouse. "Trust the path chosen for ye. It will protect ye and those around ye."

Gran reached inside the pocket of the smock she wore over her clothing when she worked in the pub and took out a yellowing black-and-white photo. Shay tried to get a glimpse of the picture, but Gran waved it around as she spoke.

"I've been carrying this around with me to show ye. I really didn't mean to leave ye in the lurch, child, but with all the goings-on with Liam and Zoey and now with Conor showing up, it just all got away from me." She placed the photo in Shay's hand. "But this is what I wanted to show ye."

Shay stared at the photo. "I have this picture, or one very much like it, in an old album of Bridget's."

"Aye, I suspect ye would. That"—she pointed to a little girl—"was yer mam's mam, Ellen, when she was about twelve, and that"—she pointed to a dark-haired girl next to her—"is me. We were the best of friends." A smile came to Gran's craggy lips, and tears formed in her eyes. She pulled out her hankie and dabbed at her nose. "This woman behind us was yer great-gran, Brigida."

"So, you didn't just *know* Bridget's family, you were friends with them."

"Aye, more than friends, though. Ye see, me mam and dada's farm was one next to theirs. When I was about ten, me mam got the TB and took to her bed. When she passed, me dad took to the drink and stopped coming home at night. Just slept where he'd fallen, coming back from Kelley's Pub in town. Me brothers and sisters were all older and had left the wee farm to go out on der own. I was the last bairn at home and pretty much on me own in those days." Tears slowly rolled down her cheeks. "One night, Brigida came to our cottage. She found me cold and shivering in the dark. There was no coal left, nothing left for me to burn to keep warm, and the porridge pot over the hearth was long since empty. Dat woman wrapped me in an old blanket of me mam's and carried me all the way back to her cottage in the pouring rain, and there I lived until I was wed to me Jake." Gran wiped her nose. "So, yes, I knew yer family, and I know of the magic ye hold within ye."

"Did you know my mother too when she was little?"

"I did. She was just as fair and sweet as ye are, me child." Gran stroked Shay's cheek and smiled. "Ye have yer family's eyes and their heart. Yer mam never doubted her gifts. She embraced them just like ye need to. When ye do, yer head will clear and all the answers ye seek will appear before yer eyes." She tapped at the pouch Shay wore around her neck. "Don't be afraid. Use it."

Shay's fingers pulled the pouch from under her shirt. She could feel warmth emanating from it as she held it in her hand.

Gran rose to her feet and smiled. "But I best be getting back to me lads. I figure I'll either be breaking them apart again or tucking them both in soon." She turned and started toward the staircase. "Remember," she called back, "I'm here to help ye grow yer wings, me dear. Call me whenever ye need me just like ye did today."

Shay stroked her hand over the long leather thong she used to hang the pouch around her neck and re-called that every day since she'd discovered the blue bottle her senses had heightened, stirring her to her core. So why now were her senses so muddled, and, most of all, why was she afraid of the power within the bottle? It didn't make sense. It had helped her see things more clearly in the past—as scary as it had been—and it was a good thing and had brought a good outcome. Perhaps she didn't want to know the answers to the questions because maybe a small part of her be-lieved that Tassi might have been the one to poison Jasmine.

"Shay?" Jen's voice echoed up the staircase. "Dean is here again and wants to talk to you."

"Now what," Shay muttered, then stuffed the pouch back inside her shirt. "I'll be there in a minute," she called back and glanced at the half-empty herb tray on the table. *I guess I'm just not meant to be harvesting today.* She trotted down the stairs but stopped midstep on the bottom rung. "Judging by the look on your face, Dean, I take it this is not a friendly visit." She looked at an equally concerned Jen. "Okay . . . what have I done this time?"

Dean, muted, held out a brown envelope.

"What now? He has served a restraining order and is suing me. What else can he come up with?" Shay scowled, took the envelope from Dean, opened it, and scanned the piece of paper. "You've got to be kidding." She looked wide-eyed at Dean. "An order to appear before a judge next Friday. Is this for real?"

"I'm afraid so. It seems you were in violation of the restraining order, and now you have to explain yourself in court."

Shay sat down hard on the nearest chair. "I only rode by her house and was there less than five minutes."

"It seems it was long enough for someone to spot you."

"Who? I didn't see a soul on the street during that time, and I'm pretty sure none of Joanne's neighbors would have reported it. I doubt they even know about the restraining order."

Dean shrugged his shoulders. "It doesn't matter who. It only matters that you were within one hundred feet of her."

"But I didn't even see her or talk to her. I was worried about Spirit because he hadn't been coming home, and I was worried about her, and I just wanted to make sure they were okay."

"Then tell it to the judge, not me. I'm just following the letter of the law, and the law states"—he gestured to the paper—"that you violated a court order and now have to appear before the court."

"But it's next Friday. That's the day the festival starts."

Dean rolled his eyes. "Do you really think Peter or the judge cares about that?"

"Well . . . no. I guess they wouldn't." Shay looked down at the paper and bit the inside of her cheek to stop the tears forming behind her burning eyes. "This is so unfair and so wrong. I was probably ninety-nine feet away."

Dean heaved out a deep breath, opened his mouth but closed it, and patted Shay on the shoulder. "You'll get through this. I have no doubt." He looked over at Jen as he pushed his sheriff's cap on his head. "See you later at home."

He started toward the door without even pausing to give Jen a kiss. Head down, he marched through the tearoom and out the front door.

Jen soothingly rubbed Shay's back. "Why don't you take the evening off and go home"

"I can't. It's nearly time for you to set out, and we can't leave Faye here on her own."

"No, Dean told me he's going to be working late, but Hunter already has a ride with his friend's parents to swim lessons because they're going out for pizza after and then back to his buddy's for a sleep over. Maddie said she has a birthday party to go to right after school, and probably won't be home until about nine. So see, I can stay with Faye. We'll be fine. You go home and rest and clear your head."

The idea of having a night off was appealing but . . . "I shouldn't. I'm so far behind in harvesting and packaging—"

"You know what? It will all be here when you come back, so stop torturing yourself. You work twelve hours a day as it is. Take some time to relax. As a matter of fact, why don't you take tomorrow off too?"

"But you don't work Saturdays unless it's a special event and that would leave Faye on her own for sure."

"Look, Dean and Hunter are going to work on repairing the back deck tomorrow, and Maddie and I were just going to hang out and have some mom-and-daughter time. We can do that here. I can serve along with Faye, and Maddie can bus tables. It's time she got a look at what it's really like being an adult anyway since she wants us to start treating her like she is," Jen said with a chuckle. "Just don't take the long way home again today and ride by Joanne's. It sounds like Peter might have cameras set up."

Shay looked at her. "Yeah, that was my thought too, and why I stayed across the street and left as soon as I could hear Tassi and Spirit playing in the backyard."

"It's just too bad your *feeling* didn't come over you sooner and make you avoid riding past there in the first place, isn't it?"

"Yes, like Gran said the other day, hindsight makes us all seers."

"She's smart, I'll give her that."

"Yes, she is," said Shay, rising to her feet. "I guess if you don't mind, I will take you up on your offer and go home early. I'll think about tomorrow, though. I'm not sure I can take that much time off. We got so far behind when we were closed after . . . well, after the Jasmine incident."

"I know, and I know how much this shop means to you, but you have to take care of yourself too, or you'll be no good to anyone."

"All right, I concede." Shay appreciatively smiled at her sister and grabbed her backpack. "There's something I want to do—no, need to do—anyway."

Chapter 23

Shay sat on her front porch, captivated by the young couple from cottage number seven's Labrador as he played with them on the beach. She chuckled at the large black dog running at the waves as they rolled out and then scampering back when the waves came crashing in again, all the while barking and yelping only to repeat his game, wave after wave. It tugged at her heart because this was the same game Spirit played whenever they went for a walk on the beach.

She was used to him not being around much during the days she was at the shop, but she had come to count on his company on her ride home or at least being met by him on the front porch, tail wagging, when she arrived at the cottage. However, lately he hadn't come home at night until after Tassi was safely tucked in. Tears burned in her eyes—she wiped her damp cheeks—but . . . she sniffed. It was all good, or at least as good as it could be. If Shay's odd pang of loneliness like now was her only problem, then Shay could count herself lucky.

She knew in her heart that it was only right that he be with Tassi now, as her life and future were on the line, and Spirit always went where he knew he was most needed at the time.

Shay settled back, drew in a wobbly breath and withdrew the pouch from under her shirt, turning the soft leather bag over in her hands. Intense warmth immediately snaked from her finger tips up through her, settling on her now burning cheeks. The fine hairs on the back of her neck prickled when the air around her crackled and groaned while she slowly removed the blue bottle from its nesting place.

She held it up, level with her eyes, and gazed at the tiny bubbles dancing in the amber liquid. With a flash of blue light, everything around her took on a crystalline appearance. Time seemed to bend, and in a moment of clarity, the two people and their dog on the beach moved in slow motion. She could see like a series of stop-motion photos, the trail of where they'd been and the steps that brought them to that moment in time.

The colors around her became so vibrant they took on a scent that she could taste and a texture she could feel. Shay knew in that moment her life had changed forever. In the past, she had held the bottle over a steaming cup of tea, and her scientific, analytical mind had found a way to explain the transformations she saw when looking at it. However, right now there was no tea. There was only her and the blue bottle and the visions melting into her mind, coming on soft wisps of fog, thick at first then fading away, leaving her with a clarity of sight she'd never experienced before.

Her skin tingled, sending prickles up her arms. A weight shifted inside her as she clasped the bottle in her hand and heard the screech of a rusted door opening, echoing in her mind.

However dangerous the journey might be, you can't turn back, a velvety whisper brushed across her cheek.

Shay drew in a deep breath and focused on the mist growing not only in the bottle but also wrapping itself around her visions. When she slowly released her breath, a clear image of the back of a woman with flowing, long blond hair appeared. The sounds of caustic laughter echoed in Shay's ears, but then the woman stiffened, and a scream replaced her laughter. She spun around, her eyes rolled back, and she dropped forward, her face toward Shay. When Shay saw whose face it was she let out a gasp. It was Jasmine Massey's.

Hands shaking, Shay tucked the bottle inside the pouch, looped the leather tie around her neck, tucked the pouch safely inside her shirt, and stared, deep in thought, out past the dog in the surf to the horizon. Jasmine's hair had been dark. Her vision didn't make sense. Who was the blonde with Jasmine's face? "Liam!" Had he told Dean his theory about Jasmine and her past?

She dug her phone out of her back pocket and tapped out a text message. Eyes glued to her screen, she waited . . . waited . . . and waited. Then she recalled he'd been in the pub all afternoon with Conor, gave up, and shoved her phone back in her pocket.

This was exactly why she had stopped using Bridget's so-called gifts in the first place. She shot to her feet and gripped the porch railing until her knuckles whitened. Not only did they scare the bejesus out of her, but the messages were also always cloaked in vagueness, and she had no idea what any of them meant. Like with her gut feelings about the fateful reading and Jasmine's ultimate death, she'd figured out their meaning too late, so what was the point of knowing anyway?

As she stared off in the distance, Shay reflected on the woman in her vision. It looked like Jasmine, but it could have been someone who happened to have similar features, like Liam and Conor did. Shay gasped at that thought. It made sense, given the lack of clues and evidence. Could Jasmine's murder have been a case of mistaken identity, meaning Jasmine wasn't the intended target? Was that what her vision was trying to tell her? *Oh, why is everything so vague?* She pounded her fist on the porch railing, her mind whirling with all the different scenarios.

Dean! She tugged her phone out again, tapped in a message for him to call her, and waited. Frantic cries for help at the same time as her peripheral vision caught a sudden burst of activity by the couple and their dog who'd been playing in the waves made her look up from her phone screen.

"Oh no!" She dropped her phone and sprinted down the steps and across the rocks and sand to reach a figure who was floundering in the waves down the beach toward the boardwalk. The young couple with the dog raced along the beach and reached the water's edge before she did.

The man then shouted a command, and the Labrador sprang into the crashing breakers, bobbed under, and when he came up, he was clasping the collar of a woman's blue shirt in his jaws. The dog dragged the woman's limp body through the surf and deposited her on the shore. The young man raced over, turned the woman onto her side, and pounded her back until she coughed and sputtered and finally waved her hand.

"I ain't dead, you know, but keep hitting me like that, John, and I will be." The woman tilted up on one elbow and sputtered some more just as Shay reached the group.

"Pearl!" Shay cried when she recognized that the sopping-wet body was her neighbor and Bridget's best and oldest friend in Bray Harbor, Pearl Hammond. "Are you okay?" She crouched beside her and swept the mass of tangled gray hair from her wild eyes.

Pearl pushed Shay's hand away and sat up straight, wheezing as she caught her breath. "I'm fine, Shay, thanks to Brody there." She gestured to the black Lab. "I don't know what happened. I came down to the beach to get some fresh air. It's been crazy busy today at the ice cream shop, and a dang rogue wave came out of nowhere. Swept me off my feet, and I couldn't regain my footing. . . ." Tears formed in her faded hazel eyes. "Here"—she waved her hand at the man she had called John—"help an old lady up."

John and the young woman with him pulled Pearl to her feet, and Shay steadied her from behind to make sure her knees didn't give out.

"Thank you, John and Ashley, and especially you, fellow." Pearl bent over and scratched the Lab's black head.

"I'm just glad we were close by and Brody seems to

have an instinct about water rescues." Ashley smiled and ruffled his head. "I guess it's a good thing he's a Labrador retriever." She glanced at Pearl. "But are you sure you're okay?"

Pearl nodded. "I'm fine, just cold and wet and in need of dry clothes."

"Well," said John, his eyes filled with concern, "it might be a good idea to get checked out anyway."

"He's right," echoed Shay. "You can't be too careful about inhaling water. It can lead to problems later."

"Will you all stop fussing, I'm fine," Pearl huffed, but her legs wobbled, and she grabbed on to Shay. "Maybe you should help me home, though, so I can get changed and back to the shop."

John looked at Shay and shook his head. "Tell you what, Pearl, why don't I go and tell your staff you won't be coming back tonight. Leslie's your assistant, isn't she?"

Pearl nodded.

"She can lock up and then, Shay, is it?"

Shay nodded.

"She can make sure someone checks you out, okay?" he added.

Pearl shooed them all with a flick of her craggy hand. "I don't know why you're all making such a fuss about this. I took a tumble in the waves, and that's all."

Ashley's brows rose, and she looked from John to Shay.

Shay smiled at her and nodded knowingly. "Come on, Pearl, let me get you home and into something dry, okay?"

"That's the most sense anybody's made in the last five minutes, but then I really have to get back to the shop."

"John's got it covered. Come on." Shay wrapped her arm around Pearl's shoulders and ushered her across the sand and rocks toward the wooden sidewalk. Shay glanced back, smiled at the couple, and mouthed, "I'll make sure she's checked out."

John gave her a thumbs-up.

"Just a minute," Pearl said to Shay when they reached the sidewalk. She turned around. "Wait!" Pearl hollered. "Thank you and please know that both of you and Brody all get ice cream on the house for the next year."

"Thank you!" John called and waved as they headed toward the ice cream shop.

"There," said Shay. "Now you can relax. See, John's gone to talk to Leslie, like he said he would, and we can get you into something dry, and then I'm calling Dr. Ward to come give you a quick once-over."

"What? I don't want a coroner checking me out, at least not until I'm dead," Pearl huffed as they went through the gate up to her porch steps.

"I know, but he's the only doctor I could think of who still makes house calls."

Pearl groaned and shot her a side glance as she climbed the steps. "Don't quit your day job, dearie, because that was a bad joke." She snickered.

"I know." Shay giggled. "I was just trying to lighten the mood. But," she added, her tone taking on a serious note, "we are going to have someone listen to your chest to make sure you didn't aspirate any water. That can lead to pneumonia and more complications if you're not careful."

"You mean because I'm old and frail," said Pearl, unlocking her door.

"No, because you're human, and it can happen to anyone." Shay shook her head in exasperation as she escorted Pearl through the door and into her small cottage. She could tell by the woman's willfulness that this was going to be a long evening spent playing tug-of-war.

"Take a seat." Pearl gestured to the sofa. "I'll be back in a minute." Her soaking-wet sneakers squeaked as she toddled down the hallway. Shay grinned; made herself comfortable in the deep, soft sofa; and gazed around the small living room.

"Funny thing about that dog, Brody, and how he just jumped into action and seemed to know exactly what to do," said Pearl as she came back, drying her hair with a towel. "You should know, though, the funny ways of dogs, since you have the best of them in Spirit." She tossed the towel onto the back of the sofa. "Although, I hear he's been spending most of his time with Tassi lately, is that right?"

"Um, yeah." Shay shifted. She really didn't want to get into the restraining order with Pearl. "But that's okay. How did you know?"

"I ran into Tassi and her mom yesterday up at the gas station on the highway. They were just coming back from visiting Tassi's grandmother in Monterey. I guess the poor dear isn't doing well and . . . it's just so sad," said Pearl, taking a seat beside Shay. "She only lost her husband of over fifty years last year, and now, well, I think she's dying of a broken heart." She smoothed the skirt of her fresh dress. "Spirit was in the backseat, looking pleased as punch with himself too." Pearl laughed. "But I bet you miss him."

"I know where he is, and I know Tassi needs him right now, so it's okay."

"Yes, nasty business that happened there in your shop, wasn't it?" She shook her head and tsk-tsked. "And to think the dang sheriff thinks a sweet little child like Tassi could have killed that woman. I tell you I could have killed that woman myself."

"What do you mean?"

"That woman who died at the tea shop. What did the newspaper say her name was?"

"Jasmine Massey."

"Yes, that's what they called her, and going by the picture in the newspaper, I'm fairly certain it was the same woman I met—oh, it must have been about three years back now—but she had blond hair then. A piece of work she was, I tell you." Pearl shook her head, demonstrating her disgust.

The cold hand of dread gripped at Shay's chest again as her earlier vision flashed like lightning bolts in her mind.

Chapter 24

Shay cradled her cup of tea between her hands and gazed over the rim at Pearl. "And you're sure that the woman you remember from three years ago was the same one whose picture was in the newspaper?"

Pearl nodded as she poured her cup of tea. "If not, then she sure looked a lot like the picture they published of the dead woman, but, like I said, it was about three years ago, so I might be wrong." She sat back and stared into her teacup. "It's funny, though. As soon as I saw her picture, the day she came into the ice cream shop came barreling back in my mind. I could even hear her high-pitched, squeaky voice ringing in my ears." She glanced over at Shay, slightly shook her head, and shrugged as she took a sip of tea.

Shay waited for Pearl to elaborate, but the woman sat silently drinking the tea Shay had insisted on making for them to help warm Pearl up. What had started out as a stall tactic so she could convince Pearl to see a doctor was now an investigative tactic to milk all Pearl knew about the woman who looked a lot like Jasmine, not only in Shay's vision but apparently also in the real-life experience Pearl had with her. The more information she could pass on to Dean, the more seriously he might take her and Liam's theory.

Shay sat forward and fixed her gaze on Pearl. "You meet hundreds of people every day, especially during tourist season, so what was it about this particular woman that stood out in your mind that three years later you still remember her?"

"She wanted to buy my ice cream shop. Or at least have that fellow she was with buy it for her, was more like it."

"That must have been Peter Graham."

"No, I know Peter. The man wasn't him."

"You know Tassi's dad?"

"Yeah, I use one of his firm's associates for all my legal dealings, so I've had the misfortune of running into Mr. High-and-Mighty a time or two."

Shay set her cup on the table. "It's interesting that only three years ago the fellow she was with wasn't Peter."

"No, this guy was old, wore expensive-looking clothes and had gray hair, not like Peter's, which was only starting to turn gray, but pure gray, and he had a ruddy complexion. Seemed sick too. He coughed and wheezed a lot as I recall, you know, like people with a chest thing do."

"And you're sure they were together, not just friends or that he was an associate of Peter's."

"Yup, he cuddled her and touched her face, kissed her all the while telling her he didn't want to buy an ice cream shop. I guess he was trying to calm her down because she was having a regular hissy fit since she wasn't getting her own way. Stomped out, she did, and he went off after her down the boardwalk. That's why I remember her so clearly. Spoiled brat that one, she was. Even when I told her the shop wasn't for sale, she kept at me and him. She told him to offer me more money and more money until I thought the old guy was going to have a stroke right there in my shop." Pearl shook her head. "Yeah, she was a piece of work, for sure."

A knock banged on the door, and Shay looked at Pearl. "Are you expecting anyone?"

"No, and I don't get much company either." Pearl rose to her feet and peered out the security peephole. "What the . . . ?" She opened the door. "Dr. Laine, what are you doing here?"

"Hi, Pearl, I hope I'm not interrupting."

"Ah, no." She glanced over at Shay. "Not really. Come in. Were you looking for Shay? Nothing's happened to Spirit, has it?"

"No, nothing like that," Zoey said, stepping through the door. "Hi, Shay." She gave her a quick nod and looked back at Pearl. "It's you I came to see."

"Me? Why? I don't have any animals."

"I know, but John Wilson and his fiancée brought Brody by the clinic so I could check his shoulder. It seems he pulled a muscle rescuing a woman from the water."

"Oh no," said Shay, rising to her feet. "Is Brody okay?"

"Yeah, he'll be fine. He just needs to try to rest his shoulder a day or two, if John can keep him away from the waves, that is. I hear it's a game he likes to play." Zoey stood awkwardly by the end of the sofa. "Anyway, John also told me that a certain woman Brody pulled from the surf was not too keen about being checked over by a doctor . . . so"—she waved a black case in her hand—"I came armed with a stethoscope and all."

"Pfft," Pearl sputtered. "First this one"—she pointed to Shay—"wants to send the coroner in to check me over. Now I get a veterinarian. I ain't dead, and I sure ain't no dog or cat."

"The coroner?" Zoey looked questioningly at Shay.

"Adam Ward was the only doctor I could think of who still makes house calls."

Zoey snorted a laugh. "Now that's funny."

"Pearl didn't think so, did you?" She glanced at Pearl, who looked like she might bolt any second.

"Pearl, I might not be a doctor for humans, but I do know what a healthy set of lungs should sound like. Let me take a listen just to make sure you're not experiencing any residual effects from being doused in the surf, okay?"

"I'm not sure why everyone is making such a fuss over a little wave," she said, taking a seat on the sofa. "Okay, do your thing Doc, but I draw the line at anything more than listening to my chest."

"Deal." Zoey grinned at Shay and took a seat beside Pearl.

Shay took the time to tidy up the tea service and rinsed out the cups, and when she went back into the living room, Zoey was at the door about to leave. "How is she? Anything to be concerned about?"

"No, everything sounds clear, but I did tell her if she has any shortness of breath, wheezing, chest pain, coughing fits, or starts to run a fever to get to the emergency room right away." She glanced down at Pearl, still sitting on the sofa. "And you promised to do that, right?"

"Yes." Pearl frowned at Shay. "See, just like I've been telling everyone, I'm fine."

"Okay." Shay strolled over to the door. "Then I think I'd better get home now too. But if you need anything, I'm right next door. Call me, promise?"

"I promise, now get out of here, both of you. I need to lie down a bit." She grabbed a throw blanket from the back of the sofa.

"Remember, call me if you have any problems," called Shay as they went outside and closed the door. "Thanks for doing this, Zoey. I feel more comfortable leaving her now."

"She's not out of the woods yet, but her lungs sound clear right now. Maybe pop in and check on her later or tomorrow if you can."

"I will, thanks. So . . . are you going to stop and see Liam while you're here?"

"No, I am not. I ran into him earlier when he and his cousin were heading—I should say *stumbling*—out of the pub, so I don't think this is the time to have a heart-to-heart."

"I hope you guys can work something out."

"I don't know if I want to."

"You're kidding."

"No, being back in my own condo has made me realize how much I missed my independence. Even though he wasn't around the last two months, everything I did still hinged on our decisions as a couple, and right now I feel . . . free. Maybe Gran knew what she was doing after all." Zoey laughed. "Well, I'd better get going. Those boxes aren't going to unpack themselves."

"Yeah, me too. My tummy is telling me it's way past dinnertime."

"See you around." Zoey waved and headed for the terraced steps up to the parking area.

Shay waved and turned but spun back around. "Wait, there was something I wanted to ask you, but then Pearl, and . . . well, it completely slipped my mind."

"Sure, what?"

"Remember the first day you saw Jasmine in the tea shop and you told me she looked familiar, but you couldn't place her?"

"Yeah, still can't, but go on."

"Could she have been a blonde when you saw her previously?"

"Hmm, maybe. Why?"

"It's just something Pearl said, and I was wondering if that's why you thought she looked familiar but couldn't figure out where you knew her from."

"It's possible, I suppose. Tell you what. I have a good friend that works for the La Jolla newspaper. She's got some great contacts. I can send her the picture of Jasmine that was in the *Monterey Times* to see if she can run it through the facial recognition program a friend of her might have access to."

"That would be great, because it got me thinking that maybe Jasmine wasn't the intended target, but this blond woman who looks like her was."

"Interesting. Okay, I'll let you know what Suzanne says."

"That would be great, thanks." Shay waved and trotted up the sidewalk toward her cottage, tucked against the hillside, but as she got closer, she slowed her pace. "Dean!" she called, but he had his back turned and appeared not to have heard her, so she ran to her porch steps but stopped when she realized he was talking to someone on the phone. Then she heard him say her name. "What's going on?"

He spun around and stared wide-eyed at her. "Call off the search party. I found her," he said into the phone, clicked off, and shoved his phone into the inside breast pocket of his sheriff's jacket. "Where have you been?" he barked, his eyes bulging.

"Ah . . ." She waved her hand toward Pearl's cottage. "What? What's going on? What search party?" she asked as she climbed the steps.

"The search party I was sending out to find you."

"Why?"

His face reddened. "Because I got a message from you. I called back *five* times and no answer. Decided to stop by and what do I find?"

She timidly shrugged.

He waved her phone in his hand. "This! Just lying there on the porch and the house wide open. I didn't know if you'd been hurt or kidnapped or . . ." His jaw tightened, and a large blue vein throbbed at his temple. "What possessed you to run off like that, especially when you'd just texted me that you had a lead in the murder case?"

"Well . . ." Shay quickly told him what had happened to Pearl and was relieved when his body language loosened. "See, I had a good reason for taking off the way I did."

"And Pearl is okay, you say?"

"Yes, Zoey came and checked her lungs and gave her strict orders to go to the emergency room if anything changed."

"Zoey?"

"It was either her or the coroner. No one else makes house calls anymore." Her words didn't garner a chuckle, like she'd hoped, but at least the throbbing vein at his temple had receded. "Pearl told me something interesting." She went on to tell him what Pearl had said about seeing Jasmine before but as a blonde and added the tidbit about Zoey recognizing Jasmine but not being able to place her.

"So maybe," Shay added, "Jasmine has a twin, or maybe there's someone else who looks like her and Jasmine was killed by accident because Pearl said this blond-haired woman was a piece of work. Have you . . . well . . . investigated Jasmine's past?"

"We don't usually investigate the victim unless they've been involved in a crime or if there are obvious reasons to do that."

"So . . . no?"

"No, but you say Pearl was pretty sure this woman in her shop was Jasmine except she was blond?"

"That's more or less what she said, but this woman wasn't with Peter Graham. It was a different man, an older man, which is weird."

"Why?"

"Because according to Joanne, her sister Karen, Peter's ex-wife, found out during the divorce proceedings that Peter and Jasmine had started their affair over two years before he filed for divorce, and they've been divorced for over a year now. I mean *if* this blonde was Jasmine and not some look-alike . . . but I guess we'll never know, will we?" She gave Dean an innocent side glance and shrugged in the hopes that he would take the bait she dangled in front of him, knowing he hated not having the answers as much as she did.

"Okay, with what you've told me, it might not be a bad idea to run a background check on her. Then at least we'll know if she has a twin sister hidden in the woodwork someplace, because as far as I know, nobody besides Peter has stepped forward to claim the body."

Not able to squelch the smile that tugged at the corners of her lips, Shay took a deep breath and gazed out at the crashing surf.

Chapter 25

Shay wavered in her emotions as she filled a travel cup with her favorite blend of morning coffee. Should she embrace a Saturday off and just enjoy it, or was it something she should feel guilty about because it was an act of pure self-indulgence? "Enjoy!" she said a bit more tentatively than the force of her conviction implied as she snapped down the lid on the cup, then headed up the sidewalk toward the main boardwalk to . . . where?

She still wasn't certain she'd made the right call by doing this, but when the sun warmed her skin and the light ocean breezes brushed against her face—something that rarely happened anymore given her schedule at the tea shop—she decided that just *maybe* Jen was right in insisting she take a break and make some time for herself.

She hummed to herself as she passed Pemberton's Beachside B&B, which was set back from the beach in a grove of trees. It had a perfect view of the harbor and the boardwalk. According to the verbal reviews of the B&B's patrons the owners steered toward her tea shop, Pemberton's was the best B&B experience they'd ever had. It warmed her heart to know that the businesses in town didn't see everyone else as competition, like they often did in larger cities, but helped each other out with referrals and recommendations.

She climbed the wooden stairs from the beach that led south down the wide boardwalk. It was clear by the crowds of tourists that the merchants in town were off to a good start for their Saturday. A pang of her earlier guilt washed over her, and she wondered if leaving Jen and Maddie to look after the morning service really had been a good idea. Faye wasn't scheduled to start work until noon, which was still two hours away, and judging by the crowds on the boardwalk, High Street would be just as busy. She really should be at the tea shop to offer another pair of hands. *What to do, what to do, what to do . . .*

"Hello, Miss Myers," said a tight voice from over her shoulder.

Shay smiled when she recognized the shy, gangly young man who'd accompanied Lilly when she'd dropped off the empty plant pots. "Good morning, Stephen. It's nice to see you again."

"You too, and when I saw you I thought I'd better let you know that I haven't forgotten about doing the Agatha Christie research for you."

"Right, the rosary bean plant." She waved it off. "That's okay. I only asked you because I thought in your research you may have already come across her using the beans as a weapon in one of her novels."

"No, but I feel bad because I told you I would. It's just that Lilly and I are still working on our lab project for Ms. Harper. That's actually why I'm here. To pick Lilly up so we can head to the lab at the college. It's not generally busy on Saturdays, so we're hoping we can get our paper finished by tonight. Then I can see what I can find out about rosary beans being used as murder weapons in literature for you."

"That's okay. You're busy. I can look it up myself, so don't worry."

"I don't mind, really. I love doing research."

"I know but . . ." She bit her lip in thought. "So, Lilly lives in Bray Harbor? I'd have thought she would live closer to the campus. You know, considering all the extra work she has to put in as Ms. Harper's teaching assistant, and if she doesn't have a car—"

"She does. She lives in Carmel, but her car's in the shop, and she works the early shift in the restaurant at the hotel here." He gestured toward the far end of the boardwalk. "So, I said I'd pick her up today."

"Oh, she is busy, isn't she?"

"Yeah." He chuckled. "I'm not sure how she manages it all, full-time TA for Dr. Harper, full-time student, and works part-time as a server, plus she's also top of her class, so I guess she can handle it."

"Good for her. Although, I know firsthand that working while being a full-time student can be tough. You seem like a good friend to her, so keep an eye out and make sure she doesn't burn out, okay?"

"I will. Even though I'm lucky and don't have to work—my parents have a bit of money—she's not as lucky. She just has her mom and their . . ." He dropped his gaze. "Anyway, yeah, I'll keep an eye on her."

"You're a good friend, Stephen."

His gaunt face broke out into a wide-mouthed grin, and his cheeks reddened.

"But I'd better be off," said Shay. "I hope you get that paper done tonight so you can both take a day off tomorrow," she said with a chuckle as she turned away.

"Miss Myers," he called after her. "If you happen to see Lilly up the boardwalk, could you tell her I'm here waiting for her?" He pointed to the Beach Side Café next door. "She should be along any minute because she's supposed to get off at ten, and it's after that now."

"I will. Bye." She waved and meandered along the boardwalk, taking in all the delectable scents of the pop-up food vendor stalls on her right. Farther up she paused and browsed through a rack of vintage dresses on display in front of Teresa's Treasures. After exchanging pleasantries with Beverly Lewis at Tasty Treats, she came to the crossroad at the end of the main boardwalk and wavered.

If she went right, she could head down the stairs and across the path that led to Land and Sea Rentals, a beach shop that specialized in bike, wave runner, and board rentals, and say hi to her old high school friend Mike Sturgis, the owner. If she went left, she'd be on High Street right by the tea shop. The temptation to stop in and check on Jen and Maddie was strong, but she knew her sister would see right through her and be insulted that Shay hadn't taken her advice and treated herself. Or . . . maybe she should go back to Teresa's

Treasures and buy that cute little 1950s-styled emerald-green sundress she'd just seen.

She turned and slammed into Lilly as she came up the top step from the hotel parking lot below the boardwalk. "I'm so sorry, Lilly." She grabbed the girl by the shoulders and pulled her closer as the girl teetered on the top step.

"It's okay. I'm okay." The girl shook off Shay's hands and pushed past her. "I gotta go," she said and scurried down the boardwalk at a brisk pace.

Shay stared after her. Something had happened to upset Lilly, and Shay doubted it was their minor collision. The girl's eyes were puffy and red as though she'd been crying. Shay glanced over the railing into the parking lot below, just as Faye Cranston tramped away from the hotel entrance. She scanned the boardwalk in the direction Lilly had gone, but she'd lost her in the crowds, then glanced back at Faye in time to see her cross the street and head toward the tea shop.

A woozy sensation gurgled in the pit of Shay's tummy. Faye was fanatical about her cutlery. Had she been in the hotel restaurant for breakfast and received a spoon or fork that she didn't deem clean or polished enough and accosted the poor server? Shay hoped that wasn't the case and it was something else, like pure exhaustion, that had spurred Lilly's teary-eyed outburst. Either way, even though it was a minor incident, it might be worth mentioning to Mia when she saw her next. If the poor girl was in a financial pinch and overworking herself just to make ends meet while at college, Mia should be aware.

* * *

A half hour later, Shay headed for home, her shopping bags swinging freely at her side. Window shopping had never appealed to her, but actually *buying* a new dress, now that was something that did lift her spirits, and she couldn't wait to get home to try it on with the open-toed shoes Teresa had convinced her would look great with the dress. After a quick stop at the ice cream shop to check on Pearl—who was doing fine, according to her—Shay had to admit it had been a morning well spent. However, now it was time to settle back and enjoy the scrumptious burger she'd also picked up from one of the food stalls along the boardwalk.

Jen had been right. She did need a day just to treat herself, and treat herself she had indeed. She sniffed the small bag containing her bacon cheeseburger, smiled as she slid onto a kitchen chair, and dug in.

As she popped the last bite of her burger into her mouth, a knock at the kitchen door made her choke. She coughed and patted her chest until the piece passed, then lifted the corner of the curtain covering the small window and smiled. "Liam," she said as she opened the door. "What are you doing here at lunchtime? Shouldn't you be at the pub?"

"I was, and then I stopped into the tea shop to talk to ye, but Jen said ye were home."

He looked questioningly at her. "Are ye sick? Yer face is bright red."

"No, I'm fine, it's just that—" She waved her hand and took a gulp of her iced coffee to wash the last of the burger remnants down. "There, is my color better?" She grinned at him, setting her drink back on the table with a relieved gasp.

"Ah . . . ya." He stepped inside the kitchen and glanced at the bits and pieces left of her lunch on the table. "Yer supposed to chew before ye swallow, though."

"I was until you pounded on the door right beside me and scared the bejesus out of me." She chuckled. "Now what can I do for you?"

"Nothing," he said and looked awkwardly at the floor.

"Nothing? You just dropped by during one of the pub's busiest times of the day for . . . nothing."

"There's something I need to tell ye, but I'm not sure how yer going to take it." He met her curious look.

Had something happened to Gran? Was she ill? Is that why he asked her if *she* was sick? Shay teetered on panic but bit the inside of her cheek to stop her spiraling thoughts and let her instincts instead of her heart rule as she studied his face. "It's not Gran, is it?"

"No," he said, taking a seat at the table and looking up at her. "Why would ye think it was Gran?"

"I . . . I, never mind, but I can sense it's something big and, well . . ." She sat down beside him and locked her gaze with his. "Just take a deep breath and tell me what it is."

Liam drew in a noisy breath, fidgeted with her drink glass on the table, and glanced away, avoiding her steady gaze.

"Just say it."

"Okay . . ." He drew in another breath. "I found out

what Conor was up to, and don't worry, he's gone now."

"Why should I worry?"

"Because . . . well, it seems that fellow I told you about that he went to work for on the Continent . . ."

"Yeah."

"I think . . . I think he might have been yer dad."

Not what she expected to hear. "You're kidding." The blood rushed from Shay's head to her already constricting chest, and she let out a sharp gasp. "That means he can identify him, though."

"Yes and no. He only knew him by the name of Doyle but said he doubts that's his real name because, over the years, he's heard him called other names and has known him to wear a number of disguises."

"Then how do you know it's him, my biological father?"

"I don't for sure, but it all adds up and makes sense when ye put the clues and the facts together."

"What clues?"

"It seems that when I was back home for the funeral, a local newspaper took some pictures of the family. Ye know my granddad ran that pub most of his life and he was a bit of a local legend. It seems this Doyle saw the pictures in the paper and noticed the similarity between me and Conor and asked him about me. When Conor told him I was his cousin living in America, this Doyle guy said he'd pay him a lot of money to come here to Bray Harbor to steal that." Liam pointed to the pouch. "He never told Conor what was inside the pouch. He only told him that the man in the picture had access to something that was his, and he wanted his property back."

"If Doyle knows you live in Bray Harbor, he knows I'm here too, that you know me, and he knows I have the blue bottle." Shay recalled what Pierre Champlain, another would-be thief, had said to her last year: *He seeks to possess what you have as much as I do.* A chill raced through Shay. "Or maybe he's always known, but since he's so bent on retaining his anonymity, he won't come to steal the bottle himself but looks for others to do his dirty work for him."

"That's what I eventually got out of Conor after a few more pints of free beer at the pub."

"What's Conor going to do?"

"He said he had full intentions of getting it for Doyle, but after hearing Gran talk about ye and meeting ye, he couldn't go through with the plan. He can't go back to the Continent or even Ireland now, so he's going to have to disappear."

"That means Doyle will be looking for him, and I'm afraid since Conor didn't make good on his deal to get this for him," Shay's voice grew fainter as she toyed with the leather tie around her neck, "he'll just send someone else for the pouch."

"Then ye'll have to be extra careful, Shay. Ye have to promise me—even though Gran is pushing ye to use yer magic—that ye won't let anyone, and I mean anyone, see ye use that blue bottle. If Doyle can turn me own cousin against me, we never know who his next errand person might be."

Shay sat upright and stared wide-eyed at Liam. "But why now? It's been over a year since he sent someone to do his bidding. What changed that he sent Conor now? There must be a reason."

Liam diverted his gaze from hers. "After Conor told me, I looked up the article on the internet. It seems besides a eulogy of sorts to my grandfather, the reporter, in giving some background on the family, named me as his grandson, of course, but also mentioned a friend of mine and how we had helped apprehend a well-known jewel thief back in America by using a little bit of Irish magic."

"Was the reporter talking about the blue bottle?"

Liam shrugged. "Probably, in a really vague way, the reporter would have had no way of knowing ye had the actual bottle, besides to most of the world, it's just a myth, remember?"

With his words the pouch warmed on Shay's chest.

"I read it as he only knew that the case had something to do with Ireland and the outcome was magical, but, and I'm guessing here. As soon as Doyle read it, he put two and two together and figured out that ye just don't have the blue bottle and blue diamond, but have discovered the power of the Early family magic and know how to use it. He must have decided he couldn't risk someone else figuring it out too, and that's why he made another move. He wants the bottle and the power for his own use." Liam leaned forward and pinned Shay with a concerned look. "I'm pretty sure if he ever gets his hands on the bottle, and figures out it won't work for him, he's going to come after ye next, to force ye to use it for his advantage."

"Then we have to figure out a way to make him come for the bottle himself, not send an errand person like Conor, and we can put an end to all this once and for all."

"Shay, this man, according to Conor, will stop at nothing to get what he wants, including murder, and now Conor's in danger too."

"Yes, but if he needs me, he won't kill me."

"But he won't know he needs ye until *after* he gets his hands on the bottle and discovers there's a reason why it's called the Early family magic. By the time he realizes it won't work for him, it might be too late for ye."

"We can set a trap for him, then. Draw him out with something he won't be able to refuse looking into himself, not through a third party, and then we can catch him before any of that happens."

"That's pretty risky."

"Maybe it's worth the risk. At least Conor wouldn't be looking over his shoulder the rest of his life, and I wouldn't have to live in fear of my own . . . father." Her thoughts immediately went to Tassi and her dad. "Yes, we have to draw him out and stop him."

Chapter 26

Liam left to return to the pub but only after Shay promised she wouldn't do anything rash and would wait until they could talk about it later and formulate a plan with Dean's help.

This felt too close to home, though, and waiting made her nervous. If Doyle was willing to use Liam's own cousin Conor as a Trojan horse, who else had he sent to do his bidding?

Shay curled into the front porch chair and cradled her hands around a cup of lemon balm tea, a citrusy-scented brew Bridget had noted in her journals as an infusion that would lift one's mood and sharpen mental functions. She sighed as the tea did its job. Could someone in her close circle possibly be on Doyle's payroll and have befriended her to get their hands on the rare blue diamond contained inside the bottle in her pouch?

Mentally, she clicked through each person: Jen, Dean,

Tassi, Joanne, Zoey, Pearl, Mia, Adam, Liam, and Gran. Just as quickly as she'd thought of them, she dismissed them all. None of them would ever want to cause her harm. She took another sip of her tea, sat back, closed her eyes, and an image of the Little White Glove Society ladies rushed into her thoughts.

"That's it!" Her cup slipped in her hand, and hot tea splashed onto her jeans. She screeched, jumped to her feet, and patted her burning thigh.

Once her erratically beating heart retained a normal rhythm and the smarting subsided, she whipped out her phone, tapped in Jen's number, and thumbed out a text: **Can you find out from Faye which one of the Little White Glove Society ladies switched their regular meeting place from Café Fleur on Fifth Avenue to Crystals and CuriosiTEAS?**

She pressed send, dabbed a tissue from her pocket over her sopping wet jeans, sat back down, and drained the last dregs from her cup. If she could figure out whose idea it was to switch venues for the group's daily get-together, it might lead to who was on Doyle's payroll. That was, of course, if her new theory was right or even close. Fingers crossed it would at least give them something to work with.

A vision of Jasmine crept into her mind, and she sat upright again. Julia had mentioned the woman pushing her way into the group, and Jasmine had attempted to push her way into Shay's life and insisted, quite vehemently, on a reading. Shay leaned back in thought. Since readings were normally conducted in privacy, Jasmine and Shay would have been alone for that.

Shay's skin prickled. Was Jasmine's plan to take the pouch then, but when that never happened, and a group reading was set up instead . . . The veins in her throat throbbed as her heart rate quickened.

Liam did say Doyle would murder to get what he wanted. Was Jasmine Doyle's Trojan horse, but when she failed to complete the job she had been sent to do, she became expendable? Shay grasped the arms of her chair, causing her knuckles to whiten as her mind raced. It was strange that Conor showed up not long after Jasmine died. Perhaps Doyle sent Conor in to do what Jasmine had failed to do.

"Oh," she moaned and slid down in her chair. She needed to know more about not only Jasmine but also Doyle if she was ever going to figure this out and get Tassi taken off the short list of suspects.

Her thoughts drifted back to the day last year when Pearl Hammond, Bridget's only friend in town, had told Shay about her biological father. Not the father who had raised Shay as his own but the man who had taken her birth mother, a fanciful young girl, into an Irish wood one day. According to Pearl, Bridget had said he was a very handsome man who'd said all the right words and turned her young head. After he proclaimed his love for her, she hadn't been able to resist his charms.

Pearl told Shay that Bridget had called him a fairy man who held a magical charm about him. Bridget also told Pearl that it was as though he'd bewitched her and made her feel like Titania, the Faerie Queen, and she had fallen willingly into his arms. But after their liaison, his true spirit came out and the hands that once held so much tenderness for her then squeezed her throat as he tried to remove the pouch from her neck. She fought him off, managed to get away and run home, only to find her mother had earlier in the day been badly beaten by the same man, a wicked fairy man, according to her mother, who had come to take the magic of the Early family and the power it had. She begged Bridget to flee and go far away so he couldn't ever find her or the pouch.

At the age of sixteen, and pregnant by this man, Bridget left her home, her family, everything and everyone she knew, and moved to America. She settled in San Francisco, thinking she was as far away from the wicked fairy man as she could get, but one day he showed up at the teahouse where she was working as a palm and tea leaf reader.

Shay shot upright in her chair. He *had* shown his face in America at least once. Now she only had to figure out a way to draw him to Bray Harbor.

For the rest of the afternoon, Shay played out in her head at least a dozen ideas on how to bring the fairy man to her. She didn't want to deal with the constant twinge at the base of her skull anymore, wondering if someone in her inner circle might not be as forthcoming as Conor had been about his true intentions. But it was no use. Any ideas she devised seemed exactly that and something an experienced thief and con man who wasn't afraid to kill would see right through. Unless, of course . . . She set aside the spatula she'd been using to stir her fried vegetables and tapped out a text to Liam.

Can you stop by on your way home tonight?
Sure, what's up?
I have an idea. Just come.
Okay, I'll be there as soon as I can get out of here.

If she could convince Liam of her plan, it might just work with his help, and they could bring Doyle out into the open and with any luck solve Jasmine's murder at the same time.

As she seized the spatula and gnashed at the sides of the frying pan, questions still haunted her: How did the poison get into Jasmine's cup? Was someone else working for Doyle? Peter perhaps? Even though no trace of poison had been discovered in his and Jasmine's hotel room . . . She dropped the pan of vegetable stir-fry she'd been cooking onto the counter with a clatter.

"But Peter had refused to allow Dean to take any of Jasmine's belongings until Dean got a warrant. That means Peter could have been stalling, giving him time to remove all trace evidence from their hotel room before Dean took Jasmine's possessions in for testing."

She needed to ask Dean if the lipstick Jasmine had been wearing the night she died was an identical match to the lipstick he took from the hotel, and not just in color and brand. Was it from the same tube and batch? Just because the lab found no traces of abrin in the lipstick tube they tested didn't mean it was the actual tube of lipstick Jasmine had been using. Peter could have replaced the tube with an identical brand and shade of lipstick.

Shay grabbed a dishcloth and scoured the counter where the sauce in the pan had sloshed over, and hoped her internal rambling wasn't just because she was sick to death of Tassi still being under house arrest, which by Spirit's continued absence seemed to be the case. If she hadn't lost her touch or intuition, there was a clue somewhere in all the puzzle pieces she'd gathered.

Despite Liam's warning, it was going to have to be done. Fingers shaking, she slipped the pouch from around her neck and turned the soft leather over in her hands. She knew the power the amulet held, but, more importantly, she knew how it made her feel whenever she used it, and it was that same power Doyle wished to possess. Somehow, she was going to have to use it against him to end his haunting danger once and for all.

Shay settled in at the table with a steaming cup of chamomile tea, the same tea she had used to see images in the past. Even though she knew by her recent experience that she didn't need the steam from the tea, she took comfort in what had worked before.

After finishing her tea and asking her question, she turned her cup, tipping it to drain. When Shay righted the teacup, she held the bottle in her left hand over the tea leaves, and drew in a deep breath.

A rapid pounding on the door echoed through the kitchen. She jerked; dropped the bottle into the cup; frantically fished it out with a spoon, trying not to disturb the settled leaves in the bottom; and leapt up to peek through the door window. "Gran?" She opened the door. "Ah . . . hi."

Gran didn't wait for an invitation to come in. Instead, she pushed past Shay, glanced at the table set for

Shay's reading, snorted, and deposited a small blue velvet case and a large black velvet one on the table.

"What's this?" Shay eyed the small suitcase-shaped boxes.

"Liam told me what Conor was up to, and how he's warned ye not to use the Early magic. So, we won't, but I've never been so *fearg*. That changeling from the Unseelie Court bewitched me boy and tried to turn him against his own kin." Gran slammed her hand on the table, and her body quivered. She raised her hand and shook a tight fist. "But he ain't seen what power this old Gran has, and with yer help we can put an end to his wicked ways."

Gran's usual faded blue eyes transformed with a fierceness that had Shay taking a step back. The old woman's eyes now blazed an electric blue, and the deep Irish slang that rolled off her tongue had Shay struggling to comprehend. "What's 'fearg' and the 'Unseelie Court'?" Shay gripped the back of her chair, and her knuckles whitened as Gran began opening the cases she'd brought.

Gran paused and looked blankly at Shay. "Fearg, ye know, mad, angry."

"Oh," said Shay, eyeing the contents of the blue box as Gran lifted the lid. "And the Unseelie Court? Do those have something to do with that?" She gestured to the gemstones arranged inside the small cubbyholes of the case.

"Nah, these are what we will use to discover if any more amongst us are here in disguise." Gran straightened to her full five-feet-two inches and turned to

Shay. "Ye have these same crystals and stones in yer shop. Have ye never used them?"

Shay shook her head.

"I told ye about the Seelies and their court, didn't I?"

"Vaguely, but what's their court?"

"I see," said Gran, sitting down hard in a chair, "we have more work ahead of us than I thought."

Chapter 27

"Okay, I think I understand now." Shay refilled Gran's teacup but continued to hover, teapot in hand. "The Seelie Court is a group of fairies known to be happy, blessed, lucky, and good-natured, the ones referred to in legends as good fairies."

"It's not just in legends, me dear," Gran sputtered with offense.

"No, I get it, but for the sake of argument, so I can wrap my head around this . . ."

Gran shrugged and from the look on her face was clearly humoring Shay.

"But," Shay continued, "there is also another group of wicked, dangerous fairies called the Unseelie Court?"

Gran nodded. Her lips pressed tight in agreement, and she gestured to the box of crystals and gemstones. "That's what dese are for. Dey will show us who among us is disguised as a member of the Seelie but has wicked intentions."

"It sounds to me like this Seelie Court of fairies broke into two factions, and it's what we generally refer to as the battle between good and evil nowadays."

"Aye, it is that." Gran lifted the lid of the black velvet case, removed a large object swathed in black velvet fabric, set it on the table, and pulled back the cloth.

The large crystal ball perched on an ornately carved wooden base mesmerized Shay, and she sat down hard in her chair. "Wow," was all she managed to utter.

"Ye have one of dese. I've seen it in yer back room."

"I know, but mine is just a crystal ball. It doesn't have a hand-carved base like that one."

"Ah, yes." A smile formed on Gran's craggy face. "This one is very old. Ellen's mam, yer Bridget's grandmam, gave me friend Ellen the blue bottle on her sixteenth birthday. Since me own mam had passed along with any family legacy she might have had, Ellen's mam felt bad for me and gave me this on me sixteenth birthday."

"So, in a way it's part of the Early family legacy too."

"Aye, just like that blue bottle." She gestured to it lying on the table. "The same one that Ellen then passed down to yer Bridget on her sixteenth. So ye see, all these are very old links to yer Irish ancestry, and it's time ye learned how to use them."

Shay glanced at the case filled with gemstones and looked at Gran. "I know what those are. I was a gemologist and geologist before I took over the tea shop."

"Aye, but do ye know what powers dey have?"

Shay shook her head. "Haven't a clue."

"'Tis time ye learn then. Ye see, crystal balls and

gems have been used by yer ancestors, the Celtics, or Druids as they be known, since time itself. Because dey believed dese stones possessed supernatural and magical powers. Da first crystal balls were made of finely polished crystal quartz. Nowadays, though, many use glass balls, but these old ones, well, dey hold a power that the glass doesn't have." Gran reverently stroked the crystal ball.

"It must work a lot like when I gaze into the blue bottle and see images in the amber liquid that surrounds the blue diamond."

"Aye, ye have the most powerful of all crystal balls right there in that pouch ye carry."

"Okay, a year ago I wouldn't have believed this, but after using it on occasion, I think I understand. What I don't understand is how those"—Shay gestured to the assortment of gemstones in the blue case—"have anything to do with this." She pointed to the top cubby. "Like this purple one, the amethyst, or the black tourmaline, or the black obsidian next to it."

"Amethyst is known as one of de most powerful crystals for a psychic connection. It opens up de mind and allows a seer to access information dat the five senses don't pick up on." Gran shifted the box closer to her and gestured to the black tourmaline stone. "Dis one is a very powerful stone. It absorbs dark energy from other crystals or from yer surroundings." She glanced at Shay. "It's a good idea to cleanse yer crystals with this stone often."

"And what about this rose-colored one, the rose quartz?"

"Ah . . ." Gran smiled. "De stone of love and calming," she said as she tenderly stroked the velvet fabric of the cubby where the gem was nesting. "De turquoise is for communication, and the green malachite is for strength and confidence." She pointed. "The orange citrine is for manifestations, and the clear quartz like in me crystal ball is for cleansing as it amplifies energy, which is why 'tis used most often. But ye'll come to learn that the simple act of holding any of dese"—she waved her hand over the remainder of the collection of gemstones in the tray—"will help ye read da person seeking yer help too."

Shay took a deep breath, sat back, and eyed the tray of stones through the lens of the psychic world of tea leaves and palmistry instead of the scientific world of geology. "There's so much to learn, isn't there?"

"Aye," said Gran, "but we'll do baby steps just like ye have with the reading of the leaves and—"

They both jumped when a loud knock rattled the kitchen door.

Shay patted her chest to squelch her palpitations as she rose and pulled back a corner of the curtain on the door window and peeked out. "Dean?"

"The sheriff?" cried Gran. "Hurry, dear, get de bottle back in the pouch and hide it, quick!"

"It's okay," whispered Shay. "He knows about it."

"He does?" Gran looked at her in amazement.

"Yes," Shay continued in a hushed voice. "He took over lead in the investigation last year and—"

"Shay," Dean hollered through the closed door, "are you going to let me in or what?!"

"And he *is* my brother-in-law." Shay flashed Gran a sheepish grin as she flung the door open. "Hi, what brings you by at dinnertime? Did Jen send you out for takeout after her long day and you thought you'd—"

"No, I haven't made it home yet. Mind if I come in?" Dean removed his sheriff's cap and gestured inside.

"Sure," Shay said, stepping aside. "Dean, you remember Liam's gran, don't you?"

"Good evening, ma'am. Yes, and it's nice to see you again," Dean said with a nod and a smile, and then he looked at Shay. "Can we talk"—he glanced down at Gran—"somewhere private?"

Shay straightened her shoulders and pinned him with a curious look. "Gran's well aware of everything that's going on, even the lawsuit Peter's bringing against me for practicing witchcraft. Whatever you have to say, you can say in front of her."

The door behind Dean flew open, sending Dean careening toward Shay and knocking her back a step. In a flash, he swiveled around, gun drawn, and aimed at the figure looming in the doorway. "Liam?!" he shouted and holstered his firearm. "What in the heck are you doing barging in like that?"

"Ah . . ." Liam glanced from Gran's face, drained of all color, to Shay's even paler one and to Dean's blazing, fierce eyes. "I . . . um . . . saw yer patrol car parked out in Shay's parking spot and thought . . ." He glanced at the table. "Are we having a tea party?" The tips of his ears reddened to match the color creeping over his cheeks.

"You're just lucky that I didn't shoot you, barging in like that." Dean breathed heavily, clearly trying to control his burst of adrenaline. "Dang you, man. Do you know how many times I've had to draw my gun and . . . just don't ever do that again."

Liam swallowed hard. "I'm sorry, but I thought—"

"Just don't do it again," Dean tersely repeated.

"No, sir, I won't." He looked awkwardly at Dean and then at Shay. "I just thought ye were in trouble and—"

"Why don't we put the kettle on, Shay," said Gran, rising to her feet. "Then we can all have a nice cup of calming tea, and the sheriff here can tell all of us what brings him by this evening."

Shay hurried over to the counter and glanced back over her shoulder at Dean and Liam, who were seated across from each other and avoiding eye contact. Gran slid up to her side and whispered, "I've never seen me boy behave like that for a lassie."

Shay looked at her and shrugged, then matching her hushed tone said, "It's not the first time he's busted through the door like a SWAT team."

"I think me boy has feelings for ye."

"No, we're friends. He said we're like kin."

"Kin perhaps from the same county, but not kin as in family ties." She glanced at a still red-faced Liam. "I tell ye, he has deep feelings for ye."

"No, he's in love with Zoey."

"Pfft," she sputtered. "He's not, and that union was never meant to be."

"Why not? They're perfect for each other," whispered Shay, filling the teapot with boiling water.

"Because she's a nymph of the woods and he's of royalty in the Seelie high court, like ye are. Take me word for it, child. Think of der breakup as a fairy wink."

"A what?"

"Ye know. A coincidence dat's not a coincidence but a push by da fairies in the direction yer supposed to be going in."

"Yes, but no matter what the fairies think, relationships are about timing, and I just don't think this is our time." Shay was taken aback. Gran had some great insight, and she valued her knowledge, but times like this she couldn't help but think the woman was bonkers. Wood nymphs and high courts, really?

Shay shook her head. What was Gran thinking? Besides, she wasn't ready for another relationship. Her ex had stripped her soul blind, and with Liam just getting out of one, no . . . Bad timing for both of them, and no matter what, she couldn't allow herself to entertain Gran's notions. Liam was someone who she knew could really break her heart, so no, she couldn't handle that right now. "I really think you're making too much of this. He was a police officer for years. It's in his DNA to protect, and he feels protective of me since . . . well, what happened last year."

Gran scoffed as Shay moved toward the table and set a tray laden with four fresh cups and a pot of steaming chamomile tea down. She removed Gran's used cup along with the cup she had prepared earlier for her reading and started back to the counter. When she went to set hers down, she glanced into it, and then looked at Gran. "Um, can you tell me what a tea leaf pattern that looks like a kettle means?"

Gran's face paled, and she paused in passing around the cups and looked at Shay. "It means death, me dear."

Hand shaking, Shay held the cup out for Gran to see.

"Is this yers?" Gran asked gazing into the cup.

"Yes, from earlier when I was going to use the blue bottle, but it's the same pattern I saw in the bottom of Jasmine's cup the night of the group reading just before she . . ."

"Speaking of Jasmine," Dean piped in, "that's what I came here to talk to you about."

Dean's words were lost in Shay's jumble of thoughts as she peered into the cup again. This was impossible, right? There was no way her leaves could be identical to Jasmine's. She must be mistaken. Shaken, she set the cup on the counter and covered it with a kitchen towel to preserve it until later and glanced questioningly at Gran, who was peering back at her under a heedful eye. "Sorry, Dean. I got sidetracked." Shay softly laughed as she and Gran joined them at the table. "What were you saying about Jasmine?"

"Is everything okay, *a chara*?" asked Liam, his eyes filled with concern.

"Yes, it's just something I saw earlier when I was going to do a reading and was puzzled by it. Everything is okay now, though." She smiled reassuringly at him and at Gran.

"I see"—Liam gestured to the bottle and pouch on the table—"that ye were going to use yer gift tonight? I thought we talked about that." His gaze went from concerned to reproach in a flash.

"I was, but Gran . . ." She looked helplessly at the old woman. "Gran stopped by with—"

"I brought the child some other ways to try, but enough of this inquisition." Her eyes snapped with authority, clearly letting Liam know she wasn't putting up with this any longer. Gran folded her hands in front of her on the table. "Now, the sheriff here has something to tell us about the young woman Jasmine." She shot Liam another warning glance. His ears turned bright red, and he slid down a touch in his chair and hung his head.

Gran set her gaze on Dean. "Ye were saying?"

"Ah . . . yeah, I was." Dean's gaze flashed between an unruffled-appearing Gran, and the bristling appearance Liam had about him, and settled his gaze on Shay. "I looked into Jasmine Massey's background, but I couldn't find anything going further back than three years."

Liam shot upright in his chair, finally over his scolded little-boy pout. "How can that be?"

"Don't ask me. There's no driver's license issued in the name of Jasmine Massey, no Social Security number, no tax returns, no bank information, nothing. Even the lease on her fancy condo in Carmel is under Peter Graham's name."

"Did ye run her fingerprints?" asked Liam.

"Of course we did."

"And nothing there either?"

"Nothing in our jurisdiction at least, so I've forwarded them to the FBI to run through their database." Dean sat back and folded his arms across his chest.

"However, if she had no priors, it will come back empty, just like our search did."

"Could she have been in a witness protection program or something?" asked Shay.

"I guess it's possible, but if she was, the FBI won't give me anything no matter what the fingerprint results show."

"You mean they won't even tell you if she was even though she's dead now?"

Dean shook his head. "There's always the possibility that she was in hiding on her own, though."

"Like running from someone in her past?" asked Shay.

Dean nodded and shrugged. "That's one possibility."

"What's another?" Shay looked from Dean to Liam.

"She was in hiding," Liam said, "because of something she'd done three years ago."

"Yes," added Dean. "Then the fingerprints will definitely tell us if she was charged with something, and it might give us a lead to finding out who wanted her dead."

Chapter 28

Shay sat at the kitchen table as Gran tidied up their tea service and Liam stood out in the backyard chatting with Dean before he left to go home for a late dinner. Her mind replayed what Dean had told them about Jasmine, and a thought struck her. She whipped out her phone and tapped in Zoey's number. Her call went straight to voice mail, so she thumbed out a text: **Hi, I was wondering if your friend turned up anything about Jasmine like if she recognized the photo you sent her. Let me know. tx**

Liam came back in and looked at Shay, then at Gran. "Now, do you two mind telling me what you were doing before Dean arrived and why ye have the bottle out of the pouch?"

"It's nothing. I was here, *alone,* so no prying eyes would have seen it, and I was about to do a reading when Gran came in with all these." She waved her hand toward the boxes on the table. "We got side-tracked. That's all. Nothing *nefarious* was taking place, if that's what you think." She went over to the cup she'd set on the counter earlier and removed the towel she had covered it with.

"It's just that I worry about ye, *a chara*. We don't know who else this Doyle character might have sent, and with Peter charging ye with practicing witchcraft . . ." He scrubbed his hand through his thick black hair. "It's probably best ye don't—"

"Don't what? Live as I please in my own home?" Shay snapped. "Why not? Do you see anyone else here besides you, Gran, and Dean, all of whom are well aware of the bottle? So how is me using it in private putting anything at risk?"

"She's right, boy." Gran leveled a steady eye on him.

Liam's shoulders sagged. If Shay weren't so spitting offended by his overbearing protectiveness of her as if she were some ditz who couldn't make her own decisions, she would have laughed at the image before her. It seemed Gran was able to turn this robust once-police detective back into a simpering twelve-year-old boy with just a few words. The woman really did have a special power.

Shay shot Liam a look of reproach too, and then peered into the cup. Her thoughts raced as she studied the patterns she'd created earlier, and she looked over at Gran, by the sink. "Gran, have you ever done a reading and had the tea leaves in your cup take on an identical pattern to that of someone you did a reading for?"

Gran straightened her back, slowly set the dishcloth on the sink divider, and turned toward Shay, her face tense. "It seems ye have mirrored another's reading."

"It looks like it." Shay held the cup out toward Gran.

"This is exactly what I saw in Jasmine's cup before she . . . well, you know. What does it mean?"

Gran steadied herself against the sink counter and hung her head.

"Gran, what does it mean that her reading showed up in my cup?" Shay's voice teetered on the verge of panic when she saw the haunted look in Gran's eyes. "Has it ever happened to you?"

Gran shook her head. "No, me dear, but I know others who have crossed between the thin veil and had similar experiences."

"What does it mean?" With her heart pounding against her chest wall, Shay frantically glanced at Liam, who gave her a bewildered shrug, and then locked her gaze on Gran. "Does it mean I'm going to die too, the same way Jasmine did?"

"No, me dear." Gran stepped closer to Shay and took her hands in hers. "It only means that ye've crossed through the thin veil between the physical world and the world on the other side. Some say magic, some say spirit world, and it seems Jasmine was able to communicate with ye."

"Did the blue bottle cause this . . . this thinning in the veil?"

Gran's eyes took on a distant stare, and she shook her head. "No, me dear. 'Tis the time of the year that some like ye, who experience the emotions of others, empaths, as they be known, seem to live between de two worlds. Der are certain times of de year when the veil thins, with the strongest of dese being late September up until about early November. It's called Samhain, which means summer's end, and 'tis celebrated on November first. Dat's considered the start of the Celtic new year. It signals death and rebirth with the end of the harvest season and da beginning of a dark winter season. De celebrations actually begin on the eve of October thirty-first."

"You mean Halloween?"

"Dat is the modern, Westernized version of it. Ye see, a powerful Celtic ritual was made into a party night, but dey did keep a wee portion of the ideas alive."

"How so?" Shay slid onto a chair beside Liam. Gran's knowledge fascinated her, and she felt like a small child listening, breathlessly, to an old legend, as so many of her ancestors would have.

"Ye see, the Druids, or Celtic priests, believed that the presence of otherworldly spirits made it easier . . . to make predictions about the future. Bonfires and feasts were held at the end of October, just before winter. Dey believed it was a time of the year when doorways to the otherworld opened, permitting beings and souls of de dead to come into our world. Many who attended dese celebrations would dress up in costumes, animals or mythical beasts, in hopes of fooling the spirits who might want to harm them."

"And Halloween evolved out of this?"

"Aye, but so much has been lost with Halloween. The only rituals kept are the tradition of dressing up and going door to door. Ye see, in Druid times peasants would wear masks and such and carry sticks when they went from house to house on Samhain Eve, collecting food for the feast and threatening to do mischief if dey were not welcomed or did not receive a contribution toward the feast."

"Trick or treat, to say the least."

"Exactly, but here I blather on and ye only wanted to know what the veil was."

"Please go on." Liam leaned forward on his elbows. "This is fascinating, Gran. I haven't heard these stories since I was a child and had forgotten them." He frowned. "But how does this relate to Shay mirroring a dead woman's tea leaf reading?"

Gran pursed her lips. "Like I started to say before I went off—must be part of me age, getting lost in the old ways sometimes—but 'tis the time of de year when de veil is at its thinnest, and seers who have the powers that Shay does are more receptive. Now this poor girl Jasmine, or whoever she was—and it doesn't matter what she did in the past—has the same needs as anyone who has come to an unfortunate death, and dat's a need for someone on this side of the veil to know what happened to them so she can find some closure and her spirit can move on. It's clear she's reaching out."

Shay peered into the cup again and shook her head. "As far as I can see there is nothing here that tells me anything more today than the night of the group reading. Except, of course, now I know the *P* doesn't stand for proposal or Peter or pregnant but poison."

"Ah, but the answer is der, me dear. Ye only need to look deeper."

"Deeper? There is nothing else, and now that I know the tea leaf clump that looks like a kettle means death, it still doesn't tell me anything I didn't know. She drank the tea, and she died."

"Remember, me dear. Death doesn't always mean physical death. It also means death of ideas or old ways and beliefs. It really means changes are coming." Gran leveraged herself to her feet with the help of the table edge and pushed the case of assorted gems toward Shay.

She reverently picked up the crystal ball, set it down in front of Shay, and smiled. "These have all been cleansed so ye are free to use them," she said as she tapped the lid of the assorted stones. "Look for one that speaks to ye, the one that is right for this moment, the one that feels right when ye hold it in yer hands. Most importantly, think about that poor woman who died. Can ye feel her in the stone? Does she speak to ye? If not, pick up another and work through the box until ye find the one she is trying to connect to ye through. Ye'll know it's the right one. Ye'll feel her warmth from its touch or vibrations like a tingling sensation and waves of water traveling up yer arm." Gran gestured to the crystal ball. "But, if ye would rather, I could teach ye how to use this?"

"Another time," said Shay, staring at the case of gems. "It all seems so much right now."

"It does that, and"—she glanced at the clock above the sink—"'tis time for this old lady to go home anyway and leave ye two to work this baby step out." She turned from the doorway and steadied her gaze on Shay. "The veil is thinning, honor yer ancestors."

She hustled off, leaving her two cases behind with instructions for Shay to open the lids and store the cases next to a window so the sun and moon could shine on them, which would both charge and cleanse the crystals and gems after each use.

Shay reached for the pouch, slipped the tie over her

head, allowing it to rest comfortably on her chest, and tucked it inside her shirt. "Okay, I guess we'll try Gran's way since you don't think I should use mine."

"It's just because of what Conor said about Doyle, and Peter and . . ." Liam steadied his gaze on hers. "I couldn't bear it if something happened to ye."

Shay recalled what Gran had said to her earlier about Liam having feelings for her, and she met Liam's gaze. He was the one who'd said they were like kin, being from the same county in Ireland and all, and she had figured that was why he was so invested in what happened to her. However, the sensations that swept through her as his gaze seemed to caress her very inner being proved that perhaps Gran was right about his deep feelings for her.

Her fingers played with the tie around her neck and she shifted in her chair. "Liam, you said we were like kin because we came from the same county, but . . ." She broke her gaze and glanced at the case of gemstones on the table.

"But what?"

"Never mind, it's just something Gran said earlier, and I was wondering."

"What did she say?"

"Nothing, it doesn't matter anyway because you're with—"

A sharp knock on the door stopped her midsentence. She got up and peered through the window. "Zoey?"

"Zoey, here now?" Liam shifted and looked up at Shay. "Why?" he whispered.

Shay shrugged. "Shall we find out?"

"No." Liam grabbed for her arm but was too late.

Shay swung the door open. "Hi, Zoey," Shay said, glancing at the armful of papers Zoey clutched close to her chest. "Um"—she glanced back at Liam, cowering in the corner—"did you need to speak to me or . . ." She gestured behind her.

Zoey peered around the door frame, smiled weakly, and then pulled back. "I wasn't expecting to find *him* here," she whispered.

"It's nothing," Shay said quickly. "He and Gran were by for tea, and Dean showed up, and Liam was just leaving, weren't you?" She gestured with her head at him to leave.

"No," said Zoey, "it's fine, really, and since he is here"—she motioned with her head toward the papers she held—"and given his background, he might also find these interesting."

Shay gave Liam a quick side glance, and he gave her a slight shrug as he rose to his feet. "Okay, sure, come on in." She stood back and closed the door behind Zoey. "Can I get you some tea or coffee? Maybe some wine?"

"No thanks." She glanced awkwardly at Liam, who was looking like he'd rather be anyplace other than in Shay's kitchen. "I'm just heading out . . . for a late dinner . . . and . . ." Her gaze changed from awkward to apologetic as she met his eyes. "I can't stay long." She straightened her back and looked at Shay. "But I got your message. Actually, I was on the phone with Suzanne when you sent me the text. She had sent these." Zoey gestured to the papers. "There's a lot here, and Suzanne had a few comments of her own to add when I spoke to her, so I thought it would be easier if I printed them off rather than forward them to you so you'll have her comments too. It all makes for some pretty interesting reading about Jasmine. . . ." Her face reddened as she met Liam's gaze. "But I have to run." She waved toward the back of the cottage. "I . . . I . . . someone . . . is waiting." Hands shaking, she set the stack of papers on the table and turned toward the door.

"Do . . ." Liam cleared his throat. "Do ye have a date tonight?"

Zoey's hand paused on the doorknob. She didn't turn around. She only nodded and whispered, "Yes."

"I see," said Liam, his voice a raspy mumble.

"Um . . ." Shay squirmed. Liam's face reddened, and Zoey still stood with her back to them, her hand still hovering over the doorknob. Shay coughed and said, "I just have to . . . um . . . get something from the other room." Shay gestured with her thumb as she slithered out of the kitchen and into the living room.

Shay tried to busy herself all the while keeping an ear bent toward the kitchen. All she could hear were low murmurings of voices, nothing raised, no outbursts of emotions, and then she heard the sound of the door closing. She tiptoed to the kitchen door and peeked around the door frame. Liam stood facing the door, fingers tucked into the front pockets of his jeans, and he slowly turned toward her. "That's it, then," he said, his gaze downcast.

"What do you mean, that's it?"

He raised his head and met her inquiring gaze. "It seems she didn't just need more space than she had with me and Gran. She needed a lot of space from me and is . . ." He swallowed hard, and his Adam's apple quivered. "She's dating a fellow she met while I was in Ireland."

"What? No, I know she missed you. There's no way she was seeing him while you were away."

"Nah, according to what she just said they didn't date then. She'd just met him at the animal shelter one day when I was away. I guess he went in to adopt a rescue, and they got to talking. She swears that was all there was between them even after he adopted the dog and took it into her clinic for a series of appointments to get advice on training and such. Until . . . well, recent developments between me and her and . . ." His voice trailed off to an inaudible murmur.

"I'm so sorry, Liam. I really hoped the two of you could work out this little hitch."

He ran his hand through his hair and nodded. "I did too. I thought once she was settled in her condo again, we'd go back to the way it was before. When we were . . ." He shored himself up. "It doesn't matter. It's done now." He poked absentmindedly at the pile of papers on the table. "Let's see what she brought us, and maybe we can help Dean close this case, and ye can get Tassi back where she belongs."

"Whoa!"

"Whoa, is right," echoed Shay. "We have to get these to Dean as soon as possible."

"Yeah, it seems our Jasmine Massey wasn't Jasmine Massey after all, but a woman named Kendra Reid. At least that's what she had gone by in La Jolla, California," said Liam, flipping to another one of the pages in his pile.

"Yeah . . . I read that too," Shay said, her voice no more than a hoarse whisper.

Liam raised his head and searched her gaze. "What's wrong, *a chara*?"

"Nothing."

"Then why do ye look like ye've just seen a ghost?"

Shay let the page she was holding slide through her fingers onto the table. "It's just that these pictures of La Jolla are hard to look at."

His gaze dropped to the images on her paper. "It looks like a beautiful place to me. Never been there meself, but after seeing these I think I want to go." He slightly shrugged. "So what is it really that's got ye so pensive now?"

"It's just that . . . before my parents were killed in a boating accident eighteen years ago . . ."

"Yes . . . and?"

"And . . . they were part of a research team for the Scripps Institution for Biological Research in La Jolla . . ."

"Okay . . ." he said hesitantly.

"Ah, it's nothing." She waved off his look of concern. "They just used to take me and Jen sometimes when they had to work over a weekend and . . ." Tears formed in her eyes. "We had some wonderful mini family vacations there. That's all, and it was a long time ago so..." She sniffled, pushed those memories back into the corner of her mind, picked up another paper in her stack, and focused on it.

Liam reached across the table and gently squeezed

her hand. She couldn't look up to meet his gaze because she knew the tears she bit the inside of her lip to contain would spill down her cheeks if she did. Instead, she kept reading, one page after another, until the pictures and the memories they induced were nothing but a fading memory of better days.

When she came to a page with a newspaper photo of a blond Jasmine Massey that had a caption underneath it, she squirmed in her chair excitedly and squealed. "Listen to this: 'Kendra Reid, aged thirty-four, wanted by the FBI for theft by deception and grand theft and fraud. Also wanted in questioning regarding the death of restaurateur George Sullivan, aged sixty-eight, of La Jolla. If you have any information on Miss Reid's whereabouts, please contact the San Diego Police Department's fraud unit immediately.' You know, I hate to disturb Dean on an evening at home with Jen and the kids, but—" She glanced up at Liam and snapped her mouth closed.

He was half turned with his arm resting on the back of his chair, his chin cradled in his hand, and staring blankly out the window into the dark.

"Maybe you should go home and call it a night."

"What?" He snapped to attention and blinked at Shay.

"I said you've had a rough evening. Maybe you need to go home, and we can relook at this tomorrow with Dean."

"No." He swiveled in his chair and straightened up. "I was just thinking."

"I know, and I also know the conversation you had

with Zoey tonight took you by surprise, and you probably need time to digest it. So maybe in the morning, after a good night's sleep, we can reconvene?" She winced, sensing his pain ran far deeper than he'd ever let on to her.

"I'm fine, time to move on." He locked his gaze with hers. "Ye did and now look at ye." He gave her a weak smile. He shook his head as if he was refocusing and picked up the paper on the top of the pile he'd been reading through, then let the paper slide from his fingers. He sat staring down at them, then lifted his head. "Ye know, I think I will go home. I need a stiff whiskey and a good night's sleep. Sorry to leave ye with this, but I'm just . . ." He swallowed hard. "Do ye know what she said to me?"

Shay shook her head, a little afraid of what Zoey might have said. Had her friend suspected that what Gran wanted Shay did too, deep down, at the right time, that was? She held her breath and waited for him to continue.

"She said, 'If I can feel this way so quickly about John, it tells me that with you I wasn't in the right relationship to begin with.' Can ye believe that? All this time and she meets this winery owner over a rescue dog, and now she thinks she and I weren't right to begin with, and she's better off with him?"

"I know it's hard"—Shay slowly and quietly let out her breath—"but look at it this way. Zoey didn't continue to live a lie and pretend you and she had more than she felt. She was honest with her feelings. It hurts, I know. But better to learn that now than in a few years and be left feeling like everything you thought you had had been a lie and a betrayal of the most intimate kind."

Shay smiled softly. She knew exactly how he was feeling. She'd been there with her ex and his two-year affair, but more than that, she could feel Liam's heart breaking as if it were her own and she wanted nothing more in this moment than to wrap him in her arms and soothe his pain. But instead, she said, "You go. I'll make sure Dean gets this tomorrow, first thing."

Chapter 29

Shay sat mutely as Dean flipped through the stack of articles she'd dropped down in front of him before he'd even had time to open the tab on the lid of his take-out coffee. She bit her tongue to stop "I told you so" from rolling off it as she twisted her fingers into knots on her lap. His silence was killing her. She edged toward the front of her chair to get a better view of which page he was reading.

"See that photo of George Sullivan?" She pointed to an older gentleman with gray hair in the picture.

"Yes." Dean looked at her from under his lowered brow.

"I bet if you show it to Pearl Hammond she could identify him as the man who was in her ice cream shop with the blonde who looked like Jasmine. The timing was about right. Those articles are from three years ago, and since there was an all-points bulletin out for this Kendra Reid—"

"Shay! Let me finish reading, okay?"

Shay blew out an exasperated breath and sat back, scanning the small office to try to focus on anything else but Dean taking forever to read the information she'd provided. A slight smile came to her lips at the picture of him and his family behind him, and her smile grew at the photo of her and Jen beside it. He had been right when he'd said they were family and they would get through this together.

"Do you think that the APB issued for Kendra Reid and the fact that she was never apprehended was the reason you couldn't match her prints to anyone in the system? With her change in name and hair color it's not surprising we couldn't find any background on Jasmine Massey."

"It's a possibility," he said, flipping to another page.

"Have you gotten to the newspaper article that says George Sullivan, who was a big deal in La Jolla, it seems, since he owned five major seafood restaurants in the area, died under suspicious circumstances and the blonde, who looks like Jasmine, was wanted for questioning?"

"Yes, and the article says the coroner ruled his death as heart failure."

Shay edged to the front of her chair again. "But it also says that George Sullivan checked into the Grande Colonial Hotel with a woman matching the description of Kendra Reid, and when housekeeping went to clean the room the following day, Miss Reid was gone and George Sullivan's body was discovered in the bathtub. The coroner initially ruled the death as heart failure, but the police still wanted Miss Reid to come forward and answer some questions. Would they want to speak to her if they really thought his death was natural causes?"

Dean closed the file, folded his hands together on top of the papers, and pinned Shay with a look of reproach.

"Okay." She slunk down in her chair. "I guess I'll leave it with you and . . ."

"That's a good idea." He stood up and gestured toward the door. "Thank you for all this, but now I need to finish reading it and try to make sense of the information."

"Okay." She grabbed her backpack from the floor beside her and rose to her feet. "I . . . I just thought I could offer some insight."

"And I thank you. I really do, but I'll take it from here."

She looked from him to the pile of papers, thankful she'd made her own photocopies to read over again later, because Dean could be pretty tight-lipped about an ongoing case, and she needed answers. Tassi and her future were at stake.

"Look, I have a lot of work to do here, so I trust you can see yourself out?" he asked.

"Yes, and thanks, Dean." She paused at the door, glanced back as he sat down, flipped the file folder open, and began scribbling notes on a pad beside him, an act that brought a smile to her lips. It was just as Jen always said about him: You have to plant the seed, let it take hold and make him think it was his idea, and then you'll end up getting exactly what you wanted. Smart woman her sister was, and it showed how well she knew her husband because she appeared to have been right in this case, at least.

She glanced at the clock above the front desk of the squad room, and her heart quickened. Where had the time gone? How could it already be past ten? Shay crossed her fingers and hoped that Jen had the Little White Glove Society ladies under control and that her sister would forgive her for being so late.

She darted outside, clipped her bike helmet on, raced toward First Street as she flew around the corner, glided down the hill toward High Street, then gasped when she realized it was Sunday. The Little White Glove Society wasn't expected at the teashop today. She giggled at the disbelief that taking a Saturday off had messed with her internal calendar so badly. Although, that Saturday off had held a number of surprises and produced more than one major event in her life. It was no wonder she thought it was Monday.

Still laughing at herself, she arrived at the corner of First and High Street when a surge of fiery energy rushed through her. She flinched, jerking back on the foot brake of her vintage bike, forcing it to come to a skidding halt. She'd stopped so fast that had she not grounded herself with a double foot plant on the cobble-stone roadway, she would have gone careening over the handlebars. However, road rash was the last thing on her mind as she squinted, trying to understand the scene that was playing out in the parking lot of the beachside hotel one block down the hill from her.

She strained and blinked, then blinked again. Yes,

there was no doubt about it. Faye Cranston and Lilly were deep in conversation. The fiery energy between the two women sparked and flashed around them, and a bitter taste inundated Shay's tongue. She could actually taste the sour venom the two women exchanged, and the pouch against her chest grew warm.

She started to propel her bike forward but then stopped as a thought struck her. This was the second time in as many days that she'd witnessed the two women in a verbal altercation. At least the one the previous morning had appeared so, given Lilly's tear-filled eyes when Shay had literally bumped into her. She knew Faye was particular about her table settings, but two days in a row to accost the poor girl? No, there had to be something else going on.

She studied their bristling energy and body language. Faye wagged a finger in Lilly's face, but instead of cowering away like one might when being confronted by an irate customer, Lilly leaned into her, clearly standing her ground. Shay's sleuthing antennae quivered. They were familiar with each other, and it appeared that their relationship went deeper than that of a server and a customer. The heat from the pouch intensified and sent unwelcoming tingling sensations through Shay's upper body. She needed to speak with Mia.

Shay turned her bike to head to the tea shop and couldn't believe her eyes. Mia rushed out of Cuppa-Jo's with two take-out coffees clutched in her hands and headed toward Adam Ward's car parked along the curb. Shay shivered as she wondered if she had conjured this or if she had sensed Mia was in the area and that's why she felt compelled to speak to her. Either way, here the woman was.

"Mia!" she called and waved as Mia was about to enter the passenger's seat. "Wait, can we talk a minute?!" Shay pumped hard on the pedals to launch forward and glided up to the side of Adam's car. "I can't believe it. I was just thinking of phoning you, and, well, here you are." Shay laughed as she came to a stop. "Hi, Adam." She bent down and waved through the open car door at her old school friend and Mia's husband.

"Hi, Shay," he said with a wave.

She smiled at him and then righted herself and met Mia's curious gaze. "I just wanted to ask you about your teaching assistant, Lilly."

"Is there a problem?" Mia passed a coffee cup to Adam and took a sip of hers, meeting Shay's gaze over the rim of her cup.

"Uh . . . no, well, I'm not sure." Shay glanced back over her shoulder toward the street corner, then looked back at Mia. "Did you say her last name was Sullivan?"

"Yeah, why?"

"Is she from La Jolla, by any chance?"

"Her college application says she's from San Diego, and La Jolla is a suburb, so yeah, I guess so. Why?"

"It's just that . . ." Shay gripped the handlebars of the bike she still straddled and took a deep breath. "Do you know if her father was George Sullivan, the restaurateur who died a few years ago?"

"Yes, he was, but why all the questions, Shay?"

Shay took another breath and relayed to Mia what

she'd witnessed the previous morning and just a few moments ago between Faye and Lilly. "I'm just worried about the girl. Her friend Stephen told me she works as your TA and also part-time at the hotel restaurant. Add on being a full-time student, and I'm afraid that my employee is making everything worse for her."

She told Mia about Faye's obsession with her place settings and how she was afraid the woman was harassing Lilly about a less-than-faultless service she might have seen in the restaurant. "I know you think the world of Lilly, but if she's still grieving her dad's death and . . . oh, I don't know, but something feels off."

"I can have a talk with Lilly tomorrow to check in with her. Would that make you feel better?"

"Yeah, it would, thanks." Shay glanced back at the street corner again when the cold hand of dread replaced the annoying niggle at the base of her skull.

"Are you okay?" asked Mia.

"Mia," Adam said, leaning across the passenger seat, "we have to get going. The brunch starts soon."

"Yes, I know." Mia waved him off, keeping her focus on Shay. "Your face went pure white. Are you okay?"

Trust your instincts. A whispered breath caressed her ear. Shay nodded and met Mia's worried gaze. "Is her mother's name Faye, Faye Cranston, by any chance?"

"No, that doesn't sound familiar. I've spoken to her a couple of times on the phone when we were arranging Lilly's scholarship, but her name was . . ." Mia looked up in thought.

Adam tapped his fingers loudly on the steering wheel. "Mia, can I remind you that as the head of the department you're giving the opening speech. You really can't be late."

"I know, just a second." Mia's forehead furrowed, and then she snapped her fingers. "No, it wasn't Faye. Her name is Loretta Sullivan. Why?"

"Really?" Shay's hopes deflated. "It's nothing then. It's just something the woman who's working Tassi's shifts said to me her first day about her husband, George, who died, and I wondered if . . . well, never mind." Shay waved it off. "There mustn't be a connection. I'm sure there's more than one George in the world who owned restaurants, right?" she added with a soft chuckle.

"It is a common name." Mia tossed her purse onto the console of the car, and she scooted onto the passenger seat. "But I trust your instincts, and if you think Lilly is having problems and this woman is making it worse, I'm happy to talk to her. I do know Lilly and her mom are struggling financially since her dad passed, and I'd hate it if this Faye woman could be the reason Lilly quits a job that fits so nicely with her college schedule."

Shay wanted to shout, *Don't trust my instincts because clearly I can't,* but instead she said, "Thanks, Mia." She crouched over and looked at Adam. "Sorry, I didn't mean to hold you guys up."

"That's okay," Adam said. "I'm with Mia on this one. Trust your instincts. If you're worried about Lilly, there must be a good reason."

"Look, we're just headed to the college now," said Mia. "One of my department professors is retiring. There's a faculty brunch for him, but after it's over, I'll drop by the plant conservatory. Lilly is usually there most afternoons, and I'll talk to her then instead of waiting until tomorrow, okay?"

"That would be great, and thanks so much." Shay waved as Adam pulled his dark blue Tesla away from the curb, and then she walked her bike across the road to Crystals & CuriosiTEAS. After fastening the lock to the back support of the bench, she rushed inside, scanned the tea shop, and smiled guiltily. "Hi, Jen, sorry I'm so late."

Jen glanced up at the clock. "It's Sunday. We don't open till ten, so you're not that late." Jen craned her neck to see behind Shay. "No Spirit again?"

Shay shook her head. "It seems Tassi still needs him more than I do." She sighed. "But with any luck, this will be over soon, and she'll be back. I'm just so grateful you could come in today since Sundays are supposed to be her days to work, not yours."

"Faye said she'd work too, so if it's not too busy, I might just sneak out of here early."

"Whatever works." Shay swiped her hand on the counter, swooshing tiny crumbs to her palm, then deposited them into a garbage can. "I just saw Faye in the hotel parking lot, and it appeared as though she was harassing Mia's student. You know, that girl Lilly, the one who picked up the plants for the college and also works part-time in the hotel restaurant?"

"I remember Lilly, but what do you mean Faye was harassing her?"

"I don't know exactly what's going on, but I can definitely tell there's something wrong between them. My gut tells me there's more to it than Faye being finicky and taking her obsession for a perfect place setting out on the girl, but so far there doesn't seem to be a link other than server and customer. I just don't know how to approach Faye to find out if that's the problem or if there's something else going on."

"I don't think you should."

"But, Jen, I just saw Mia, and she told me the girl is really struggling financially since her dad died a few years ago. She works mornings at the hotel restaurant, and her schedule fits perfectly with her college one. I'd hate it if Faye was the reason the girl quit her job. She needs it to stay in college."

"And what are you planning on saying to Faye? You can't come right out and tell her that her obsessive-compulsive behavior has to stop immediately because it's affecting Mia's student, can you?"

"No, but what if it's something else?"

"Then it doesn't concern you anyway. Look, Faye told me she sees a therapist, so leave it alone and let her work out her own issues."

"Even if until she does work it out she's hurting someone else?"

"Then ask yourself what could you possibly say to Faye that wouldn't hurt or offend *her.*"

"I guess there's no right way to approach this, is there?"

"No, there isn't," said Jen. "I understand the need to step in and do something when we see someone getting hurt, but you also have to be careful and not overstep personal boundaries, especially if it's a mental health issue like Faye's. Leave it to the professionals."

"Then how do the professionals know there is a problem? Faye would have to be the one to tell her therapist, and I doubt she's even aware that her behavior is hurting Lilly."

"That's the catch-22, isn't it?"

"But I can't stand by and say nothing. You should have seen Lilly after their altercation yesterday."

The bells above the door rang out, and Faye stepped inside, grinning at them.

"Be careful what you say, is all I'm saying," whispered Jen before she turned to Faye. "Good morning, we're so glad you could work today."

The rest of the morning flew by. First the regular Sunday after-church group came in, and then the tourists poured through the doors, eager to try samples of the tea blends Shay had set out as part of her usual Sunday promotion since Sundays could be a hit-or-miss day after the peak summer season ended. However, with the festival less than a week away, she shouldn't have worried. All the bags of tea blends she'd worked hard to replenish were flying off the shelves. Normally this would have been good news as she heard the constant *ching* of the cash register. Her thoughts, however, weren't on daily profits but on the imposing woman who effortlessly worked the floor and served tea and goodies as though every single customer was a guest in her own home.

She glanced over at Faye for the hundredth time, looking for an opening to approach her about Lilly, but realized Jen was right. What could she possibly say to this woman that wouldn't offend her? Jen had said to leave it to the professionals, and Mia was just that, so if she talked to Lilly and found out there was a problem, she could help Lilly deal with it and Shay would have a better idea what to do or say to Faye going forward. With that rationalization, the weight of her thoughts lifted and Shay smiled.

She slid up to her sister's side at the cash register. "Jen, I'm going to have to go upstairs and do some quick harvesting so I can make up some more bags of blends tonight."

Jen smiled as she handed her customer his change. "Sure, we'll call if we need you."

"After I'm done, you can probably head home if you still want to get out of here early."

"We'll see, but I just called home, and Hunter's playing video games and Maddie's still in bed." She shook her head in disapproval.

"It sounds like she's turning into a full-fledged teenager right before your eyes." Shay laughed.

"Yup, and I don't think I'm ready for that." Jen smiled at the next customer in line.

"Okay, I'll be back as soon as I can."

Shay headed upstairs armed with her wicker harvesting tray and set to work clipping and snipping leaves and flowers and digging up roots. She was so engrossed in her work that when she heard footsteps behind her she shrieked and spun around. "Oh . . . Mia, Adam," Shay said, patting her erratically beating heart. "I'm sorry, I don't usually greet visitors to the greenhouse by yelling at them."

"It's we who should be apologizing," said Adam. "We didn't mean to creep up on you, but Jen said it was okay if we came up. I hope it is."

"Of course it is." Shay looked at Mia. "Does that mean you had a chance to talk to Lilly today?"

"No." Mia flashed Adam an awkward glance, and he nodded, urging her on. "She wasn't there today, which is weird for her, but it got me thinking, so I went back to my office and looked up her student file. . . ."

"And?" asked Shay.

"I probably shouldn't be telling you this, confidentiality and all, but . . ." She glanced hesitantly at Adam, who jerked his head in a slight nod of encouragement, and she steadied her gaze on Shay. "You asked if her mother's name was Faye Cranston."

"Yes."

"And I said it was Loretta Sullivan."

Shay's heart knocked against her ribs.

Mia fleetingly looked at Adam for reassurance. He smiled and she drew in a deep breath. "It seems her name *is* Loretta. Loretta Faye Sullivan."

Shay's brows rose.

"It could be just a coincidence." Mia winced.

"Maybe," Shay murmured, her thoughts reeling. What was it she had heard about coincidences? Something like, they were the occurrence of events that happen at the same time by accident but seem to have some connection. From her own experiences Shay didn't believe in coincidences. There was always a connection—one simply had to look for it—and the tightening in her chest over Mia's words told her Faye's behavior toward Lilly wasn't merely the coincidence of Lilly's mother and Faye Cranston sharing the same name.

Chapter 30

Shay slowly wandered over to Jen at the back counter but her gaze remained steadily focused on Faye clearing a nearby table.

"Is everything okay?" Jen asked distractedly as she continued to sort through the daily receipts.

"I don't know."

"Was it something Mia and Adam said? They acted like it was urgent they speak to you." She glanced at Shay. "I hope you don't mind that I sent them upstairs."

"No, that's fine."

"Okay." Jen shrugged and closed the till drawer and stared out the front window as Adam and Mia got into their car. "You know, I don't think I've seen him since their wedding. I'd forgotten how handsome he got as he grew older."

Shay broke her focus off Faye and tracked Jen's sight line to the street. "He couldn't stay a gangly teenager forever."

"I know, but"—she sighed—"do you sometimes wish you and he—"

"No, we were just school friends."

"Really? I always thought you guys had a special bond."

"I guess we did for a few years, but we were young, and after Mom and Dad died and my life changed, so did his, and our friendship just sort of . . . never mind, that was a long time ago." She looked over at Faye. "Excuse me. I think I'll give her a hand clearing tables."

"Are you done upstairs then?"

"For now," Shay said as she grabbed an empty bin from a side cart and headed over to Faye. If her gut feeling was right, it would answer a few of her questions about what she'd witnessed between her and Lilly, and she had a feeling that Faye's mental health had nothing to with it.

"Wow," said Shay, "I can't believe the rush we had there, can you?" she asked Faye, picking up an empty saucer and cup and set it in her bussing bin.

"It was crazy for a minute, that's for sure, but Jen and I work well as a team." Faye added a stack of four plates into Shay's bin.

"That's great. Teamwork is so important." Shay smiled at her as she struggled to find the opening she needed to broach a possibly sensitive subject. "The service industry is a tough one, but . . ." She paused in wiping the table down. "Why am I telling you? You're the one here with the most experience." She chuckled.

"Yeah, I have a bit." Faye gave a short laugh and moved on to the next empty table.

Shay grabbed her cleaning cloth and the bin and shot over to Faye's side. "Although, I imagine when you first started serving it took you time to catch on, right?"

"I guess, but offering good service should come naturally. That is, if a person has been brought up right and taught their manners. Like you and Jen, you both know what it means to provide good customer service, and you're making it work here."

"Yeah, but I don't think everyone is as lucky as we are." She gave Faye a side glance. "Take, for instance, that young girl, the student from the college."

"What girl?"

"The one who came in to pick up the plants?"

Faye's body stiffened as she reached for a plate.

"You know"—Shay snapped her fingers—"what's her name? Mia's student. Lilly? I heard she works at the hotel restaurant, and you mentioned you eat breakfast there most days, so you must know her, right?"

Faye shook her head. "Can't say as I do."

"The cute girl with brown hair usually in a high ponytail?"

"Oh, her." Faye fleetingly glanced at Shay before turning her back and moving to the next table. "Yeah, I don't know her," she said, without looking back at Shay. "She's just a server there. Not very good, though, and I usually avoid sitting in her section." Faye blew out an audible breath, tensed her shoulders, and began wiping the table.

Shay stood behind her, holding the bin, and squirmed

when the amulet pouch grew hot against her skin. Shay came around in front of Faye and set the bin on the table. "You know what, I think I'll leave you to finish up here and go back upstairs to harvest some more herbs."

"Sure, whatever," Faye said, scrubbing at a spot on the table without so much as a glance at Shay.

Shay backed away, keeping her gaze on Faye. All the signs were there that she was uncomfortable speaking about Lilly, but Shay's gut feelings weren't enough. She needed Faye to admit what Shay suspected, but the woman's face was as unreadable as the energy she produced. It showed Shay nothing. There was no hint or acknowledgment of the altercations Shay had witnessed over the past two days, no glimmer of even being familiar with Lilly, let alone any hint or indication that she was the girl's mother.

Shay spun on her heel and headed back upstairs, where she slunk onto the chair in her small alcove office in disbelief that her instincts had let her down, again. She had been so certain that Faye and Lilly's relationship was more than customer and server. However, it appeared that she had jumped to conclusions, seeing something she *wanted* to see, and not what was really there. After all, her instincts had been off recently. So, perhaps it was as she had originally thought—that Faye was just being a difficult customer and Lilly was the unfortunate recipient of her angst.

She gazed at the Polaroid picture of Bridget holding her as a newborn that she'd framed and kept on her desk and moaned. "Oh, Bridget, I might look like you, but I'm far from being like you, it seems. Seer? What a joke." Shay shook her head.

A folder in her in-basket with a red arrow sticker protruding from a page inside it caught her eye. The title tab on the side of the folder indicated it was Faye's personnel papers, and judging by the arrow sticker, there was something Jen wanted Shay to see before it was processed for payroll and tax.

Shay grabbed it and flipped to the page that Jen had marked with the sticker pointing to the line that asked for maiden name. Faye had written *Cranston*. Shay sat back and studied the other information Faye had filled out, particularly the answer to the question, Have you ever gone by any other name? Faye had answered no.

She absently tapped her finger on the paper in thought. There was no mention of her married name or a different surname at all anywhere in the papers, and the fact that Jen had left this out for Shay to review meant she must have questioned this too since Faye had said on a number of occasions that she had been married to a man named George. If that was the case, either her maiden name or her married name would appear as Cranston, but not as both.

Faye certainly wasn't of the generation that didn't assume their husband's last name. That trend started years later. So why was the only surname on her personnel forms Cranston and had she answered no to going by any other name?

Shay stared down at the folder recalling her earlier conversations with Mia and mentally drew a line between everything she could remember.

Lilly's last name was Sullivan, and—according to

Mia—her father had been George Sullivan, a restaurateur who had passed away a few years ago.

Faye's husband was also a restaurateur who had passed away a few years ago and was also named George.

Lilly's mother's name was Loretta *Faye,* and now this omission by Faye of ever having gone by another name on her form, which clearly was a lie, all added up to one too many so-called coincidences. Combined with what Shay had observed taking place between Faye and Lilly the past few days, regardless of Faye's recent dismissive explanation downstairs, Shay would bet money that Lilly and Faye *were* mother and daughter and Faye was none other than Loretta Faye Sullivan, née Cranston.

The question was, why didn't Faye want anyone to know, even going to the extent of denying knowing the girl? What could have possibly happened when George died that drove such a wedge between mother and daughter that she wouldn't even acknowledge their family ties?

Shay's thoughts flashed to Peter and Tassi and how he had lashed out at anyone and everyone after Jasmine died, including his own daughter. From experience, Shay knew grief could do strange things to people, and they often looked to someone to hate or blame to cover for their grief. Did Faye, for some reason, blame her daughter for her husband's death or . . . Shay gasped. Did Lilly blame her mother for driving her father into the arms of another woman?

She reread the forms to make sure she hadn't missed anything, because it broke her heart to think that perhaps Lilly, in her innocence, hadn't yet learned that a woman couldn't steal another woman's man unless *he* wanted to be stolen. Shay's heart recoiled. She had learned that the hard way through her husband's betrayal.

She stopped reading and pushed the folder aside. Was that why Shay had seen them arguing? Was Faye trying to mend the gap between them but Lilly, in her youthful stubbornness, refused to bend? That could be why Faye, brokenhearted over her daughter's estrangement, hadn't acknowledged her daughter. It wouldn't be easy to explain to virtual strangers that her daughter blamed her for her husband's infidelity, which led to his death in a hotel room he'd booked into with another woman.

Nausea settled in the pit of Shay's stomach like a rock. If this was the case, didn't the girl know how lucky she was to even have a mother still alive? Not a day went by when Shay didn't wish she could change fate and have her mother and father by her side. The rock in Shay's stomach started to twist. She needed to stop these two women from continuing to make possibly the biggest mistake they would ever make in their lives, and one they would eventually come to regret. A life filled with regret cannot be reversed after a loved one's passing. By then, it's too late for a do-over.

She knew of course that all this was pure speculation on her part, and her instincts were something she hadn't been able to trust in weeks, but what if? Her mind raced as her fingers trailed over the leather tie around her neck, and then she sat a little taller in her chair. No, her instincts had been correct the whole time. As Gran had pointed out to her a number of times, once everything had played out, it had shown her she had been on the right track. She'd only been reading the signs wrong. It made her wonder if now she was second guessing herself . . . again.

Shay's phone pinged out a text alert, and she reached inside her apron pocket. No phone. When it pinged again, she glanced in the direction of the sound and saw the dim light of her phone screen illuminated on the potting table, where she'd left it earlier.

She went over, picked it up, and read a text from Dean:

I thought I'd let you know I took the newspaper photo of George Sullivan to Pearl Hammond, and she identified him as the man who was in her shop three years ago with the blond version of Jasmine. If we can trace Kendra Reid's steps to Bray Harbor from La Jolla, we might be able to find out who wanted her dead. More to follow . . .

Shay nodded and smiled with a sense of ease. This meant that not all her instincts had gone haywire, but then it made her think. Just *maybe* she was right about Faye, too. . .

But before she went down any more rabbit holes, she needed to confirm something, so she typed out a question:

Could you run a background check on Faye Cranston to see if she has ever gone by any other name?

I can't legally unless it's related to the case.

It could b—

Her finger hovered over the *e* when she heard a noise in front of her and glanced up. "Faye? Is everything okay downstairs?"

"Yes, it's fine. I . . . um . . ." She glanced over her shoulder toward the office. "I see you've been looking at my personnel file." She flashed Shay an accusatory look.

Shay swallowed hard, pressed send, and shoved her phone into her apron pocket. "Yes, I was . . . getting your banking information so we can pay you," Shay said quickly and forced a smile that she hoped reached her eyes, but in case it didn't, she averted her gaze. "I was just going to harvest some more flowers." She reached for the shears and wicker basket beside her. "Are you interested in learning how to take cuttings for our teas?"

"Not particularly."

"I see. I . . . I thought maybe that's why you came upstairs." Shay inwardly cringed with the heat of the pouch on her chest. "Then what can I do for you now?" She met Faye's piercing gaze, hoping to deflect it with one equal in her attempt to feign innocence.

"It's just that after Dr. Harper, Mia, left"—Faye took a step toward Shay—"you asked some pretty strange questions, and I was wondering what she came in to talk to you about?"

The fine hairs on the back of Shay's neck bristled at Faye's pointed line of questioning, and she edged around the end of the potting table, fighting to keep her voice even. "It was nothing. She only had a couple of questions about the plants I donated to the college."

"What about them?" Faye snapped and took another step toward Shay.

Shay didn't miss the fact that the harsh tone of Faye's voice didn't match the fear that filled her eyes.

"Um . . . nothing really." She tried to lighten her voice. "But that's what made me think of Lilly, I guess, and why I asked you about her since she is Mia's teaching assistant, and you appeared—"

"Is that the only reason you asked about the girl?" Faye pinned her with an intent look as she picked up a gardening trowel from the table and turned it over in her hand, all the while her gaze never wavering from Shay.

"Faye," called Jen from the bottom of the circular stairwell, "we just got three tables of four in. I could use a hand down here."

Faye jerked, looked over her shoulder, and then slowly turned and set the trowel back on the table. "I guess I'm needed downstairs," she said, her tone as flat and cold as her eyes were. A slight smile twitched at the corners of her thin lips. She started for the stairs but paused at the alcove office, glanced over to the desk, and looked back at Shay. A wry smile twisted her face before she descended the steps.

"Whoa." Shay blew out a pent-up breath. She was used to the flashes she got when she was around bad energy, and she had had one heck of a flash with Faye's. It was clear Faye had a secret she wanted to keep buried. Shay shivered at the sight of the trowel on the potting table where Faye had left it. The question was, what was her secret and how far was Faye willing to go to make sure it stay just that?

She lifted the pouch off her chest when the scorching heat emanating from it became unbearable and held it in her hand away from her body while she tried to clear her head. As her thoughts untangled, she recalled Julia Fisher had made it clear that Jasmine wasn't a welcome addition to the prestigious Little White Glove Society, which meant someone in the society must have sponsored her. She typed out a message to Julia, the one person who she knew for certain didn't get along with Jasmine and who might be willing to disclose the details on how Jasmine's membership came about.

Out of curiosity, whose idea was it for Jasmine to join the Little White Glove Society?

Shay shoved her phone back into her apron pocket and scurried downstairs. By the time she reached the bottom, she winced and quickly released the hold she had on the pouch when its heat seared her fingers. She flinched again when it slipped back down onto her chest, and she hurriedly flipped the leather cord over her head and allowed the pouch to dangle freely from her hand.

She hesitated when she reached the round table in the center of the back room. Should she trust her instincts and take the warming of the amulet as an indication that she was on the right track with her hunch? Unless of course, the heating sensation of the bottle in the pouch was purely a response to her skin's fight-or-flight reaction and magnifying her own nerve endings, which, after witnessing Faye's odd reactions and the malicious look in her eyes, wouldn't surprise her.

Chapter 31

Shay glanced down at the pouch dangling from her fingers as her adrenaline-induced spiraling thoughts subsided, but then she had another thought, and her heart rate quickened again. It couldn't be a coincidence that the woman in George Sullivan's hotel room at the time of his death was the same woman who three years later had died in front of her, could it? Her phone pinged out a text alert, and she fished it out of her pocket and read the reply from Julia.

It was Faye. She told us she got talking to Jasmine one morning when she went for breakfast at the hotel restaurant, and Jasmine complained to her that she was bored and lonely sitting around all day while Peter looked after his business in Bray Harbor. Faye told the group that as she was soon to be the wife of a highly influential lawyer on the peninsula that we should consider inviting her to the group. Why is this important?

I was just curious how she joined since no one seemed to like her.

Cora, the mayor's wife, did, and she's in charge of the group, and none of the rest of us had a say in the matter. As soon as Cora heard who Jasmine's boyfriend was, she jumped at the chance to invite her. My guess is that since Cora's husband has political aspirations beyond being the mayor of Bray Harbor, she thought Peter Graham could open doors for him and what better way to get through him than through his girlfriend, right?

Right, thanks, chat soon. xx

"Phew." Shay shook her head. Clearly Cora wasn't the only one who had an ulterior motive for inviting Jasmine to join the Little While Glove Society. Faye was the one who had dangled the carrot she knew a social-climbing woman like Cora couldn't refuse.

From the beginning, Shay had known that Tassi could never kill anyone. The only logical explanation had been that Peter Graham had slowly poisoned Jasmine because no one besides Tassi had contact with Jasmine's tea or cup that night. Now, however, it appeared as though someone else may have played a part. The question still remained, though: How did they do it without being seen and leaving no trace?

Shay studied the low shelf at the back of the room where the crystal collection Bridget had used in her readings was still stored. She crept over to the door leading out into the tearoom, opened it a crack, made sure Faye was busy, and then quietly closed it. She leaned her back against the door, drew in a series of slow mind-clearing breaths, set the amulet pouch on the table so its heat wouldn't distract her, and edged toward Bridget's crystals.

"Okay, Jasmine, Gran said you were reaching out because you had something you wanted us to know," she whispered as she scanned the shelf of crystals, having no clue which one to start with. "Come on, speak to me because you hold the key that none of us can find."

Then she recalled that Gran had told her to touch each crystal to find the one that Jasmine spoke to her through. Even though these weren't exactly the crystals Gran had been talking about, it was all she had, so she hoped the same process would work on these.

She closed her eyes and focused on Jasmine, but worrying thoughts crept in that this might not work anyway since these stones hadn't been cleansed in the sun and moon ritual like Gran said they should be. Hoping for the best, she took another deep breath, kept her eyes squeezed tight, and mentally crossed her fingers. Since Bridget would have been the last person to use these, maybe a little of Bridget's energy would help Shay select the right one for what she was about to do.

Once an image of Jasmine was fixed in her mind's eye, Shay opened her eyes, and her fingers clasped a large piece of uncut amethyst—known to promote psychic gifts—but it didn't produce any of the effects Gran had told her would come if it was the right stone. She moved her hand over to the piece of calcite quartz crystal, known to bring one closer to one's higher self, and still nothing. Even when she clasped the crystal ball, which according to Gran was the strongest psychic conductor of all, she felt nothing—no warmth, tingling, or vibrations, and definitely nothing like waves of water traveling up her arm, as Gran said there would be.

"Pfft," she blew out in frustration, sat down hard in a chair at the table, and stared at the shelves of Bridget's crystals. "Now what, Bridget?"

She toyed absentmindedly with the amulet pouch beside her on the table as she glanced around the room. There was a shelf of candles Bridget had also used in her readings, but Shay knew nothing about them, and they weren't something Gran had brought into any of her lessons. Best to leave well enough alone right now. Who knows who or what she might conjure up using them?

She shivered but quickly realized it wasn't her thoughts about messing with something she didn't understand that made her tremble. There was no doubt about it. The temperature in the room had dropped, and she was shivering cold even as the pouch grew warm again in her hand. The bottle inside the pouch was heating up even though she wasn't wearing it. This was something that had never happened before, and disproved her theory that the heating of the bottle was a response to her heart rate and nerve endings, which if they weren't prickling before, they sure were now as the room grew even colder.

A velvety whisper brushed across her cheek, *Trust your instincts.* Gran's words also rushed through her mind. *Ye have the most powerful of all crystal balls right there in that pouch ye carry.*

Shay's hand closed around the pouch, but it was as though someone else's hand had replaced hers, and she knew that Bridget was with her, guiding her, just as Shay had longed for her to do.

Shay took another series of deep breaths to calm her racing mind—it was only too bad that calmness didn't reach her fingers, which still trembled as she tried to unfasten the tie that held the bottle inside the small leather pouch. Once successful, she slid the bottle onto her open palm. As soon as the glass touched her skin, a sensation of a slow-burning fire spread through Shay, setting her nerve endings sparking and cinching around her heart like a vice grip. She glanced toward the door to double-check she had closed it, and then opened her palm, attempting once again to clear her mind and focus only on the blue bottle she held.

A flash of blue light illuminated the room, and the screech of a rusted door opening echoed in her mind. The fine hairs on the back of her neck prickled, and the air around her crackled and groaned. After another spark of light, Shay squinted into the bottle. Everything from the night Jasmine had died was in front of her. It was exactly as it had been that evening. Shay was even seated in the same chair as she was now. Zoey was on her right. On the other side of Zoey sat Jasmine, then Faye, and then Nadine, the librarian. Next to her was Dot Simpson, then Cora, Millie Patterson, and then Julia on Shay's left.

As the mist in the bottle continued to lift, the details became clearer. It wasn't as though Shay were watching a movie unfold before her eyes. It was more like she was there again, watching, but this time as an impartial observer. She could even smell the aroma of fresh-brewed chamomile and black oolong tea.

She watched herself explain the tea leaf-reading process to the group, heard all the conversations around the table, saw the horror in Tassi's eyes when Julia made the comment about Jasmine being pregnant, except this time, Shay wasn't hindered by seeing only what happened near her. She saw the elbow nudge and eye roll Nadine gave Dot when Jasmine started apologizing for making the group late.

It was little exchanges like that between the women Shay had missed because her attention had been focused elsewhere. But this time around, Shay wasn't encumbered by her own body and perceptions. She had the advantage of being an overseer.

She squinted and took in the actions and interactions of each woman at the table. As she moved clockwise from Julia around to Faye there was nothing untoward occurring. She paused when Tassi handed Faye a fresh napkin so Faye could continue her obsessive ritual of cleaning the cutlery before she used it. Then Tassi moved on to fill Jasmine's cup. When Jasmine questioned the tea, everyone's attention, including Shay's, then became focused on Jasmine and Tassi's verbal exchange about the eye of newt and hemlock.

The advantage of sight that the bottle was giving Shay now allowed her not to become distracted by Jasmine's verbal outburst but gave her the ability to focus on Faye, the woman who had brought her husband's lover into the group, the lover who would soon die after this incident.

Then she saw it, the key that had been missing the whole time. While all the attention was on Jasmine and

Shay's conversation about tea selection, Faye continued fussing with her place setting. However, instead of polishing her own cutlery with the new napkin Tassi had handed her, Faye polished Jasmine's with her old crumpled up one stored in the palm of her little white-gloved hand. After giving it a good rubbing, she set Jasmine's spoon back in its place and shoved the old napkin into her pocket.

After Jasmine relented and allowed Tassi to pour the tea, she picked up her spoon, stirred her tea, and drank it as Shay instructed them all to do. When Jasmine collapsed on the table, causing plates and cutlery to fly about, Faye hit the floor, seized Jasmine's spoon, tucked it into her bag, and joined the rest of them in the ensuing chaos before the ambulance arrived.

Shay blinked when an image of the rosary bean plant took over her vision and jumped when the door to the tearoom flew open. Faye stood in the doorway, a teapot clutched in each hand.

"It was you," Shay whispered hoarsely. "You poisoned Jasmine."

Faye stepped inside the back room, and with a kick of her shoe heel attempted to close the door. Her eyes narrowed, and she pinned Shay with a look of contempt and smirked, "You're kidding, right?"

Shay set the bottle down, braced both her hands on the table, met Faye's piercing glare, and rose to her feet. "You used beans from the rosary plant I had upstairs. What did you do, crush some that Tassi missed when she cleaned up and cover Jasmine's spoon with the fragments, giving her a lethal dose?" Shay's gaze never wavered from Faye's. "Tell me, was it Lilly who told you how deadly they are? Is that why I saw you arguing with her? She knew you took her expertise and used it to kill someone."

Faye flung her head back and cackled out a sound that sent tidal waves of tremors rocketing through Shay. Then, just as quickly as her outburst had come, she fell silent, pinning Shay with a defiant stare. A mocking smile slowly formed on her lips. "No . . ." Faye quietly hissed, her tone cool and flat as she took a step forward. "And kindly leave my Lilly out of this."

"But I saw you arguing with her, not once but twice. . ." Shay slithered a step sideways to put more distance between them. "It looked pretty heated from where I stood." She glided another step to the side as Faye edged around the table toward her. "The girl was in tears. . ." Shay's mind filled with a flash of memories: the day Lilly told her how excited the college was to acquire the more potent specimen of rosary bean plant from Shay's greenhouse, the moment Stephen told Shay that Lilly worked at the hotel restaurant, and Jasmine's words about feeling unwell. With another flash of kaleidoscopic patterns, those images merged with the scene of Faye wiping Jasmine's spoon at the reading.

Shay staggered a step back. "Lilly wasn't an innocent in all this, was she? Given her education, she was the mastermind and the one poisoning Jasmine all week at the restaurant." She pinned Faye with a look of disbelief. "And what? When Jasmine announced at the group reading that she and Peter were going back to Carmel the next day, you panicked and thought you'd rush things along with the more toxic beans you got from my conservatory? Or were they from Lilly?" Shay's fixed stare never wavered. "What were the arguments about? Was Lilly mad because you took away her thunder, or mad because it made her mother a cold-blooded killer too?"

"You think you have it all figured out, don't you?" Faye took a step closer to Shay. "Well, let me tell you, Miss Smarty-pants. You couldn't be more wrong about Lilly than you are. We argued because she has some perverse sense of entitlement, like too many people, including that Kendra Reid—Jasmine—or whatever name she was going by."

The dark depths of Faye's revulsion sucked all the light from her eyes, leaving them empty and haunted as her aura blasted out rays of red and black. "Lilly actually thought that now since I am working she should be able to quit her job at the restaurant and focus on her position at the college and her grades. Can you imagine? She actually thought she should just be able to concentrate on school, and after what we'd been through?"

Faye took another step around the table. "That woman Jasmine stole everything I had worked hard for during the past thirty years. Out of the blue, she comes into the restaurant, swinging her hips, and with a bat of her eyelashes, she sucked every penny out of my George, killed him, and left me and Lilly with nothing, absolutely nothing. Jasmine made sure she got it all. When she died, Lilly thought that since we finally had our revenge, her work was done. She could quit her job and go back to being a full-time student, of all things, but . . . " Faye's voice drifted, and she set a haunted disembodied gaze on Shay. "The girl has no idea what hard work is. I do, and you know, and Jen. . . Yes, especially Jen. I see it every day with her, but these young people . . ." She erratically shook her head. "No, they have no idea what working twelve hours a day, looking after children, and keeping house on top of it is like." Her gaze dropped. "No wonder my George was taken in by that . . . that floozy. I was a haggard mess."

Shay had little experience with what is often referred to as crazy talk, but she was certain this was exactly what was meant by the expression. "You can't blame yourself for his wandering eye, and you certainly can't blame Lilly." Shay hoped that if she could keep Faye calm and bide time, she could work her way around the table closer to the door, which was still open a crack, then make enough noise to get Jen's attention away from the customers, letting her know there was a problem back here. "So now what?" she said, eyeing the distance to the door. "Because I don't think you really want Lilly to have the same sort of life as you've had, worked to death and finding no pleasure in it, do you?"

Tears formed in Faye's eyes, but she lifted her head, her eyes flashing with venom again, and took another step toward Shay. "No," she sneered, "but she needs to learn what true sacrifice is."

"Then what you're saying is all this was your idea and you forced Lilly into doing your bidding for the sake of revenge on your shattered life?" Shay inwardly cringed as the woman's outburst of fiery energy filled the room. She slid another step and caught the toe of her sneaker on a chair leg.

Before Shay could regain her footing, Faye was around the table, eye to eye with her, her hot breath coming hard and fast. "Enough of this!" she screamed. "Let's see if this will scramble those inky feelings Jen is always going on about you having!" She laughed sardonically and brought the teapots in her hands crashing down on either side of Shay's head.

A bolt of white light blurred Shay's vision, shooting her backward, and her head exploded in searing pain. In a haze-like awareness, Shay wondered if she was hallucinating since she could hear snarling and growling on the floor beside her. The drone of a disembodied voice faded in and out. She struggled to get to her feet, but strong hands kept pushing her back down. Her arms thrashed out, and her fists pounded on the source of her imprisonment, only stopping when Liam's face came into focus.

"*A chara*, are ye okay?"

She squinted, struggling to focus her vision, and breathed a sigh of relief when an image of Spirit pinning Faye to the floor came into focus. She blinked and gazed up, meeting Liam's anxious expression as he hovered over her. "Don't tell me he did that dancy-prancy thing again."

"He did. Came right into the pub and all."

"You two always have a way of making a dramatic entrance, don't you?" She gave a short laugh, grabbed the back of her head, and moaned.

Chapter 32

"There's a good crowd out there," Shay said, gesturing to the window. "Do you think Maddie and Hunter can handle it on their own?"

Jen looked outside at her children operating the refreshment table on the sidewalk and grinned. "It looks like they've recruited a couple of their friends to help, so I think they'll be just fine. See that little girl with the bow in her hair?"

Shay nodded.

"That's Hunter's latest crush, and judging by the way she's making moon eyes back at him, I think everything is under control for now."

"Let's just hope it doesn't get so busy in here that we can't keep an eye on things out there, since we're still short Tassi, and now that Faye's . . . well, indisposed."

When the overhead bells jangled out their greeting, Shay glanced over at the door and gasped. "Dean Philips," she cried, "don't you dare eat all the treats. We won't have enough to last through the festival." She flashed him a look of reproach when she saw him clutching one cookie in his right hand and two in his left.

He popped the last bite of a cookie into his mouth and quickly thrust his other hand behind his back. "My daughter insisted," he mumbled through bits of cookie crumble. "I couldn't very well say no, could I?"

Shay shook her head and looked at Jen. "He's all yours. You deal with this."

"Gee, thanks," Jen grunted. "Just what I need, another kid to look after today."

"Ah, but you do it so well." Shay grinned and grabbed her backpack from under the sales counter. "But I have to go, or . . ." She glanced over at Dean, happily munching on another cookie. "Have you come to drive me to the courthouse?"

"Nope," he mumbled, taking another bite.

"Then I really have to get going or I'll be cited for delay of court on top of having to explain why I broke the terms of my restraining order."

"Nope," mumbled Dean, shaking his head and popping the last bit of cookie into his mouth.

"What do you mean, nope? Has the judge already decided to throw me in jail without even hearing my side?"

"Nope." Dean swallowed hard as he brushed cookie crumbs from his hands. "You don't have to appear in court today, or any day, at least not in relation to any of Peter Graham's previous charges."

"I don't understand. I'm supposed to appear before a judge in"—Shay glanced at the wall clock—"thirty minutes."

"No you aren't. Peter rescinded the restraining order, dropped his lawsuit against you, and stopped his custody petition."

"He dropped everything?"

"That's fantastic news!" Jen grinned and glanced from Shay to Dean. "Does that mean Shay doesn't have to stand trial for practicing witchcraft?"

"That's exactly what it means. It seems when Peter delved deeper into the terms of Tassi's inheritance, he discovered the lawyer who drew up her grandfather's will was better than he is. I guess there's a clause in it that supersedes any custody outcomes." He shrugged. "So, it didn't matter if he had custody or not. He still can't get his hands on a penny of the money."

"I don't get it. Why not, if he has custody of Tassi?" asked Jen.

"It seems that in the case of any custody dispute, the money automatically goes into a trust fund to be overseen by Tassi's grandfather's company's board of directors until she's of legal age. Her grandfather was no fool. He knew exactly the type of person Peter Graham is."

"Then all of his actions had absolutely nothing to do with him lashing out in grief," said Shay, shaking her head in disgust. "It was only ever about the money."

"Meh." Dean folded his arms across his chest and leaned against the end of the bookcase in front of the counter. "I think to begin with he was grieving. He and Jasmine had been together for nearly three years, but it sounds to me like after the initial shock wore off he saw it as a blessing. Jasmine was pretty high maintenance and a drain on his bank accounts, and if there's one thing Peter Graham showed through all his actions it's that money is his driving force."

"That's for sure," said Jen. "I would love to have been a fly on the wall when he found out Jasmine—or Kendra, or whatever other identity she went by over the years—was a seasoned con woman and he was only one of her many rich victims."

"You know"—Shay looked at Jen—"this is why I can never call myself a psychic. My emotions get all jumbled up with my instincts, and I can't seem to separate them." She turned her attention on Dean. "Because all this time, I was so sure that due to Peter's actions, combined with the fact that we couldn't figure out how Jasmine's teacup had abrin in it when there wasn't any in the teapot, he had to have been the one poisoning her and it had to have been in her lipstick."

"It was the only theory that made sense at the time, so don't beat yourself up, because I was thinking the same thing." He revealed an out-of-character awkward eyeroll. "But when did you figure out it was Faye, and why didn't you say something to me before about her?"

"Because it was only a hunch, one of my inky feelings." She flashed Jen a grin. "And I wasn't positive about anything until the day she attacked me with the teapots."

"Yeah, that was quite the day," said Jen. "I thought at first the food dehydrator had exploded on you or something when I heard Faye shouting, but when Spirit and Liam burst through the front door and made a mad dash back there, well, that's when I called Dean."

"I, for one, am glad you did. I had a gut feeling

about her earlier that day when there were so many dis-crepancies in her personnel file. Then how bent out of shape she got with my questions about Lilly and how nervous she was that Mia had said something about the rosary bean plant that had been upstairs. But it wasn't until Jasmine showed me—" She glanced uneasily at Dean, then swallowed hard. "I mean it wasn't until I did a reading and figured out how Faye got the crushed beans into Jasmine's cup that I knew for sure."

"Well . . . it's a good thing you did it, whatever it was." Dean eyed Shay suspiciously. "Otherwise, she might have gotten away with it, and Tassi would have ended up with a murder conviction hanging over her head the rest of her life."

"Yeah," said Jen, "the poor kid is still going to have scars, though. It must be tough finding out her own dad did everything in his power to prove she was guilty of Jasmine's murder and went out of his way to build a case for his custody suit by discrediting everyone she knew in town. Then when the real killers were appre-hended, he walked away from it all."

"Walked away from *her*, you mean," Shay said with a sneer, showing her contempt for the man, and then looked questioningly at Dean. "Can he be charged with anything now?"

Dean shrugged. "It all comes down to intent and—"

"Yes, and like you said before, intent is hard to prove. Poor Tassi, it must be tearing her apart to dis-cover her father never cared about her, just the money she was going to come into."

"I'm sure she's hurt"—Dean shrugged and stepped aside, giving Shay and Jen a full view out onto the street through the window—"but she seems to be handling it okay, don't you think?"

"Tassi!" Shay squealed and dashed out the door. "I can't tell you how much we've missed you," Shay cried out. Tears streamed down her cheeks as she swept the girl into her arms and hugged her for all she was worth.

"I've missed you so much too." Tassi sniffled and hung tightly on to Shay.

Shay took hold of Tassi's head and nestled it into her shoulder when the girl began sobbing. "Oh, my friend, it's so good to have you back with us." Shay held her out at arm's length and looked into her eyes. "Just know, you are loved and appreciated, now and always."

Tassi nodded and glanced down at Spirit, sitting by her side. "I couldn't have survived this without him." She gave his head a gentle pat. "He really saved my sanity. Thank you for sending him to me." She sniveled and wiped her nose on her jacket sleeve.

Jen, who had joined the reunion, reached over to the refreshment table, grabbed a napkin, and handed it to Tassi, gesturing to her dripping nose. Tassi awkwardly obliged and wiped it.

"That's better." Jen grinned. "But I see we're going to have to house-train you again," she added with a short laugh as she reached out and pulled Tassi into her arms for a hug. "You've been missed around here, girl, that's for sure."

Shay glanced down at Spirit. His tail wagged and his ears perked as he watched with hopeful eyes. On his face was a smile as big as Shay's as she gave Tassi another hug, just to make sure this was all real. "I'd like to take credit for sending Spirit your way, but I can't. It was all his idea to keep you company and act as your protector."

"He didn't do a bad job protecting you either, when you needed him the other day, did he?" said Jen.

"No, he didn't." Shay bent down and ruffled the fine fur on his neck and kissed his head. "You just seem to know when and where you're needed, and that's something very special about you, isn't it, fella?" She laughed when he set his paw on her arm. "Yes, you are something pretty special, aren't you, boy?" She gave his head another ruffle and stood upright.

Tassi's eyes widened, and she looked from Jen to Shay. "So, it was true, not just people talking? He really did save you from death by teapots?"

"Well . . ." Shay sputtered and glanced at Jen. "I wouldn't say I was in that much danger. I could have handled Faye's attack. It's just that Spirit got there before I could use any of my kung fu moves on her." She crouched into a martial art fighting stance, hands raised in a karate chop, and laughed. "See, I had it all under control, didn't I, boy?" She glanced down at Spirit, who whimpered, lay down, and buried his head under his paws. "Pfft, thanks for the vote of confidence."

"No, seriously." Tassi pinned Shay with a worried look. "You could have died."

"I didn't, though, and the last thing you should be doing right now is worrying about me. It all worked out, and the real killers were found."

"So, that means Lilly was arrested too?"

"Yes," said Shay, "she was. After Dean finally got Faye to confess to her part in the whole scheme, Lilly copped to tainting Jasmine's coffee every day with crushed rosary beans when she had breakfast in the hotel dining room. When she got hold of the rosary bean plant here from the shop and discovered it was more potent than the one she'd been using, she and her mother came up with the idea of giving Jasmine a larger dose at the group reading."

"Yeah," Jen said, "it took a few days, but it all finally came out. It seems that Faye, being the master manipulator that she was, threatened Lilly by telling her she wouldn't sign her scholarship application if she didn't go along with her plan to kill Jasmine."

"And Lilly agreed, just like that?" asked Tassi.

"Yeah, it seems that she had become as bitter and resentful as her mother, especially when it came down to the fact that she might have her college education taken away from her on top of everything else they had lost to Jasmine. Now they're both looking at a lengthy prison sentence."

"That's too bad." Tassi sighed. "Lilly seemed like such a nice person. Her mother always struck me as a bit off, but . . . it's hard to believe they were really a mother-and-daughter assassination team."

"Me word! Am I seeing things?" cried a familiar sing-song voice from the door of Madigan's Pub. "Is dat me Tassi girl come back to us?" Gran cried out as Tassi grinned and dashed over to her.

"Hi, Gran!" She wrapped her arms around the old woman. "It's great to see you're still here. I was afraid you'd be gone by the time this was all over with."

"And where da ye think I'd be going? Da good Lord isn't ready for me quite yet, I don't think."

"No!" said Tassi, her voice quivering with panic. "I didn't mean that. I meant I was afraid you'd move to San Francisco before this all came to an end."

"Ah, dat's good. Ye had me a little worried that ye'd seen something in me life I wasn't prepared for. But don't ye worry, girl, this old Gran isn't going nowhere soon. Too many people here need me, and me daughter-in-law, Liam's mam, has herself a new buachaill, and—"

"A buachaill?" asked Tassi.

"Aye, a boyfriend, and the last thing she needs is me interfering in her new relationship. She's had it so hard since me dear son passed. 'Tis a good thing for her now."

Shay, overhearing this, couldn't resist an eye roll. It was too bad Gran hadn't had that same mindset when she'd moved in with Liam and Zoey. Things might have turned out much happier for him. It tore at her heart to see the way he'd been moping around since they'd broken up. Speaking of Liam, she flashed him a smile when he came out of the pub carrying a box of sample cups, and dropped them on the table beside Carmen, the bartender, who was operating a mini streetside beer station.

He returned her smile, his eyes locking with hers, sending a wave of warmth racing through her. Then Tassi squealed, "Liam!" He rushed toward her, beaming, gave her a hug, and then left her and Gran to continue their reunion and walked over to Shay, beside her refreshment table. "How's yer head today?"

"Better," she said, rubbing the sore spot on the back of it. "No concussion, so no harm done. Adam said I would have a bruise for a couple of weeks, but . . ." She shrugged.

"Good, ye had me worried."

"I'm fine, but I have been meaning to talk to you." She glanced over her shoulder at Maddie and Hunter, right beside them. "Um . . ."

Liam gestured to the road, which was cordoned off to traffic for the weekend, and jerked his head.

"Sure," she said and the two of them stepped off the curb and made their way to a spot out of earshot. "I wanted to ask you about that thing we talked about before everything went crazy with witness statements and everything—"

"You mean about Conor and asking him if he'd help us lure Doyle to Bray Harbor."

"How did you know what I was going to say?"

"I guess yer not the only one with inky feelings." He laughed.

"Wow, Gran was right. You are a member of the High Seelie Court, aren't you?"

"Nah, I just figured since we never talked about it again, ye'd want to know what he said."

"Yes, I do. Is he going to help us?"

"Yer the seer, ye tell me." He nudged her arm and gestured toward the pub door.

"He's here?" Shay couldn't believe her eyes. Conor stood at the table with Carmen, passing out samples of beer as though it were something he did every day. "I can't believe it. Does that mean he's agreed to help us even though it could make him a target now too?"

"Like I said, ye tell me. Do ye think his intentions are genuine or is he going to play us to get his hands on that"—he gestured toward the tie on her neck—"and sell it for a hefty price himself or turn it over to Doyle like he was hired to do in the first place?"

Shay focused on Conor, closed her eyes, and pictured him in her mind, mentally crossing her fingers that her feelings were back on track now that Faye and Lilly had been apprehended, and the murder case was closed. A sense of well-being flushed through her, and she smiled. "No flashes, no dark energy. I think he might really want to stop Doyle from doing to others what he's done to Bridget and so many others over the years, including him."

"Let's hope ye're right, *a chara*, but until we know for certain, do not trust him."

"Let's give him the benefit of the doubt, okay? He did come back, and he's not hiding from Doyle anymore, so that must mean something, right?"

"If he's playing us, then he doesn't have to hide from Doyle, right? And if he's not"—Liam raised his brows—"it means Doyle will just send someone else to do his bidding while he continues to hunt Conor down."

"Do you think so?"

"Aye, I know men like Doyle. He won't stop until he gets what he wants and will kill anyone who gets in his way, which is why I'm surprised Conor came out of hiding and is out here now in broad daylight like he is. He might as well be wearing a target on his shirt, if he's being true to his words with me, that is."

"Conor's not a fool either. He knows the risk. Maybe that's part of his plan to get Doyle to come here himself."

"What do ye mean?"

"Maybe he wants Doyle to think he's still working for him. After a while Doyle will get impatient and come here himself to find out what's taking Conor so long to get his hands on the amulet. You did say Conor has worked for him a long time, so Doyle must have a certain level of trust and isn't going to kill him until he finds out what the problem is first."

"Is that the seer in ye speaking?"

"Just a hunch, so give Conor a chance to prove himself, and if I'm wrong, then we'll deal with Doyle another way." Shay shuffled from one foot to the other and glanced at Liam. "But there was something else I wanted to ask you."

"Sure, what?"

"It's just that tomorrow night there's the dance over on the boardwalk, and—"

"Liam!" Teresa Boyer, the owner of Teresa's Treasures on the boardwalk, called and waved from the curb.

He nodded at her in acknowledgment and looked back at Shay. "Sorry. Ye were saying?"

"I just wanted to ask you if—"

"Liam!" Teresa called again and smiled apologetically. "I have to get back to the shop, so I just have a minute!"

His gaze wavered between Shay's expectant one and Teresa's hopeful one. "I'd better go. She probably wants to firm up the plans for our date tomorrow night."

"Your date . . . tomorrow night?"

"Yeah." He grinned sheepishly. "She asked me to go to the festival dance with her. I didn't want to say yes since Zoey and I have only just broken up, but then I figured why not? Zoey will be there with her new laddie."

"Yeah, why not . . ." she muttered and hung her head, hoping the cobblestone street at her feet would open up and swallow her.

"We can talk later, okay?"

"Yeah, later." She managed a weak smile as he left her to meet Teresa.

That's the story of us, isn't it? Shay sighed. *Bad timing all the way around.* She shook her head to try to clear it and gazed up High Street, hoping the sights and sounds of the day's festivities would ease the crushing in her chest, but gasped when a burst of intense energy seized her. She scanned the street for its source and paused when her eyes locked on Madam Malvina.

The black-haired woman waved her over from her table on Cuppa-Jo's patio.

This wasn't good. If this woman was half the psychic she said she was, there was no doubt that she had sensed Shay's school-girl theatrics regarding Liam just now on the street. Shay shored herself up, walked toward her and hoped for the best—like that Madam Melvina was oblivious to actually reading people's energy no matter what she peddled to her customers.

"I'm surprised to see you here on a Friday," Shay said, taking the chair Malvina pulled out for her. "Did you close your shop in Monterey for the day?"

"You might say that." The woman flashed her a smile cloaked in mystery as she took a sip of her coffee.

"Okay." Shay gulped.

Was this the woman's way of telling her she knew what Shay had been thinking a few moments ago, or was there something else behind her mysterious smile? Shay always did have a hard time following Malvina's line of thought and too often put her foot in her mouth when she tried. It was probably best to go with conventional social exchanges until she could figure out what was behind the veil of ambiguity Malvina appeared to be shrouded in. "So how are you enjoying the festival so far?"

"Oh . . ." The woman played with the handle of her cup after she set it on the table. "I'm not here for the festival."

"You're not?"

"No, I'm here on a . . . little shopping trip."

"Ooh, that sounds like fun. Did you buy anything good? I know there's lots of unique stalls set up on the boardwalk for the weekend."

"Yes," she said slowly, "I was down there, and actually . . . I'm glad I ran into you."

"You are? Why? I don't have any more stock to sell you from the shop, if that's what you're hoping for."

"Nooo, it's just that I wanted to be the one to tell you so you didn't hear about it from your friend. What's her name? Julia Fisher?"

"What would you be worried about that Julia might tell me?" Shay's eyes widened. "You don't mean that you bought property in Bray Harbor, do you?"

"See, you are good," Malvina said with a sardonic chuckle. "Yes, as a matter of fact, I just signed the purchase agreement for the cheese shop down on the boardwalk."

"Hmm . . ." Shay said thoughtfully. "I didn't know their building was for sale. Does that mean you're going to change careers?"

"No." She wrapped her hands around her coffee mug and clicked her polished black fingernails on the ceramic surface. "They're moving locations to a larger space on Fifth Avenue. So," she focused her penetrating gaze on Shay, "I'm going to relocate my psychic shop from Monterey to here."

Shay swallowed hard.

"In fact, we're not only going to be business neighbors. I managed to convince Julia to sell me one of the cottages she uses as an income rental property, and after some negotiation, shall we say, she agreed. It appears that we'll also be neighbors at Crystal Beach Cottages."

Madam Malvina smiled, pushed her cup away, and rose to her feet. "But I have to run now. Orion is going to be thrilled by the news that the deals went through. You know, he really has a thing for that girl Tassi who works for you. Cheerio; have a good day." She flipped her black shawl over her shoulder and sauntered off up High Street.

Once Shay had digested the fact that her life was once again going to change in a dramatic way, she stumbled across the road to Crystals & CuriosiTEAS; took a deep breath; looked at the golden letters on her windows that advertised teacup readings, palm readings, and protective and healing stone treatments; and grabbed the tea sample table for support.

"Are ye okay, child?" Gran set a tray of tea samples on the table and placed her hand on Shay's arm.

"Yeah, I will be."

"What did that black-haired, black-hearted woman say to ye to put ye in such a state?" Her eyes flashed from a look of concern to a fierce glare.

"Nothing really," Shay said with a shrug. "She just gave me some news that might mean I'm going to have to make some changes around here, that's all."

"The only thing ye need to change is learning to trust yer instincts, and then everything will be as right as rain. Ye'll see."

Shay glanced over at Conor, who was working the pub's sample table, then in the direction Madam Malvina had gone and winced when the amulet on her chest sent off a red-hot burst. "I don't know if my instincts are good enough to get me out of what I sense may be coming."

"Don't ye worry, child. I'll be here as long as ye need me."

She then held out her arms and Shay crumpled into them. This feeling was what she had missed in her life. The warmth and love of the mother who had raised her but was taken from her, and the love of the mother she would never know. She hung on to Gran for all she was worth, feeling their hearts beating as if they were one. She never wanted this feeling of belonging to end. Tears seeped from Shay's eyes as she pulled back and stared into Gran's faded blue ones filled with tears. "Thank you," Shay hoarsely whispered.

Gran sniffled, gave her a knowing smile and a wink, and then tottered off to help Maddie and Hunter pass out tea samples and goodies to customers.

Shay watched them for a moment, her heart bursting

with gratitude, and then she glanced through the tea shop window at Tassi and Jen, who were just as busy inside, and a soft smile tugged at her lips. "Thank you for all this, Bridget," she whispered, "but especially for sending Gran."

She took a wistful glance over at Liam by the pub table, drew in a deep breath, and pushed from her mind the fleeting image she had of him holding Teresa in his arms tomorrow night on the dance floor. Then she thrust her head high and marched into the tea shop. With the warmth from the pouch resting over her heart, she was secure in knowing she at least had it, and Gran, to help her through all of what the future might hold.